The Cornish Dukes

Born to inherit, destined for love!

Vennor, Eaton, Cassian and Inigo grew up together
on the coasts of Cornwall, knowing that one day
they would inherit their fathers' weighty titles and
the responsibility that comes with being a duke.

When Vennor's father is shockingly murdered, that
day comes sooner than expected. All four heirs
are forced to acknowledge that their lives are
changing. But the one change these powerful
men might not be expecting? Love!

Enjoy this tension-filled new quartet by
Bronwyn Scott

Read Eaton's story in
The Secrets of Lord Lynford
Available now

And look for Cassian's,
Inigo's and Vennor's stories
Coming soon!

Author Note

Readers, as we start off a new series, there is so much that could go into this author's note. It was hard to choose. I am excited about the theme of innovation that runs through this series. Each story centers on the idea of creating a legacy and thinking about what we leave behind, how our lives matter and how we can choose to make them matter. Eaton's story picks up where *An Invitation to a Cornish Christmas* leaves off—with the establishment of a music school. Eaton is a man who appears to have it all, but in truth he lacks the one thing an heir to a duke ought to have, and it's reshaped his life and how he views his legacy. Spoiler alert—Eaton is infertile. He cannot sire an heir.

Male infertility is not widely discussed in the Regency, but physicians had been espousing it as early as the fifteenth century in texts like John Tanner's *The Hidden Treasures of the Art of Physick*. Semen analysis did not become used until 1860, so I acknowledge that Eaton's informal semen analysis is fifty years in advance of formal nineteenth-century medicine, but not improbable to have done. The microscope existed and was already analyzing bacteria.

I hope you enjoy Eliza and Eaton's story. Tune in to my blog at bronwynswriting.Blogspot.com for more interesting tidbits behind the story.

BRONWYN
SCOTT

---

*The Secrets of
Lord Lynford*

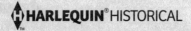

HARLEQUIN® HISTORICAL

Recycling programs
for this product may
not exist in your area.

ISBN-13: 978-1-335-50523-1

The Secrets of Lord Lynford

Printed in U.S.A.

www.Harlequin.com

Bronwyn Scott is a communications instructor at Pierce College in the United States and the proud mother of three wonderful children—one boy and two girls. When she's not teaching or writing, she enjoys playing the piano, traveling—especially to Florence, Italy—and studying history and foreign languages. Readers can stay in touch via Facebook or on her blog, bronwynswriting.Blogspot.com. She loves to hear from readers.

Books by Bronwyn Scott

Harlequin Historical

Scandal at the Midsummer Ball
"The Debutante's Awakening"
Scandal at the Christmas Ball
"Dancing with the Duke's Heir"

The Cornish Dukes

The Secrets of Lord Lynford

Allied at the Altar

A Marriage Deal with the Viscount
One Night with the Major
Tempted by His Secret Cinderella
Captivated by Her Convenient Husband

Russian Royals of Kuban

Compromised by the Prince's Touch
Innocent in the Prince's Bed
Awakened by the Prince's Passion
Seduced by the Prince's Kiss

Visit the Author Profile page
at Harlequin.com for more titles.

For Jeff, who is very much the embodiment of the legacy of Richard Penlerick in this story and this series. Throughout his life, Jeff loved others unconditionally and gave generously of himself for the betterment of his world. He left this earth the week I finished this story, and it is safe to say our world is vastly improved because of him and the lives he touched.

Prologue

London—June 18th, 1823

Death had officially come to Mayfair. Richard Penlerick, Duke of Newlyn, and his Duchess were buried, and the funeral witnessed by the *ton*'s finest that morning in the hopes of bringing closure to the tragedy that had stunned their exalted world a week earlier: a peer—a *duke*, no less—and his wife, stabbed to death in an alley after an evening theatre performance.

Eaton Falmage, Marquess of Lynford, closed the front door behind the last of the funeral guests, wishing he could just as easily shut the door on the week's horror for the sake of those who remained within the Newlyn town house on Portland Square. But for them the journey into grief was only just beginning. Now that the pageantry of death was over, the real mourning could commence, as he and those closest to the Penlericks could give free rein to their emotions.

Eaton found that inner circle, a collection of friends

he'd known and loved since childhood, gathered in the library, a male conclave of power and strength, both of which had been lent unreservedly this week to Vennor Penlerick, the heir.

Vennor stood by the sideboard, pouring brandies, a rare blond in a room full of dark-haired men. He glanced in Eaton's direction, his eyes asking the question.

'Yes, they are all gone,' Eaton offered in low tones. 'I had the servants sweep the halls for stragglers.' He gripped Vennor's arm in a gesture of assurance. 'We are entirely alone. At last.'

The week had been nightmarish for all of them, but none so much as Vennor, and it showed. Despite his immaculate grooming, Vennor bore the unmistakable signs of strain and grief. To lose one's parents without warning, even at twenty-eight, was devastating. Vennor had been strong all week, the ideal heir, the consummate host to those who'd imposed their company and their own grief. Eaton took both the glasses. 'Come, sit, you needn't be on display with us.'

The group had gathered around the cold hearth. Someone, Inigo perhaps, had culled chairs from about the room and arranged them in one central place to accommodate the group known throughout the *ton* as 'the Cornish Dukes': heirs from four long-standing ducal families whose patriarchs had grown up together in the wilds of Cornwall and in turn so had their four sons. The bond between those fathers and their sons was legendary, as was their loyalty to one another.

That impressive connection had been on view

throughout the week for all of London to see, as if to say 'let no one doubt there are no lengths to which we would not go for one another'. The fathers had taken their leave discreetly a half an hour ago to give the four friends privacy to grieve together, as they would no doubt be doing themselves at another undisclosed location. They had lost their dear friend just as Eaton and the others had lost a man they'd looked upon as an uncle and mentor but Vennor had lost a father and a mother all in one blow.

'Thank you, Eaton. I'm glad the guests are gone.' Vennor took the brandy and slumped into the chair beside Inigo. He favoured them with a tired smile. 'I had no idea my father's friends possessed so many daughters of a certain age. I knew it would happen, of course. I just thought people might have the decency to queue up *after* a period of mourning. I don't think I can tolerate one more offer of marriage wrapped in a condolence. I can't bear to hear one more time that my father was a good man who'd want me to look to the future as soon as possible. Dear lord, some of them weren't even subtle about the fact that I'm an only child and the Penlerick nursery is a veritable ghost town in *immediate* want of infants.' There was none of the usual humour underlying Vennor's words. There was only anger today, as well there should be. The deaths of Richard Penlerick and his wife were violent, senseless crimes.

Eaton's chest tightened at the thought. *Thank God it hadn't been his own father in that alley.* The guilt of such a sentiment gripped him, as did the reality. It hadn't been his father *yet*. One day, though, it would be; an accident, old age, God willing *not* a crime, but the terrible moment *would* come. Not just for him, but for all of them. Eaton looked about his circle of friends: dark-haired, strong-jawed Cassian, heir to the Duke of Hayle, enigmatic Inigo, Boscastle's scion with the pale blue Boscastle eyes handed down from generations of Boscastle Dukes. Were they thinking the same? That this scene would be re-enacted in variation three more times as each of them assumed the titles to which they'd been raised? They would all lose their fathers. It was an inherently deadly business being a duke's son.

The morbid aspect of that 'business' had Eaton staggering emotionally as much as the visceral quality of the murder had him reeling, along with the rest of the *haut ton*. If a duke could be murdered in cold blood at the theatre, no one was safe. People did not like reminders of their mortality. Rich people especially. It was a brutal prompt that not even piles of money could stop death. It was never a question of 'if', but merely 'when'. Just as long as it was not yet. He wasn't ready to lose his father. But this week had proven age was no barrier to death, to the ending of an existence. Life was finite.

Penlerick's death had been a wake-up call to the difficult knowledge that a man's legacies were all that would remain of him to remind others he'd been here on this earth. Eaton recognised that perhaps he felt the hard truth more keenly than the others. With the smallest amount of luck, his friends would eventually leave behind children, heirs to their legacies, while he would not. Ever. No amount of luck, large or small, would change that for him. His legacies would be of the inanimate sort: schools, hospitals, places that would continue to do good long after he'd left this life. But there would be no sons or daughters to tend them. It was a truth Eaton didn't enjoy facing. There'd always been time to delay facing it, but Richard Penlerick's death proved his logic had been faulty. Not even time was on his side.

Vennor raised his glass. 'A toast, to all of you and your support this week. I could not have borne up without it.' He nodded to each of his friends. 'Here's to friendship in good times and bad.'

They all drank and Eaton fetched the decanter to refill glasses. He poured another brandy for Vennor. It was better to stay busy in order to keep his thoughts from straying too darkly. This was what he did best— taking care of the others. It was what he'd always done. How ironic that that particular talent would not be lavished on a family of his own. 'You've done your duty splendidly this week, Ven. You can get tap-hackled to the gills now if you want. There's no one to see, no one to judge.' It would do Vennor good to get shamelessly drunk and let loose the emotions he'd kept on a tight rein since the news had come, but Eaton feared Vennor had other ideas.

Vennor shook his head. 'There's too much to do. Father had important legislation in the House of Lords. It would be a shame to see it falter now. I will take up his seat as soon as it's allowed. Until then, I mean to direct things from here so we don't miss a step. It will be my tribute to him.'

Eaton exchanged a worried look with Cassian. Going to work would only suppress the grief, ignoring it instead of dealing with it. Cassian leaned forward. 'Why don't you come to Cornwall with me and rusticate a bit in Truro? It's what everyone expects and it will get those matchmaking mamas off your back for a while. As you said, there is a period of mourning to observe—it would be entirely natural if you didn't take up the seat until next year.'

'*I* expect it of me,' Vennor cut in sharply. 'Besides, there's more than legislation to look after. If I am here, I can see justice done.'

'Justice or revenge?' Eaton questioned. In his opinion, Vennor needed distance from the crime if he was going to come to terms with his loss, not to immerse himself in it. 'You needn't interfere. The Watch will handle everything.'

'And I will handle the Watch,' Vennor answered firmly. 'I will find my parents' killers and bring them to justice.'

Eaton's gaze slipped unobtrusively around the circle gauging the group's reaction. He wasn't the only one concerned about Vennor's course of action. The thugs who had mindlessly murdered Newlyn and the Duchess had left behind no clue. They might never be caught. He didn't want Vennor disappointed. At what point did serving justice become an obsession? Would Vennor recognise that point when it arrived? How could he leave his friend alone to manage his grief, knowing that Vennor would obsess? Yet how could he stay away from Cornwall much longer? He had plans, too; his school, the musical conservatory, was set to open this autumn. His *legacy* was waiting. He'd not intended to stay in London long this year. He'd come up to town with the intention of supporting Marianne Treleven's debut as a family friend, and then returning to Porth Karrek immediately. But it only took one look at Vennor's face to make the decision to stay. His friend couldn't be left on his own or he'd work himself into oblivion.

'If that's what you're going to do, we'll stay with you.' Eaton scanned the group to see heads nodding in agreement. They would all put their plans on hold for their friend.

'No, that's not necessary,' Vennor argued. 'Eaton, your conservatory needs you. You cannot spare any more time away from home. I know what a sacrifice it would be for you, don't tell me otherwise. My father would not approve. He supported your school and he'd not want it delayed on his account. You've devoted the last five months to preparing—you even cancelled your trip to Italy and I know how much that meant to you.' Vennor shook his head. 'I won't have you throw it all over just to play nursemaid.' He fixed Cassian with a stern look. 'I won't have you staying either. You can't build your Cornish pleasure garden from London. Besides, your fathers will be here. I'll hardly be alone.'

It wasn't the same, though, Eaton thought. When grief closed in, Vennor would want a friend his own age, not his father's compatriots. Yet how like Vennor to think of others first. They all had their gifts and that was Vennor's. He understood people the way Inigo understood money: intuitively. But Vennor could not be allowed to win this argument.

Eaton was about to launch his rebuttal when Inigo settled it. 'We'll be here. Father and I have banking business. We would be staying regardless to see how Parliament handles some new investment legislation.'

'Inigo can stay. I will allow that. Are you satisfied, Eaton?' Vennor smiled his gratitude and the knot of worry in Eaton's gut eased. Inigo would look after their friend with the same dedication with which he did everything else.

In the wake of the decision, silence claimed the group. Brandy glasses were nearly empty again and the business of helping Vennor take on his ducal responsibilities was settled. Eaton was aware of the mantel clock ticking, loud and insistent, a reminder that it was time to move on, that there was nothing more that could be done now. It was time for the four friends to say goodbye and go their separate ways. He and Cassian would leave early tomorrow for their journey home to Cornwall. Inigo would settle back into his London habits. Vennor would establish new routines.

Nothing would be the same.

Vennor would be invested as a duke the next time they met, with the accompanying ducal responsibilities. Vennor would marry soon and that would change the equation entirely. This was a last moment, the ending of a chapter. Part of the adventure of living, Eaton supposed, although it didn't seem very adventurous at the moment. On the contrary, it seemed sad. Something was being mourned in this very room as they took another step deeper into adulthood, another step further away from their childhood. A piece of Eaton's soul rebelled at the notion. Hadn't he lost enough already? Need he lose that, too? But it was inevitable that he would. It was the way of life for dukes. His friends would marry in time, not only Vennor. Would they all still be close even when their affections were shared with another beyond their circle? When a wife and family claimed their attentions? Their fathers had managed it. But perhaps that was because they all had wives and family in common. Eaton would likely never marry. Would that decision make him an outsider? They would never intentionally exclude him, but it might happen accidentally.

Cassian shifted in his chair, casting a quizzing glance at Eaton. *What next?* They were all looking to him. He would have to be the one to do it. Among the four of them, he was the ringleader, the adventure master. A swift bolt of memory took him, of blue skies and rolling surf, of four boys who'd spent summers combing the Cornish beaches, playing at being smugglers, or pirates, sometimes soldiers fighting the French fleet, or treasure hunting. He remembered the summer he'd found the map, the last great summer before the trajectory and expectations of his life had subtly veered. Of course, the four of them had not known it would be their last, any more than Richard Penlerick had known when he'd sat down for breakfast a week ago that he'd not see his bed that night. It had been a good summer, full of real adventure, even if they'd never found the treasure. He must have led them through every tidal cave along the Porth Karrek beaches. There'd been bonfires and camp outs, nights of star gazing and the whispered secrets of newly minted adolescence. They had all looked to him then and they were looking to him now to take the next step, to help them say goodbye.

Eaton raised his glass, searching for words against the emotion crowding his throat. They needed hope right now, they needed to know that as much as things were about to change, the things that mattered would stay the same, a piece of constancy they could cling to in a world that only promised uncertainty. He was suddenly hungry to be home at Falmage Hill, home in Porth Karrek surrounded by the familiar: his new school, his orangery, his favourite paths in the Trevaylor Woods, his science experiments, his hound, Baldor. He'd been gone too long. 'It's time, gentlemen. A last drink for the road. If there's one lesson this week has taught us, it's that life is surprising and short. We are guaranteed nothing. We already drank to the past, let us now drink to the future. Here's to our pursuits. May all of them be served through the best of our efforts in the time that we have. My friends, here's to making every minute count.' Especially when every minute was all one had.

Chapter One

Porth Karrek, Cornwall—September 1823

Every minute mattered now that the school's opening was upon them. Eaton pushed up his sleeves and gripped the oak table. At the other end, his headmaster, the renowned composer Cador Kitto, gave a nod and, with a mutual grunt, they lifted the heavy table. Around them, workmen painted and swept with feverish urgency. School began in three days and some students would arrive early to be on hand for the open house in two. The past few days it had been all hands on deck, even his—*especially* his. Eaton didn't believe in leading idly. He refused to stand back, shouting orders to others, without lending his own efforts to the project. Besides, staying busy made it possible to forget other unpleasant realisations, albeit temporarily; that Richard Penlerick was dead, life was short and there was nothing he could do about either.

They manoeuvred the table into place at the front of

the room and set it down with a relieved thud. Damn, but good oak was heavy. Eaton swiped at his brow and Cador laughed. Eaton groaned. 'Did I just smear dirt across my forehead?'

'Yes, but no matter. There are no ladies about to see you.' Cador winked.

'Just for that, you can unpack the books.' Eaton chuckled.

'Oh, no, I've got instruments to oversee.' Cador wiped his hands and nodded towards the door at the arrival of Eaton's secretary. 'Looks like you've got business to attend to.'

Eaton turned, stifling a sigh. He far preferred physical labour to the never-ending tedium of paperwork, especially when there was so much to get done, so much to forget. It was too easy for his mind to wander into difficult territory when he was doing paperwork. He found a smile; it wasn't the secretary's fault. 'What is it, Johns?'

'There's someone asking to see you, my lord.' Johns was young, hired to help with the record-keeping and correspondence at the school, and today he looked every inch of his mere twenty years. Johns shifted from foot to foot, his cheeks tinged a fading pink which Eaton didn't think was due to the exertion of the stairs. Whoever was waiting had been quite insistent.

'Do they have an appointment?' Eaton looked about for a rag to wipe his hands on. Johns would have to learn how to be a better gatekeeper.

'No, my lord.'

'Has one of the boys arrived early?' Eaton gave up

on a rag. His mind was already working through options. There were rooms ready on the third floor if needed and the cook could be called in to prepare food a day earlier than planned, although provisions weren't expected to arrive until tomorrow…

Johns cleared his throat. 'It's one of the patrons, my lord. One of the widows.' Johns's tone was urgent now. Some of the insistence that had been pressed upon him by the unexpected visitor was now being relayed.

Eaton relaxed, although he did wonder what had upset his secretary. Two of the school's patrons were wealthy widows and he couldn't imagine either of them being the source of such angst. 'Is it Mrs Penhaligon? Has she come to see that her piano is properly installed?' Austol Penhaligon's widow had donated her expensive Sébastien Érard double action keyboard piano, much to Cador's delight. The other, a Mrs Blaxland, was an extraordinarily rich woman from Truro, whom Eaton had never met. He'd assumed her age, which must be considerable, had brought about an inability to travel. Her husband, Huntingdon Blaxland, had been sixty-five when he died and that had been five years ago. She likely let her money do the travelling for her these days. Thanks to her generous donations, the boys would have the finest music instructors Cador Kitto had been able to find, acquired from the Continent on his summer honeymoon.

Soft fabric rustled behind Johns, giving Eaton his only warning before no-nonsense female tones announced, 'No, not Mrs Penhaligon, I'm afraid.' Apple-green skirts and shiny chestnut hair swept past Johns with an imperious air that smelled of peach orchards and vanilla, the very best and last of summer. 'I'm Eliza Blaxland.' She ran a gloved hand along the surface of the oak table, collecting dust on the pristine tip of one finger. 'And you, Lord Lynford, have some accounting to do.'

Eaton gave her an assessing stare. *This* haughty virago was Eliza Blaxland? What had the elderly mining magnate been doing with a woman like her? She was no frail grey-haired widow, practising philanthropy from her armchair. This was an elegant, sophisticated woman in her early thirties with decades of life and fire still left to her, a woman who valued being in control. If so, she'd have to adjust. He was more than happy to take her money for the school, but not her orders. He was the Marquess of Lynford and his deference was given sparingly. He could not be bought, nor could he be intimidated. 'Accounting, Mrs Blaxland? In what way? I was unaware we had an appointment, let alone any accounting to do.' He was usually the one who did the intimidating. How interesting that she thought the interaction might go differently. She needed to learn that her cheques did not allow her carte blanche in the school and that included showing up two days early for the open house.

She was not daunted by his cool reception. Instead, she returned his assessing stare with one of her own, making him acutely aware that she was entirely his antithesis. While he stood before her sans waistcoat, jacket and cravat, shirtsleeves wrinkled and rolled with a belatedly remembered smudge of dirt on his forehead, *she* was all elegant summer perfection in her apple-green walking ensemble of India muslin, matched head to toe from the brim of her green-crepe chapeau Lyonnaise to the peeping toes of her green half-boots. 'I disagree. You are two days from opening and this place is a madhouse.' She held up the dusty finger of her glove in reminder. 'My money did not pay for chaos.'

Eaton summoned up a smile from his repertoire, the one known for successfully impressing older, more conservative women who occasionally found his love of adventure a tad too liberal—until they tried it for themselves. 'I assure you, all will be in order for the open house.' She was not convinced. Her gaze roved about the room, taking in the painters, the movers, the sweepers, casting doubt and disappointment wherever her eyes landed. Eaton grimaced. He needed to get her out of this room. There were plenty of spaces that were finished. It was too bad she hadn't found him in one of those. 'Might I offer you a tour, Mrs Blaxland?' The woman was likely to poke her nose into all the rooms on her own—at least this way he could keep an eye on her. He could control a tour, although it would cost him an hour of work to squire her around. Still, better an hour of work lost than a lucrative patron. Disappointed patrons often bred other disappointed patrons. 'On our tour, we can discuss whatever it is you're doing here.' It was a subtle reminder that she was the one in the wrong, the one who'd shown up uninvited.

He gestured to Cade, giving her no chance to refuse. 'Let's start with an introduction to our headmaster, Cador Kitto, lately from Vienna. He's composed at the Hapsburg court.'

Cade, with his wavy blond locks and Continental élan, bowed over her gloved hand with a courtly aplomb that made Eaton envious of the man's slender elegance. 'A pleasure to meet you at last, Mrs Blaxland. Our students will benefit greatly from your patronage.' A little dose of Cade could go a long way in smoothing ruffled feathers—at least that was what Eaton was hoping for, particularly when he didn't know what had ruffled her feathers in the first place.

'What you describe as chaos, Mrs Blaxland, I consider progress. Allow me to show you.' They left Cade and the busyness of the classroom behind. He toured her through the students' rooms on the third floor, showing her chambers with neatly made beds, braided rugs, dust-free wardrobes and bright white curtains hanging at the windows. The rooms smelled of lemon polish and linseed oil. 'Mr Kitto's wife designed the dorms,' Eaton explained, making no effort to hide his pride. 'She believes the homelier the place feels, the more comfortable the boys will be here.'

'And the less likely they will be to leave,' Mrs Blaxland translated in more blunt terms. 'Tell me, how is enrolment? Do we have enough boys to fill these chambers?'

Eaton shut the last door behind them and directed her back towards the staircase. 'We have two-thirds of the rooms accounted for, which I think is excellent for a first semester.' Twenty-one boys ranging in age from seven to fourteen would be arriving the day after the open house. 'Once word spreads regarding the quality of student and the superiority of musical education we offer at the Cornish Academy, we will reach capacity soon enough,' he assured her, but her sharp green eyes met his assurances with questions.

'Do you have quality students?' she asked pointedly. 'I think the challenge of such a school is not the idea of it, but the location, as I've mentioned before in correspondence. Why would a person of any talent want to travel to the wilds of Cornwall for a musical education when one could be in London? Or go abroad? I fear those who have choices will not choose the academy at Porth Karrek.'

She was bold-tongued, her comments blunt and bordering on rude. Perhaps that was simply how it was in business circles where money mattered more than manners. Eaton chose to be impressed with her analysis rather than offended by the implication that the academy would only be capable of drawing mediocre students.

'The talent you seek will come if you and the other patrons tell them to. Quality enrolment is all of our obligation.' Richard Penlerick had been adamant on that issue. He'd been promoting the academy in London just days before the murder. 'One cannot simply throw money at a project and expect that to be enough to ensure success.' The words came out harshly against the sudden tightness of Eaton's throat, but he wouldn't apologise for them. If Eliza Blaxland took his response as a scolding, then so be it. He wasn't entirely sure he didn't mean it as one. He was the son and heir of a wealthy family. If it had only been about money, he could easily have bankrolled the school entirely by himself. He didn't need patrons' funds the way a struggling orphanage in St Giles did. He needed the names and reputations behind the funds.

Eaton cleared his throat and offered Richard Penlerick's often-voiced sentiment. 'The quality of our students will depend on the quality of our patrons. That is why I sought you out in particular. You are well known in Cornish circles for your appreciation of education.' Even if those circles had failed to convey how young she was.

At the bottom of the stairs he showed her into the drawing room where the Sébastien Érard piano stood in pride of place. 'This is where our recitals will be held. Mr Kitto will perform at the open house, of course.' He smiled, reminding her he'd done his part in securing a well-known musician for headmaster, one with a name that would draw talented students.

He allowed her to appraise the Sébastien Érard with her sharp eyes before he got to the heart of the matter. 'Surely all of this checking up could have been handled at the open house. Why have you really come, Mrs Blaxland?' Did she have a student she was hoping to get admitted? Did she have an instructor who needed to be hired? Whoever they were, they would have to earn their place here, no matter how much money she donated. Kitto wanted only the best. They wouldn't attract the best if they took in just anyone.

She gave him a polite smile he did not mistake for friendliness, although it did serve to warm him none the less. 'I have found in the years of running my late husband's mines that scheduled appointments can often result in misleading impressions. When one arrives unannounced, one sees a clearer representation of the truth.' She was already a fortress of perfection in her dress and in her speech, but in her directness she was nigh on impenetrable. Eaton felt the urge to penetrate that directness, to lay siege to its walls.

'You mean an ambush, Mrs Blaxland?' Sparring with her was quite a warming exercise indeed. A part of him that had been dormant since returning from London was waking up.

'An ambush assumes someone can be taken by surprise, that someone lets his guard down,' she countered smoothly. 'If one is always prepared, one cannot be caught unawares.'

When was the last time Eliza Blaxland had been taken unawares? From her cool façade, he would guess it had been a while, if ever. It was hard to imagine anyone got anything past her. Eaton would take that as a challenge—not that he wanted to take advantage, but he would like to surprise her, just to prove to her that it could be done. How would she react when things were out of her control?

He studied the flawless perfection of her face, its smooth contours with its elegantly set nose, green eyes and that mouth—that gorgeous pink mouth with its full, kissable lower lip. His gaze lingered there while his thoughts drifted. What would bring a crease to those perfect features? What might fluster her well-ordered world? Had old Huntingdon Blaxland ever flustered her, aside, perhaps, from dying? Would a kiss be enough to offset that world? She was a widow, after all. He could presume she'd been kissed before. Would she like to be kissed again? He found he would like to pursue that course of action. Between Richard Penlerick's death and the school, it had been a while since he'd felt a spark of interest.

They were hardly the thoughts one ought to have about a wealthy patroness, yet when the patroness was so aloofly, coolly attractive, it seemed a natural progression of thought to wonder, what if? They returned to the main hall, the front door just feet away, providing a less-than-subtle opportunity to bid Mrs Blaxland farewell and get on with his day. 'If there's nothing else, I'll leave you here. As you have already ascertained, there's much to be done.'

'There is one more thing.' She gave him another long perusing stare with those intelligent eyes. 'I thought you'd be older. I was unaware Bude's heir was so…young.' She was implying that perhaps he might not be up to the task of overseeing a school, that a man of his age and station was better suited to the frivolous pursuits of London.

'Twenty-eight is young?' he queried with a sardonic cock of a dark brow. It was an odd remark coming from a woman who couldn't be more than thirty-three, but time and age were different for females. 'It's been some time since anyone has thought of me as young. Good day, Mrs Blaxland. I will look forward to seeing you at the reception.' He gave her a small bow in farewell. 'I assure you that you needn't worry. I am in my prime.' He'd been unable to resist the final remark. Intuition suggested that no one teased Mrs Blaxland and someone ought to. People didn't build impregnable fortresses around themselves without reason. He was intrigued as to what her reason might be.

'You most certainly are,' she acknowledged with a slight, indifferent nod of her head, but beneath that cool exterior, something akin to interest sizzled and flared in her gaze before it was snuffed out by practice and perhaps practicality. But it was too late. Eaton smiled over his little victory. She'd already given herself away. Eliza Blaxland wasn't as unaffected or as distant as she appeared.

Chapter Two

It had been a long time since she'd been surprised—not since the day Huntingdon had left for the office and never returned. Five years, eight months and three weeks, to be precise. Eliza sat back against the leather squabs of her coach and let out a deep sigh. In the intervening years, she'd become used to being the one doing the surprising; she'd had to if she meant to keep the shareholders on their toes. But Eaton Falmage, Marquess of Lynford, heir to the ducal seat of Bude, had done all the surprising this afternoon. The ambush had been her idea, hers to control, but she'd not been prepared for *him*. Eliza reached for her fan. From the first glance of his dark eyes, his heat had nearly incinerated her glacial cool.

Years of practice had made her confident in the belief that her skills would rise to any challenge, that her icy façade could not be cracked, that she was impervious to the powers of men. Lynford had challenged her today, though, not only as a patron, but as a woman.

The former, she could deal with. Patronage was simply one of many business arrangements she conducted. The latter, however, well…that was different. She hadn't been a woman—a real woman with real feelings and affections—since the day her husband died. For her daughter's sake and her own sake, she couldn't afford to indulge such a fancy.

When men looked at her, they saw a female facsimile—one that dressed elegantly, spoke with cultured tones, and danced divinely; one they often sought to possess—but the illusion fell away when she sat across from them at the boardroom table and delivered her verdicts in those cultured tones. Some men called her a snake in the grass, a viper waiting to strike, others called her a Siren, luring men to smash themselves against the icy granite of her façade. But today, Lynford had been formidable, a veritable Odysseus, undaunted by her surprise visit and undaunted by her.

She wished she could say the same. Eliza plied the fan a little faster. He was not only younger than she'd anticipated, he was also younger than *her* by five years. He was taller, broader, endowed with dark eyes that looked into a person's gaze and long, powerful legs. Oh, how she loved a good pair of legs on a man and his had been on blatant display with no coats to hide them. In fact, his tight breeches and open-necked shirt had hidden nothing. He'd been in utter, unmistakable déshabillé, yet he'd not once apologised for his appearance or attempted to cover it up. The primal woman in her, so rarely unleashed, had rattled the bars of her cage, thrilling at the masculinity on show, a reminder that she wasn't dead after all. It was an uncomfortable revelation.

Eliza closed her eyes. It had been so long since she'd felt anything akin to desire, or its milder counterpart, attraction. What a shock to discover it after five years of sexless living where she didn't dare act either too much of a man or too much like a woman for fear she would be ridiculed for overstepping herself or taken advantage of for *being* herself. But what a most inopportune time for that discovery. She would have preferred Lynford to be a man nearing middle age, bearing a paunch at his stomach and silver at his temples with a conservative, tired air about him. She knew how to manage those men.

Her husband had been such a man, thirty-seven years older than she when they wed. Those men populated the Blaxland Mining Corporation board of shareholders, but Lynford exuded alertness, energy, a fresh boldness. He thought himself infallible and perhaps rightly so. He was a duke's son. He was used to asserting himself, used to ordering the world according to his desire. He was not a businessman, a man like her husband had been, who limited the scope of his world to balance sheets. And Lynford, unlike her husband, was most definitely in his prime.

She had no such experience with a man like that: a man who looked at women and openly admired their beauty, a man who didn't patronise, a man who matched her directness with his own. Nor could she allow herself to acquire such an experience.

The one flicker of attraction she'd felt today had

been nice in its own way, a reminder that she was more than a moneymaking automaton, but she could not fan it into anything resembling a flame. She had a daughter to raise and mines to run, her husband's legacy to preserve so that her daughter would never know want and penury as she had simply because she'd been born female. Such pursuits did not leave room for passion. Such a task required that she walk a tightrope. One false step and all she'd worked for and all she envisioned for the future could be so easily lost.

Neither did such a pursuit serve her as a patron for the school. She hoped by donating generously to his school, in return, Lynford would support her bid for establishing schools for children in the villages up and down the coast wherever there was a Blaxland mine. To mix business with fleeting pleasure could jeopardise that connection.

Hence the reason for her visit today—to see if Lynford was worth the investment. Could he get the job done, or was he another lazy dilettante? She wanted to see that everything was well in hand for the opening reception. She would do her part to make sure the conservatory succeeded. Her own plans depended on it, as did keeping her own reputation intact. The trust of her shareholders was essential now as the Porth Karrek mine prepared for expansion. She'd learned early on after taking the reins of her husband's business that one could never have too many friends, but a woman could have too many lovers—even just a single lover was often one lover too many. A misguided affair at this juncture could cost her everything, just as it had her mother, a widow left with a daughter and a fortune and no sense about how to manage the latter.

The outcome had been obvious: her mother and her money had been soon parted thanks to an affair that had blinded her to the incompetence of her lover. Eliza had been fourteen when that had happened and she'd vowed she would never put her heart above money. Nor would she put herself in a position where money wasn't readily available. She'd set out the next day to learn all she could about managing funds, starting with the bookkeeper for the family's mine. Knowledge was power. She believed that education could keep the wolf from the door and it could buy her independence so that she needn't rely singularly on a marriage to save her. There were too many women like her mother who hadn't a clue how to manage their own freedom, who needed men. Eliza was determined to avoid her mother's mistakes. This time, for this woman, Eliza vowed it would be different. She was far too astute to fall prey to the charms of a handsome lord.

Two days later, the Academy Open House

This time, it would be different. Eliza entered the conservatory's drawing room with that mantra firmly entrenched in her mind. Tonight, she would be ready for the oh-so-attractive Eaton Falmage. His good looks and confident manner would not catch her by surprise. She knew what to expect now and this time they wouldn't be alone—a point emphasised as soon as she arrived. The room was practically a crush and a very well-dressed one at that, with men in dark evening clothes and women in silks populating every corner of the grand salon. It was a far more robust turnout for the academy's opening than she'd anticipated. This was no mere gathering of a board of directors and a few patrons. But then, perhaps the outstanding attendance stood to reason. When a duke's heir gave a party, everyone wanted an invitation.

Eliza unfurled her fan and began to stroll about the room, looking purposeful. No one need pity her aloneness. She'd made an art of it. Over the years, she'd become accustomed to attending events on her own and others had become accustomed to it, too. She arrived alone, she left alone. She'd learned not to be afraid of her own company. She actually rather enjoyed it. There was no conversation to worry over, no egos to flatter or polite compliments to muster. She could survey her surroundings at leisure, study her options and make her own choices as to how she spent her time and who she spent it with. At the moment she wanted to spend that time with Lynford. Congratulations were in order. A private smile skimmed her lips in satisfaction as she assessed her surroundings. Lynford had succeeded against what had looked like overwhelming odds. One would never guess that two days ago the place had been in varying states of chaos.

Eliza scanned the room, her gaze glancing over the masculine decor done to perfection in shades of muted teal and beige against a backdrop of walnut panelling and chair rail that ran the perimeter, interrupted only by a bank of French doors opening to the gardens beyond where paper lanterns winked. She made a mental note of the gardens—those gardens might provide a convenient escape from the crowd should she need it.

Her gaze hurried on, still seeking as it brushed over the multi-armed brass chandelier at the ceiling, the coveted Sébastien Érard, lid raised, at the front of the room—neither item enough to halt her rampant gaze. These were not the things she was looking for. She'd nearly completed her visual circuit of the room when she found him at last, standing at the fireplace, just feet from the Sébastien Érard. It was time to test her hypothesis.

The fan in her hand halted its oscillation, her mind flooding with a certain sense of satisfaction. *He* was what she'd been looking for. Lynford stood in profile, talking with a group of men, all dressed alike in dark evening clothes, yet he was no more like them than the sun was like the moon. She knew instantly her mantra was wrong. This time was *not* going to be different after all, unless one counted the fact that Lynford was fully clothed. He was no less handsome for the more formal attire. Eliza began to ply her fan in earnest.

His dark, tangled curls were tamed tonight, carefully styled into compliance, perhaps painstakingly so given the extent of their unruliness the other day. His jaw was smooth-shaven, setting off the strong planes of his face, the wide, almost simian flare of his nose, the broad, high sweep of his cheekbones beneath his dark eyes; in his face, the elegant classical construction was unabashedly at war with the harsh masculinity of his primeval ancestors. In evening clothes, the result was devastating. He stood out, a powerful stallion among the herd, a man born to lead no matter what his age.

Tonight, authority's mantle sat comfortably on his broad shoulders, not an ounce of that breadth fabricated, even if the rest of his body gave the impression of wanting to be out of doors tramping the moors and cliffs of Porth Karrek. His was not an indoor physique. Not that she should be assessing such things. Her attendance at the conservatory's opening reception tonight was all business and business did not mix with pleasure. *Ever.* Hadn't her experience with Miles Detford taught her that much? She had too much to keep her busy between the mines and the school. She could not allow herself to be distracted with useless speculation about the Marquess of Lynford. She certainly could not allow herself to be caught staring. He might interpret a stare as interest.

Too late. She didn't look away soon enough. Lynford caught her gaze and returned it with a wide smile, broad like his shoulders and just as genuine, the kind one gives when one is truly pleased to see someone. That worried her. After their last visit, why would he be pleased to see her? She watched in horrified fascination as he excused himself from the group gathered at the fireplace and moved towards her. There was no escaping; she was well and truly flushed out. What could he possibly want? She should be annoyed by the thought that he'd demand anything of her, but there was only intrigue where annoyance ought to be—another reminder that she was very much alive and very much a woman.

He snared two glasses of champagne from a passing tray as he approached. 'Mrs Blaxland, it's so good to see you.' He offered her a glass, his smile unwavering. 'I trust everything meets with your approval. No dust on the tables. Your gloves will be spared this evening.' She had the sensation that Lynford was laughing at her, that there was a private jest, some innuendo involved.

'I've only just arrived.' Her cool tone insinuated there was still time to be disappointed. Would he let her have the lie? Or would he make her accountable for the shameful truth: that she'd been there long enough to take notice of things and the only thing she'd noticed was him? Eliza sipped her champagne, thankful to have something to do other than admit he'd trapped all her attention, that for all her earlier concern about the state of the school, she'd given the issue only the smallest fraction of her attention, while her gaze had raced around the room, gliding over the details in its hurry to find him. Even in a room full of men, all clad similarly, he'd managed to stand out, managed to capture her eye *and* her thoughts to the exclusion of all else. That was a dangerous position to be in. It made her vulnerable. It was time to go on the offensive.

'Whatever you want from me, you must want it badly, given your champagne and your smiles, Lord Lynford. So, let's have it.' She gave him a smile of her own, one full of directness.

'Ah, you like champagne. Duly noted. I shall make a note.' He smiled wickedly. Lynford *liked* the edge. She'd not expected that. She'd meant for it to be off-putting, but instead a spark leapt in his dark eyes.

'What makes you think I want anything other than your approval?' he drawled.

She laughed at that. 'My approval or my acquiescence? You will not get the latter. If you are looking for it, then you misunderstood my concerns the other day. I was worried you might not finish your preparations in time, *not* that I wanted you to fail.' Eliza tapped his sleeve with her fan. 'I have every hope this school will succeed. I do not sign on to doomed ventures.' True, she had wondered if he could do it, if he could bring everything together in time. But she'd not wanted him to fail. Failure did not suit her purpose. 'This school may be the touchstone. Perhaps people will see the value in other types of schools. I've been contemplating opening grammar schools for my miners' children so that they might grow up with the opportunity to develop a broader range of skills than their parents.' She paused here, wondering briefly if she should go on. Not everyone shared her views, not even her own board. 'And with those skills, have more choices about how to make their living.'

Lynford's eyes were two thoughtful dark stars. For a moment, she feared she'd offended him. What would a ducal heir think about empowering miners with education? Would he even understand the necessity? Perhaps she'd overplayed her hand? But Lynford nodded and smiled, his dark gaze intent. 'I would enjoy speaking about the subject further, Mrs Blaxland.' He clinked his glass against hers. 'Here's to successful ventures in all their forms. Speaking of which, you might be able to aid our cause tonight.'

Ah, there it was. The real reason for his approach. Eliza stiffened in anticipation. Her instincts had not been wrong. He did want something, but she owed him. If he hadn't called her out on her lie, she couldn't call him out on his. 'I was hoping you would say a few words tonight as one of our most generous donors.'

A speech? She sipped her champagne, her mouth suddenly dry despite the cool liquid. He wanted *her* to make a speech? Of all the cruel and unusual punishments she could think of, this was by far the worst. 'A speech?' She choked on the idea.

'It's hardly Pericles' Funeral Oration, Mrs Blaxland, just a few words. Something like, welcome to the school, we are so excited to begin this venture, etcetera, and then lead in to an introduction of Mr Kitto, who will perform afterwards.' *And* he wanted her to introduce the famous Mr Kitto, a man she'd briefly met once? It was as if Lynford had looked into her soul and pulled out her worst fear. She could face down a boardroom full of stockholders, she could stand her ground against men who didn't think a woman could do successful business in their world, but speaking before a crowd without preparation was entirely different. There would be no heat of the moment guiding the interaction. A speech was a planned, formal affair. People would be staring at her—*a lot* of people—and they would be judging every word, every gesture. She'd spent years earning the right *not* to be judged.

'You *are* prepared for such a contingency, aren't you?' Lynford solicited. 'Surely, as our largest benefactor, you've anticipated such a request? I have it on good authority that preparation is the best protection against surprise.'

There was an echo of their previous interaction in his words and she knew: this was tit for tat.

This was an ambush.

Chapter Three

Eliza studied Lynford, seeing his gambit all too clearly now. 'Is this revenge, Lord Lynford?'

He grinned, mischief lighting his eyes. 'This is just business, Mrs Blaxland. Something akin to unplanned visits, I am sure you understand.' He relieved her of her empty glass and deposited it on a passing tray with his before offering his arm. 'I would like to introduce you to a few of the board members, some of our parents whose sons will perform tonight and our other donors.'

'You need a hostess,' Eliza quickly deduced. It was a large request that looked much smaller when compared to giving a speech. Perhaps he'd planned it that way, knowing she'd be less likely to refuse. She'd often used that same strategy with her shareholders when asking for an approval of funds.

'Mr Kitto's wife, Rosenwyn, was to play hostess, but she's indisposed,' Lynford explained with a melting smile. 'These events need a woman's presence to smooth out conversations between strangers.' She'd not meant to draw attention to herself tonight. Playing hostess and making a speech would put her at the centre of the festivities. Still, she could turn this to her benefit. His introductions would pave the way for other discussions she wanted to have later about schools for the miners' children. She caught sight of Cador Kitto's blond head, a trail of students behind him with instruments, and her pulse sped up. It was almost time for the programme, almost time for her speech.

She was going to make Lynford pay for this.

'Shall we?' Lynford steered her towards the front of the room where the new students and Kitto were settling into position.

'Are you sure there isn't someone else who should speak?' She tried to avoid it one last time. 'Perhaps Mr Burke?' He'd been a pleasant, well-spoken man in the last group they'd visited and another generous benefactor of the school.

Lynford shook his head and gave her one of his disarming smiles. He'd been using them liberally tonight with the guests, but that made them no less effective. 'No, I want *you* to do it.' She knew what that meant: an ambush for an ambush. He covered her gloved hand where it lay on his sleeve and gave it a conspiratorial squeeze. 'You will do wonderfully.' He leaned in, giving her a teasing whiff of clean, autumn male, the woodsy scent of English oak mixed with the sweeter note of hazelnut. Good lord, that scent was intoxicating. It reminded her of strength, of bonfires beneath starry skies when she was younger, when she didn't carry the world on her shoulders, when autumn was a time to laugh and dream. His voice was a husky whisper at her ear, a tone better reserved for the bedroom. 'I have every confidence in you. You are not a woman who knows how to fail, Mrs Blaxland.' Then he slipped away from her, his long strides taking him to the front of the room, the very presence of him compelling people to quiet their conversations, to find a seat and anticipate what came next.

She envied him his confidence, the ease with which it was assumed whereas hers was a hard-earned façade; once acquired, she had dared not lay it down for fear she might never be able to pick it up again. This was not the life Huntingdon had imagined for her, but this was the life she had, the life she'd chosen out of necessity.

At twenty-eight, she'd gone from running their home to running a mining empire, from sponsoring parties to sponsoring schools and other educational causes. If there was one thing the past five years had taught her, it was that education was everything. She'd transitioned into her husband's position only because she'd had the skills to do it. She could read, she could write, she could do sums, she could keep a ledger and myriad other things. She could think critically and she'd spent her marriage listening, learning and planning ahead against the inevitable: an eighteen-year-old bride would doubtless outlive her fifty-five-year-old husband. The majority of her life would be spent in widowhood. The only question was when it would happen and what she'd do about it.

That foresight had stood her in good stead. If this life was not the one imagined for her, it was a far better one than what she would have had. Without those skills, she would have been passed from relative to relative; her husband's legacy, his mines and her daughter Sophie's inheritance would have been taken out of her hands and put into the care of an apathetic male relative. She'd seen it happen to women around her, women like her mother, who lost everything when their husbands died, even the very control of their own lives. When Huntingdon had died, she'd reaffirmed her vow that would not happen to her. She would secure her freedom at all costs and her daughter's, too. Now that she had, she would see to it that others had the opportunity to develop the same skills.

Lynford finished speaking and gestured that she should come forward. She rose and smoothed her skirts, her head high. She wouldn't let anyone see how this unnerved her. Lynford was right. She didn't know how to fail. She knew how to fight. That gave them something in common. He no more wanted to see her fail in this speech than she'd wanted him to fail in having the school ready. It occurred to her, as she stood before the guests, that she and Lynford were compatriots whether they wanted to be or not. Philanthropy, like politics, made for strange bedfellows indeed.

She was magnificent. Eaton listened to Eliza Blaxland address the guests, her cultured tones confident and strong. He watched her, looking for little tells that hinted at her nerves and finding none. Still, he stood on guard, feeling protective, as if he had the right to defend her, to intervene if she faltered. But she didn't falter. He suspected she didn't know how. It was not in her nature. Eliza Blaxland was all cool competence in her dark blue silk and pearls, her shiny chestnut hair dressed simply, elegantly, in a braid that coiled at the nape of her neck. If he hadn't seen the initial flicker of uncertainty in her eyes when he'd asked her, he never would have known she didn't welcome such opportunities.

What else didn't he know about her? What he thought he knew of her up until two days ago had been entirely wrong. An *old* rich woman, she was not. He found the prospect of righting those misnomers intriguing. He'd known widows before—women with a sharp worldliness to them—but they'd not got under his skin so quickly. Or ever. Who was Eliza Blaxland? Was she truly all cool smiles and sharp eyes, or did something hotter burn beneath that smooth, uncrackable façade, waiting for a reason to come out?

She was introducing Cade now, taking the opportunity to cede the room's attention to the school's headmaster and his musicians. When the applause began, she attempted to slip away to the gardens. If Eaton hadn't been watching, he would have missed her. Seeing her go only made him impatient to follow her out. But it would be bad form to leave before Cade got the little concert underway. Was she counting on that? Was she hoping to slip away before he could find her? Did she think to hide from him, or was this an invitation to join her? Perhaps she wanted him to follow?

Eaton took the first chance he had to drift towards the French doors and then fade unnoticed into the gardens, aware he might be too late. An initial sweep of the garden suggested he was right, but a second survey revealed her, sitting on a stone bench, face tilted to the night sky in lovely profile. 'Are you avoiding me or waiting for me?' Eaton approached from behind, his voice low. 'I thought for a moment you might have played Cinderella and slipped away before I could follow. What are you doing out here?' It was a bold question, one that demanded a direct answer in return. But why not be bold? She was not afraid of him. Even now, alone in the garden, her widowhood protected her reputation and granted her the freedom to respond as she liked.

With that freedom, she might take a lover. Had she? Would she? Did she have a lover now? A man who knew the truth behind her façade, who was allowed the luxury of seeing her without her cool armour. Eaton found the prospect disappointing. He didn't want Mrs Blaxland to belong to someone else. He didn't want someone else to know what he did not. There was that sense of exigence again, the same urgency he'd felt in the drawing room while watching her slip away. Wanting to know her, to obtain information about her had escalated from merely acquiring facts to something bordering on obsession. He wanted to acquire her. She would be a delicious distraction from the darkness that had dogged his steps since Penlerick's funeral. Perhaps she would be someone who could bring him back to life, someone who could hold his grief at bay.

It would not be the first time he'd taken a lover for such a purpose. His own lovers were women of the world who enjoyed time with him until it suited them both to move on to new experiences, new adventures. But it was the first time he'd wanted to do so with such covetousness. It was not the usual reaction he generally had towards his lovers. The intensity of that emotion must have showed in his gaze for in the next moment, Eliza Blaxland suddenly rose and made excuses to leave with far less fluency than she'd delivered her speech. 'I ought to go, it's getting late.'

Was she looking for an invitation to stay? It didn't sound like a question. It sounded like a decision. He hadn't believed she'd be a runner, but she showed every sign of wanting to do just that. How interesting. If she wasn't running from him, that only left the option of running from herself. Was she running from her reaction to the attraction that simmered between them? Did this flame that sparked between them unnerve her? How intriguing that the unflappable Mrs Blaxland could be unnerved by the nascent overtures of a flirtation when barging in on a man unannounced hadn't flustered her at all. But she'd been in control then. She'd been the one to do the barging.

'Leave? Surely you don't mean to return to Truro tonight?' The protectiveness he'd felt in the grand salon surged again. He didn't like the thought of her out on the dark Cornish roads. It was three hours on the road in daylight between Truro and Porth Karrek. A man could do the trip in a day on horseback, but it was a long day and a lonely one. Cornwall was full of wide, empty spaces, especially when one's wheel or axle gave out. She'd be miles from any help if there was need.

'I have rooms at the inn by the harbour. I need to visit one of my mines early tomorrow and then return to Truro. I've been gone from home for three days already and I am eager to return. Thank you for the evening.' Such eagerness prompted the question of who or what was waiting for her? A lover? Was she already otherwise engaged? Was that the reason she was so fluttery now? Covetousness flared alongside his protectiveness.

'Perhaps I shall see you in Truro. I often have business there.' Eaton thought he might find a little more business in Truro. Cassian was in Truro, working on plans for his amusement gardens. Perhaps a visit was in order once the term started here and Cade no longer needed him. 'Or should I be expecting any more surprise inspections?'

Her fan tapped his sleeve. 'They wouldn't be surprises if you expected them, my lord.'

'Call me Eaton, please. There's no need to stand on ceremony.' He made the bold offer spontaneously, his earlier urgency surging to the fore once more. He did not want to be 'my lord' or 'Lord Lynford' with her; he wanted to be something more intimate, more personal, something that would separate him from any other who attempted to claim her attentions. It was the fanciful wish of a schoolboy with a crush. He reached for her hand, bending over it. 'You were a delightful hostess tonight, surely you've earned the right to address me more informally.' He could count on one hand the people who had that right: Cassian, Inigo, Vennor, their fathers, of course. He didn't need both hands for that count now. He pushed back the grief that managed to edge its way to the surface at the oddest times and in the oddest ways.

'I was pleased to be of service. I hope the term begins splendidly. I'll be looking forward to Mr Kitto's reports on the students' progress. If weather permits, I might make the journey for the Christmas concert.'

He doubted her on both accounts. 'Don't lie to me, Mrs Blaxland. You did not want to give that speech tonight and the weather in December is too questionable.'

'I was being polite.' She withdrew her hand in a deliberate gesture.

'I prefer you be honest.' Eaton felt disappointed at the prospect of her leaving. How could he unravel her mysteries if she was three hours away? Already he was devising reasons why he might call her back. He might need her counsel on the school, for instance; they might want to discuss her own schools in person rather than through correspondence and, when that was done, he might take her truffle hunting in the Trevaylor Woods. Eaton leaned close, breathing in the peach-and-vanilla summer scent of her, his mouth near her ear as if imparting a secret. 'And in the spirit of being honest, Eliza, I find you to be a complete revelation.'

'I assure you, I am quite ordinary.' But the words pleased her. He heard her breath catch despite her cool response and she hadn't corrected him on the use of her first name, proof that this encounter, this response, was not ordinary for her, that *he* was not ordinary to her.

'Then we must agree to disagree since I find nothing plain about you.' Eaton let his gaze hold her eyes, let her see the interest she raised in him. They were both experienced adults. They needn't play coy games. He would be honest, too. He did not want the conversation to end. 'I've been wrong about you from the start. I thought you'd be older.' He gave a low chuckle. 'It seems we have that mistake in common.'

'My husband was considerably older than I. It is a common assumption.'

'If you'd not come to the open house, I might never have known.'

'What difference did my age make when we corresponded about the school? What difference did my age make to my donations? My age is of no import.'

'Huntingdon Blaxland was sixty-five when he died.' Eaton remembered his father noting it one morning over breakfast and newspapers. His father had commented that Blaxland's death would leave a gap in the mining industry, a power vacuum. Eaton had assumed his widow was of a commensurate age. Never had he imagined Blaxland's widow was in her thirties.

'Yes, and he was fifty-five when we married. I was his second wife, of course, his first having died a few years before.' Perhaps that was why he'd thought Mrs Blaxland would be older. He'd not realised the first wife had passed; he would have been a child, after all. It was hardly the sort of news an adolescent paid attention to, even if he hadn't been recovering from the throes of his own illness. But now, it was like finding a pearl in an oyster and Eaton filed the precious knowledge away along with the champagne. It was the most personal piece of information she'd offered. His collection of facts was growing: she was a widow, a second wife; she was confident, strong, stubborn and direct; she was young, *attractive*; she liked to be in control.

She was asserting that desire now, perhaps sensing the conversation was fast slipping beyond her ability to command it. 'I fail to see what consequence any of this holds. It doesn't matter.' But it did. She wasn't as sure of herself as she wanted him to believe. Did she think he didn't see the flutter of her pulse in the lantern-lit darkness, or the way her eyes met his and then slid away? She wanted to know, as much as he did, what it would be like if they acted on the spark that jumped between them when they argued, when they challenged one another, when they were merely in the same room together. He'd been aware of her tonight long before he'd gone to her. He'd been aware, too, that she'd been looking for him the moment she'd arrived.

What could it hurt to find out? She lived miles away and was hardly in the habit of haring down to Porth Karrek.

'It *does* matter.' He slipped his hand behind her neck, drawing her close, letting his gaze linger, letting the proximity of his body signal his intentions as he murmured, 'I am not in the habit of kissing grandmothers.'

'And I am not in the habit of—'

Eaton didn't let her finish. He captured her lips, sealing her rejoinder with his mouth. They could discuss her habits—or lack of them—later.

Chapter Four

Apparently, she was *not* in the habit of completing her sentences. She certainly wouldn't be capable of doing so now. All her mind could focus on was that *he was kissing her.* The realisation rocketed through Eliza, a bolt of white-hot awareness. There wasn't a single part of her that wasn't aware of him—the sweet, sharp autumn scent of him in her nostrils, the feel of his touch on the bare skin at her neck, the press of his mouth against hers—all combining to stir her to life, perhaps for the first time.

His tongue teased hers; a slow, languorous flirt confident of its reception. His hand adjusted its position at her neck, tilting her mouth, deepening his access to her until she gave a little moan. She had never been kissed like this, as if the kiss was a seduction within itself, as if every nuance of mouth and tongue and lips communicated a private message of desire designed just for her. She felt herself wanting to give over; there was no question of resistance, no desire for it. She wanted this kiss, wanted to fall into it, wanted to see where it led. Perhaps it led to other wicked desires, other wicked feelings. But only if she let it—and she wouldn't, she promised herself.

All the reasons why began to reassert themselves, slowly coming back to the fore of her defences after the initial onslaught of this new pleasure. She shouldn't be kissing a stranger, a man she'd only met once. She shouldn't be kissing a man with whom she meant to do business. She was a mother; she had to think of her reputation for her daughter's sake. She was a business owner; she also had to think of her reputation for the sake of the mines. Kisses were for women who could afford them.

The last thought brought her up short. She pushed against the hard wall of his chest. Did he think she could afford to give away kisses? That she'd come out to the garden on purpose to signal her intention—that she was willing to acknowledge *and* act on the flicker of attraction? Had he taken what she'd intended as an escape as an invitation instead?

The white-hot burn of pleasure turned to heated mortification. 'My lord…' She should have been more astute. Widows often had a reputation for discreet licentiousness. The widows the Marquess of Lynford knew most certainly did. But she could not be one of them. It was for that very reason she'd been so careful of her own reputation for five long years. 'I fear I have given you a most inaccurate impression of myself. I apologise, sincerely. I must go. Immediately.' Eliza tried to step around him, but all the height and breadth she'd appreciated about him earlier worked to her disadvantage. He was not a man easily evaded. She should have left when she had the chance. She should not have lingered in the garden, tempting fate. She'd come out thinking to put some distance between herself and those dark eyes. But the garden hadn't been far enough.

He moved, subtly positioning his body to block her departure, a hand at her arm in gentle restraint, his voice soft in the darkness. 'When will I see you again?' It was 'will' with him, not 'may'. Lynford wasn't the sort of man to beg for a woman's attention. He went forward confidently, assuming the attention would be given. *Will.* The potency of that one word sent a frisson of warm heat down her spine. His dark gaze held hers, intent on an answer—*her* answer. Despite his confident assumptions, he was allowing that decision to be all hers.

'I don't think that would be wise. Business and pleasure should not mix.' She could not relent on this or she would come to regret it. An affair could ruin her and everything she'd worked for. The shareholders in the mines would no doubt love to discover a sin to hold against her.

'Not wise for whom, Mrs Blaxland?' The back of his hand traced a gentle path along the curve of her jaw. 'You are merely a patron of the school I sponsor. I don't see any apparent conflict of interest.'

'Not wise for either of us.' If she stood here and argued with him, she would lose. Sometimes the best way to win an argument was simply to leave. Eliza exercised that option now in her firmest tones, the ones she reserved for announcing decisions in the boardroom. 'Goodnight, Lord Lynford.' She was counting on him being gentleman enough to recognise a refusal and let her go this time, now that any ambiguity between them had been resolved.

Eliza made it to the carriage without any interference. She shut the door behind her and waited for a sense of relief to take her. She'd guessed correctly. Lynford hadn't followed her and it was for the best. He was probably standing in the garden, realising it at this very minute, now that the heat of the moment had passed. The kiss had been an enjoyable adventure. It had added a certain spice to the evening, but it was not to be repeated. He didn't know her. He didn't know the depth of her responsibilities, or that she had a child—Sophie—the true love of her life.

If he did, he'd most certainly run. A man like Lynford, a man in his prime with wealth and a title to recommend him, was expected to wed a young woman capable of giving him his own heirs. She knew precisely the sort of bride who was worthy of a ducal heir: a sweet, young girl, who had no other interests than stocking her husband's nursery. Lynford would want, would *need*, a family of his own. All dukes did. The Marquess would never seriously consider a woman with another man's daughter clinging to her skirts and who spent her days running a mining empire, any more than she would consider him as a husband.

She would never marry again. She had no inclination to give up her hard-won control over her future and her daughter's. The risk was too great, even if the cost was also great. Sophie must come first, ahead of her own personal wishes for a family. Eliza had come to such a realisation early in her widowhood and it had been both a relief and a disappointment.

It was the only thing the doting and decent Blaxland hadn't been able to give her and the only thing she would not risk giving to herself. He'd given her security and a future, but he could not give her a family. Despite ten years of marriage, there was only to be her darling Sophie between them. Another husband, another man, younger, more virile, might provide her with those children, but she did not want to turn her responsibilities over to a husband in exchange, nor could she risk her reputation with the entanglement of a lover. The well-intentioned overture from Miles Detford years ago had shown her how even the smallest misstep could weaken her position.

On either front, she had no business kissing the Marquess of Lynford in the academy gardens. She was the daughter of a mine owner, the widow of a mine owner. Her family came from business. Cits on all sides, including her late husband's. Such a background wasn't for a marquess. Eliza knew how the world worked. She could be nothing for him but a brief dalliance until whatever mystery he saw in her was solved. Men could do as they liked. But *she* would never outrun the stain and neither would Sophie.

That was the lesson she told herself as her coach deposited her at the inn. But it didn't stop her from dreaming that night of a dark-eyed man who'd called her extraordinary and kissed her body into an acute awareness of itself, who'd made her feel alive in ways she hadn't felt for years, perhaps ever. There simply hadn't been time or place for such realisations. There still wasn't. Whatever that kiss had awakened had to be suppressed. That kiss could stay in her dreams, but it could go no further. In the morning she would wake up, visit the Porth Karrek mine and return to life as usual. As earth-shattering as tonight had been, it simply couldn't be any other way for her.

It simply couldn't be this way. The lumber order for the tunnel timbers was excessive. Eliza sat back from the ledgers, hazarding a glance at the clock on the wall of the mine office. It was eleven already. The morning had slipped away while she'd grappled with the receipt, trying to make sense of the overabundance of ordering. She'd meant to leave for home by now and she was nowhere close to making that self-imposed departure. If she left it any later, she'd miss tea with Sophie. She'd promised she'd be back in time and she never broke a promise. But ultimately, she was the one who had to answer to the shareholders in a few weeks at the annual meeting, the one who would be accountable for this over-ordering.

Eliza went to the window and looked down on the bustling scene below: carters pushing wheelbarrows of ore from the mine to the sorters; sorters separating the ore; her foreman, Gillie Cardy, shouting orders. The sight of her mines at work brought a certain thrill, a certain proof that she'd accomplished something. She caught Gillie's eye and gestured for him to come up. He would know why so much lumber had been ordered.

Gillie knocked on the door before entering, sweeping off his knit cap as he stepped inside. 'Mrs Blaxland, how can I be of service?' She liked Gillie. He'd been the site manager even before her husband died. He was competent and knew the mechanics of mining thoroughly, and he'd been a friendly face when she'd first taken over.

She motioned towards the ledgers. 'I have some questions about the lumber order.'

Gillie chuckled and shook his head. 'I'm no good at numbers, ma'am. I just do what I'm told. You want someone to find a lode in the mine, I'm your fella. But if you want someone to do the books, that's not me. I know mining and not much else.' Eliza nodded. This was yet another reason her schools were vital. People needed mathematics and reading skills no matter what their profession. Education was power and protection. Without it, people were waiting to be victims.

'I've done the sums,' she assured him. 'With the amount of timber ordered we could build a tunnel twice the length.'

He twisted the cap in his hand, looking worried. 'The tunnel *is* very long, ma'am. We are tunnelling out underneath the ocean.'

Eliza stared at him in disbelief. 'We are not! We opted not to take the risk at this time.' Her stomach began to turn. The board had decided at the last quarterly meeting not to go that far.

'Pardon me, ma'am, but Mr Detford said we were tunnelling under the ocean.'

Miles Detford? He ran the Wheal Karrek mine for her. She trusted Detford, counted him as friend. Miles would never go against the board's decision or her wishes. He knew how she felt about the dangers of tunnelling beneath the ocean. Surely, there must be some mistake, that Cardy had misunderstood or that Miles Detford had been pressured by someone, because if that wasn't the case, it meant she had misunderstood—not just the decision not to tunnel, but so much more. Her board was willing to override her decisions.

If it were true, it was a slap in the face. Someone thought she wouldn't notice, either because she wasn't diligent or because they thought she wasn't smart enough. The other answer was even less appealing. Maybe whoever ordered the timbers simply didn't care if she noticed. Her wishes were to be overridden. Not everyone on the board had agreed about the tunnel. It had been contentious and hotly debated. She'd rather put the money towards mining schools. Others had not felt that way. There was no money to be made from the schools.

Eliza pressed a hand to her stomach, trying to settle the roil that had started with the realisation. After years of proving herself, it seemed things still weren't beyond that first year. Hadn't she been the one who had insisted on steam engines to replace the horses? Hadn't she been the one to institute safety protocols? The worst of it was, *she'd* thought things were better.

But they weren't. Someone was laughing behind her back, playing her very publicly for a fool.

Already, her mind was running through options. Which shareholders had conspired against her? Was it Isley Thorp or Sir Gismond Brenley, the other chief shareholders? It must have been if they had enough leverage to force Miles Detford into ordering the timbers. Miles would never have ordered them on his own. He would have defended her decision.

She returned to her desk chair and drew out a piece of paper from the drawer, penning a note with instructions. There was no question of returning to Truro until this mess was resolved. She folded the note and handed it to Gillie. 'Have a messenger deliver this to the town house with all haste.' Sophie and her governess could be here tomorrow. That would give her time to find suitable living arrangements. The inn wasn't a decent place for a young girl. But where? Who did she know in town to whom she could turn? Did she dare ask Lynford? He was her only acquaintance likely to have any connections. The thought of Sophie at the inn, driving guests mad with her exuberance, settled it. As hesitant as she was about asking Lynford, she didn't have a choice. Wheal Karrek needed her and she needed Sophie.

Decision made, she took out a second sheet and penned another note. 'Take this up to the new conservatory.' She reread the note, making sure she'd struck just the right tone, short, concise, a very businesslike message, nothing that Lynford would misconstrue as an invitation to continue what they'd started *and* finished in the garden. Satisfied, she sent Gillie off. That only left sending a note to Detford. Her stomach surged once more at the thought. She settled it with a reminder that this was all a misunderstanding. Miles would come and explain all. She'd been on her guard for so long, it was too easy to see trouble where there was none.

Chapter Five

Eliza had barely finished the note when the commotion of an arrival sounded in the yard below. Perhaps another wagonload of supplies was expected today? But when she reached the window, there was no wagon in the yard, only a lone man on a chestnut horse— a tall, broad-shouldered man, dark hair unruly and windblown. He dismounted in a fluid motion and Eliza's breath caught. Lynford was here! He'd come and immediately. He couldn't have received her message more than an hour ago.

He looked up at the window, shielding his eyes against the sun, and Eliza reflexively stepped back even though there was little chance of being seen. She was both flattered and flustered by his attention. What to do? Allow him to come up or should she go down to meet him? She would go down. *Things* tended to happen when she was alone with him. Crowds were safer. She took up her hat and gloves and paused a moment to check her appearance in the small mirror behind the door before whispering, 'Breathe, Eliza. He's just a man.'

A man who had kissed her. A man who had not been intimidated by her when she'd surprised him at the school. A man who had come to her immediately even though she'd not specifically requested it. She stopped at the foot of the stairs to collect herself. She should not be excited. This was an entirely girlish reaction. She'd summoned him for business purposes because that was the nature of their acquaintance and she knew no one else in the area who might be positioned to help her. She'd *not* summoned him because of last night. She wanted to be clear with herself on that. In fact, that had been the singular reason she'd hesitated to send for him in the first place.

She stepped outside, striding forward with confidence, hand outstretched in a mannish greeting. 'My lord, how good of you to come and how surprising. I'd expected a list of recommendations in response, not an actual visit. I hope this isn't disrupting your day?'

He shook her hand and gave her one of his broad, winning smiles. If he was put off by the masculine gesture he gave no sign of it. 'Not at all. There's nothing left to do up at the school except get in the way while Kitto tries to settle the students.' Sweet heavens, he was just as devastating in daylight and plain clothes as he was by night. Perhaps more so. Without the elegance of evening clothes, it was too easy to forget he was a marquess, heir to a dukedom and entirely above her touch. Today, he looked the part of a country squire and eminently more attainable, dressed in riding boots, tight buckskins, and a long greatcoat suited for the autumn air that blew in off the sea.

Lynford did not relinquish her hand, but covered it with his other. 'Tell me, what sort of accommodations do you require for the longer term? A manse? A cottage? An estate? I have a place in mind if you think it would suit. There's a dower house at Falmage Hill. It's not far from here. It would be close to the mine and it's well situated between Porth Karrek and Penzance. I am in residence at the main house, or else I'd let the whole estate to you instead.'

'I don't need a whole estate.' Eliza laughed. 'The dower house will be ideal.' Did she sound as flustered as she felt? The offer was overwhelming, all the more so because she couldn't recall the last time someone had lifted the burden from her shoulders. Her world was full of wolves and vultures, but here was a stranger—an acquaintance at best—who'd shouldered the weight of this one task without hesitation. This was arguably the best news she'd heard all morning. But did it come at a cost? What guarantees was Lynford looking for? Why would a man she barely knew offer such largesse?

'Are you sure, Mrs Blaxland?' Eaton's gaze narrowed, matching her own speculation. 'If so, why are you looking at me as if I were a predator?' She should have been more deliberate with what she let show on her face. She'd become sloppy in the wake of the morning's tensions.

'Are you? A predator? A girl can't be too careful. When something sounds too good to be true, I've learned it usually is.' Eliza didn't back down from his challenge. 'Truthfully, Lord Lynford, I *am* wondering why a man who hardly knows me would volunteer such lavish accommodation. What could he want in exchange? I shall pay you rent in coins and in nothing else.' She needed to be clear on this point, especially based on last night in the garden. Did he think there were additional kisses to be had? Or perhaps something more than kisses?

'You will do no such thing. I am not asking for money…or for anything else,' Lynford answered with the swiftness of an insulted man. 'As for why I am doing this, it is because I can. I have an empty house and you need one.'

Did she dare believe him? She was not used to taking men at their word. But what choice did she have? Sophie and her governess would arrive tomorrow. Eaton swung up on his horse and for a moment she thought he'd retract his offer, offended by her scepticism. Then he leaned down and offered his hand. 'Come up, we'll ride out and look the property over. You can decide then if it will suit.'

'But my coach is here,' Eliza stammered, craning her neck to look up at him. Lynford appeared twice as large atop the big horse as he did on the ground and twice as commanding.

'Send it on ahead.' Lynford answered easily, dismissing the detail. 'Stop stalling and come up, Eliza. We've already established I'm not a predator. It's a beautiful autumn day, perfect for a ride, and I promise my horse will behave.' She noted he said nothing about himself. She also noted he'd used her first name.

She should be wary. She should refuse on grounds of impropriety. What would people think if they saw her with him? The argument had no teeth. *Who* would see them? Who would care? Miners on their way to their shifts? People who didn't even know who she was? She lived quietly and Truro was further than most of these people would ever go in their lifetime. But *she* would know. But when he looked at her with that smile and those dancing dark eyes, something deep inside her began to stir, as it had last night, as it had the first time she'd laid eyes on him—that reminder that she was alive, that she was something more than a book-keeper and an overseer. She took his hand and leapt.

He settled her before him on the saddle and clucked to the big chestnut with an enviable ease, apparently unbothered by the proximity of the female sitting in front of him. Eliza wished she could claim such sang-froid. She could not. The rhythm of the horse beneath her beat a tattoo of freedom as the cliffs and fields of the Cornish landscape sped past. But neither dominated her attentions like the presence of the man behind her. She'd not counted on the practical act of transportation, such a mundane task, feeling so intimate.

Huntingdon hadn't been a rider. They'd always gone everywhere by coach. To ride astride with a man was a very different thing. There were the thighs to contend with, muscular thighs that bracketed her legs, the chest she couldn't help but press against as they cantered along the cliff road to Falmage Hill, the arm that came around her, the leather-gloved hand that held the reins resting at her hip. She could smell the wind on him, could feel it in her face, the thrill of freedom humming in her blood. It was fanciful to ascribe such poetic feeling to the ride. Lynford would likely be stunned to know how a simple act had conjured up such fanciful connotations for her.

The newly awakened wildness in her was disappointed to see Falmage Hill come into view, disappointed to turn into the drive, disappointed to slow the horse to a trot, the wind settling to a light, arbitrary breeze in her face. Eaton turned the horse down a path, giving her a tour of the drive lined by tall, impressive oaks with a green lawn extending in all directions. 'The main house is straight ahead, but the dower house sits on the west corner of the property. It has a nice view of the sea.' She couldn't care less for the sea view at the moment. She was transfixed on the lawn. Sophie would love running here. There was precious little space for a girl to run in town. A twinge of guilt pricked at Eliza. Courtesy dictated she should tell him she wouldn't be his only guest. But privacy counselled caution. She was protective of Sophie and those who came into contact with her. A woman or a girl with a fortune couldn't be too careful.

The entrance to the dower house was dominated by two thick stone pillars and a wrought iron gate that stood open, ready for them. The house itself was a square, brick manse with ivy growing up its walls and five white-framed windows decorating the second storey. The entrance was set on the right side of the house and covered with an arched arcade. Eliza found the home immediately charming, a place where a family might take a holiday. Where children might frolic in the yard with a puppy. She pushed the sweet image away. There was no purpose in torturing herself with what she couldn't have. Besides, she never took a holiday. She was too afraid of what might transpire if she looked away from the mines for a moment. Apparently, it hadn't mattered. Things had transpired anyway.

Out of nowhere, a man in livery materialised to hold the horse. Lynford dismounted and reached for her, his hands easy and comfortable at her waist. Was she the only one who noticed how much they touched? Was she the only one moved by it? The only one whose pulse thundered with each contact? One would think she was fresh from the schoolroom, not a woman who'd had a husband and a child and who dealt with men every day. There should be no mystique in a man's touch. She was helped in and out of carriages, escorted into dinners on the occasions when she went out in Truro. Touch was no stranger to her, yet Lynford's touch managed to stand out.

Eaton set her down and gestured towards the house. 'Shall we go in? I sent word ahead to the staff to start cleaning once I received your note. The worst of the dust should be gone by now.' He slid her teasing look. 'I know how you are about dust.'

'You're very…efficient.' *And confident*, she added silently. He'd been sure she'd accept his offer…and he'd been right. Was she that predictable or was he that sure of himself?

Eaton ushered her through the front door, a hand resting at the small of her back. Another touch. Another reminder that he stirred her. 'There's a parlour, a dining room and a library space you can use as an office here on the first floor. The kitchen is below stairs. The bedrooms are upstairs. I will send down staff for cooking and cleaning. I have plenty to spare with only me to look after at the big house.'

He'd anticipated everything, Eliza thought as they climbed the stairs. 'There are five chambers up here and seven beds.' Eaton led her down the hall. 'You can have your pick, perhaps a bed for every night of the week.' He laughed, coming to stop at a room nearest the stairwell. 'This one is the largest.'

Eliza stepped into the airy room, impressed. Eaton's staff had already been here. The bed linens were fresh and the window was open to let in the crisp autumn air. A small bud vase with deep pink ginger lilies stood on the table beside the bed, lending the room a personal touch, an extra detail. She was aware of Eaton behind her, his words a quiet, masculine rumble. 'Will it suit?' At the enquiry, her eyes began to sting, tears welling. She was glad she was facing the window. How would she explain that a simple question had moved her to tears?

She cleared her throat, summoning a modicum of control. 'Yes, it will do splendidly.' But she did not turn from the window. The echo of her previous thought came again: How long had it been since someone had taken care of her? The jingle of harnesses sounded in the drive, announcing the arrival of her coach and saving her from any further awkwardness. At the sound of horses, Eaton was in motion. 'I'll go down and tell them to bring your things up.' His boots sounded on the stairs and, within moments, her trunk was deposited in her room. 'I'll have one of the maids unpack,' Lynford offered.

'No, I'd like to unpack on my own. Thank you.' Eliza turned from the window, finally the mistress of her emotions. 'You've done more than enough.' He'd done so much, in fact, that she was on the brink of tears, perhaps a sad commentary on her life that such acts would have this effect, especially when he clearly viewed the efforts as basic acts of politeness.

Lynford gave her a grin and a bow. 'Then I will leave you to it. I have business to complete, but before I go, I would like to ask for your company at dinner tonight. It gets lonely eating by myself. Meanwhile, if there's anything you need, send to the house for it.'

Eliza set to undoing the buckles on her trunk. She needed to stop being overwhelmed by him. It would be too easy to fall into the trap of relying on him, of laying her burdens down. This afternoon was proof enough she needed to be wary. Men bearing gifts always wanted something and Lynford's gift was far more than Detford's bonbons and roses had ever been. Perhaps she was being too cynical. Perhaps it was just as he'd said—he'd given it because he could.

Eliza shook out her dresses and hung them in the wardrobe. Today had been upsetting. Tomorrow would be better. Sophie would be here by teatime and she'd have a clear mind with which to think about the situation with the ledgers. Until then, however, there was dinner with Lord Lynford to keep her busy.

Chapter Six

The school was still busy with move-in-day excitement when Eaton returned. It had been a bustling hotbed of activity when he'd left and, if that hotbed wasn't precisely still boiling in the late afternoon, the chaos of housing the boys and reassuring their parents remained very definitely at an energetic simmer. Trunks from later arrivals were piled in the drive awaiting the attention of footmen. Parents milled in the wide hall while instructors, strategically placed about the hall, attempted to direct the last of the boys and pair up roommates. It was a good kind of chaos, reminiscent of his own days at school. The sight put a certain nostalgic warmth in his heart. His own father had made it a point to travel with him to school for the start of autumn term the first few years he'd gone instead of consigning him to a servant's or tutor's care for the journey. Not all the boys at Eton had been that fortunate and he looked back on those times fondly. He remembered their parting ritual, that last manful shaking of hands as his father said goodbye in the main hall and pressed a secret five-pound note into his palm with a wink.

There were still a few families saying farewell in the hall, but from the looks of it Cade had everything in hand, a realisation that was both satisfying and bittersweet as Eaton slipped into the headmaster's office unnoticed.

Eaton poured himself a drink from the sideboard and slouched into a tall wing-backed chair with a silent toast. His vision of a music school had come to fruition most magnificently. Richard Penlerick would be proud. That was something for which to be thankful. It had been a tremendous undertaking accomplished in a short period of time. Today, watching students arrive and move in was something to celebrate. But it also carried a tinge of sadness to it. His part in the school was done. Cade Kitto would take things from here, as had always been the intention. Eaton knew he wasn't relinquishing his association with the school. He'd always be in the background, raising funds, recruiting patrons and students, but the school wouldn't be *his*, not any more.

Eaton twirled the stem of his glass, indulging in a moment of whimsical melancholy. The school had absorbed him entirely since December when Rosenwyn Treleven had first put the idea to him. Since then, he'd embraced the project fully. He'd cancelled his long-anticipated trip to Italy in March. He'd foregone most of the Season, spending his summer here instead putting the finishing touches on the school. It had filled his days, but that was over now. It was time to get on to the next project, whatever that might be. Urgency surged. He didn't like being at a loose end. Life was short and unpredictable, Richard Penlerick's death had proved it, but even that ghastly reminder hadn't been enough to spark an interest in a new project.

The door opened and Cade slipped inside, all smiles despite spending a trying day of student arrivals. 'I thought I might find you here.' The sight of a satisfied Cade Kitto did much to alleviate Eaton's melancholy. In many ways, this school had been for Cade and Rosenwyn. If not for them, the school wouldn't exist. 'I don't know if I've answered a thousand questions or just the same question asked a thousand different ways.' Cade laughed good-naturedly as he poured a drink. 'I think everyone is settled now.' He took a seat across from Eaton and crossed a leg over one knee. 'Here's to you. Without you, today wouldn't have been possible. You saw the potential of Rosenwyn's idea and made it a reality. You provided the house, the funds and the prestige of a name that would draw worthy students. Rose and I can't thank you enough.' Cade saluted him with his glass. 'What will you do with yourself now that the school is up and running? You'll have time aplenty on your hands.'

'I was just thinking the same before you walked in.' Eaton smiled, determined not to lose the joy of the day. 'I will have time to work in my orangery, perfect my truffle oil recipe. I can plan my trip to Italy again.' But his tone lacked conviction. None of the ideas held any appeal.

'And Mrs Blaxland? Is she settled to your satisfaction?' Cade asked with keen eyes. 'I got your note that you'd ridden out to assist her. I hope all is well?'

'Yes, I put her up at the dower house at Falmage Hill,' Eaton replied neutrally, but not neutrally enough to escape Cade's attention.

'At your family estate?' Cade's brow creased in surprise and perhaps concern.

'Yes, is there a problem with that?' Eaton asked somewhat teasingly. He'd not expected Cade to react one way or the other.

'It's just the suddenness of it all,' Cade answered. 'You hardly know her and now she's entrenched on your family's property. I would have thought a cottage near Penzance or even rooms at the Trelevenses', where she'd have female company.'

'They'd be strangers to her,' Eaton dismissed the suggestion. 'She's been a generous donor to the school. It was the least I could do and I know plenty about her.' Did he? He knew only that he was attracted to her, that she stirred something in him that hadn't been stirred in a long while. How would he explain if Cade asked what that meant? 'She's alone, she knows no one else here she can turn to,' Eaton offered obliquely. 'I helped her because I could.'

Cade chuckled, but Eaton did not miss his warning. 'She runs a mining empire. She's not helpless or without resources. Do not, for a minute, my friend, think Eliza Blaxland is a damsel in distress.'

No, he would not make that mistake. 'She is definitely not that.' Eaton had seen the flustered look on Eliza's face today when he'd offered the house. There'd been relief in her eyes and disbelief, too. For a moment she'd been able to lay down her burden. 'Perhaps that's why I did it,' he mused. 'Sometimes even the strong need a hand.'

Cade offered a wry smile. 'Like helping court musicians establish a music school?'

Eaton shifted in his chair, uncomfortable with the praise. 'The estate was from my great-aunt. She'd be pleased to see it used as a school. Quite possibly, I should be the one thanking you. The house was standing empty before Rosenwyn suggested it. As for the funds, those came from patrons. It would be a mistake to think I singlehandedly funded the school and those patrons came because of you, because of the chance to study with Cornwall's very own home-grown genius, Cador Kitto, Porth Karrek's finest musician.'

Cade leaned forward in earnest, not distracted in the least by Eaton's rebuttal. 'You know what I mean. It's not only the school I thank you for. It's everything this school represents: a chance for me to work in one place, a chance to give up the risk of the itinerant lifestyle, moving from court to court with no assurances of commissions. It's relieved me of the shame of relying on my wife's dowry for funds. I will always be truly grateful for what you've done for me. Without your efforts behind this school, Rosenwyn and I would never have been able to marry. I would have left Porth Karrek in December and returned to a life of wandering. I would never have known what it was like to have a wife and a family.'

The last was said with all the passion of a newly-wed man only a month out from the bliss of his honeymoon, but there was something else in Cade's words that caused Eaton to think he wasn't talking about Rosenwyn's five sisters when he referred to family. 'Family, Cade? Do you have something to tell me?' Eaton smiled, a few other subtle hints from throughout the last weeks falling into place like Rosenwyn's indisposition rendering her unable to play hostess for the open house.

Cade's face broke into a beaming smile. 'I am going to be a father in March.'

'That's wonderful news, for you both,' Eaton congratulated him. He and Cade had grown close in the last months, bonding over the school. He knew how much having a family meant to Cade, who'd grown up in Porth Karrek as mining poor, and to Rosenwyn, whom Eaton had known since childhood. The Trelevens and Falmages were both part of the district's society. He'd saved Rosenwyn from a disastrous marriage a couple of years ago in London and the happiness she'd found with Cade was all he could wish for his old friend. Yet there was a stab of jealousy as they drank to Cade's good news. Cade had the dream: meaningful purpose, a wife who was a partner and companion, who challenged him, who loved him, and very soon Cade would have a child to dote on as well. Envy speared Eaton, driving deep. How was it that a poor miner's son should have all those things while a duke's son did not?

Cade clapped him on the knee and rose. 'I need to get back out there and make sure all the parents have left, then the masters and students will have our first supper together as a school in the dining hall. Reverend Maddern is coming to say the blessing.'

Eaton rose with him. 'I need to go as well. I asked Mrs Blaxland to dinner. I wouldn't want to be late for my own invitation.' He wanted fresh air in his face, the power of his horse beneath him. What he needed was a good hard canter to push away his jealousy and dilute his anger over the hand fate had dealt him.

Outside, he swung up on Titan and kicked him forward, letting his thoughts race with his horse's hooves. It wasn't the idea of a marriage that sparked his envy of Cade. He could marry anytime he wanted. Candidates were thick on the ground for a man of his attributes and expectations. It was the quality of that marriage he envied. Rosenwyn had fought for Cade. She had wanted him despite the limitations of his station. She loved Cade for who he was, not what he was. It was the one thing Eaton could never ask of a woman. He could marry whenever he wanted, that was true, but it came at a cost.

He could make a woman a duchess. He could never make her a mother, could never give her a family. A measles epidemic when he was fourteen had seen to that. But it was not him society would be unkind to. Society never believed it was the man's fault when there were no heirs. Debutantes were raised for titles and aristocratic motherhood much like heirs were raised to be aristocratic studs. He would not burden a wife with a foregone conclusion of failure she could do nothing about. What woman of his circle would care for *him*, live for *him* without the promise of a family? No one he knew, quite honestly. So, he remained unwed and would choose to remain unwed.

In terms of the ducal succession it did not worry him. He had his younger brother to see to the line. But in terms of his own personal journey, he minded very much. He would make the journey of life entirely alone. No wife. No children. No one even to confide in. Naturally, the family had kept this a secret. No one knew except their close circle of friends and they were sworn to secrecy. He would reach a certain age when society would begin to speculate about him. There would be questions: Why didn't he marry? A duke's heir was duty-bound to wed. His source of intimacy would be reduced to a collection of temporary relationships with temporary women to see him through. Who else would want the broken heir to the Duke of Bude?

Eaton let Titan's hooves eat up the ground, let the wind push against his thoughts. He did not want to wallow in his own misery. He was lucky in other ways. He would rejoice instead in the little thrills, the small joys that were available to him, like dinner with a beautiful woman whose pulse raced when he was near.

What was she doing, dressing up for dinner with a marquess? Staying in his home—well, on his property—spending time with him alone? All this, *after* she'd allowed him to kiss her. If he offered her an affair tonight, she'd have only herself to blame. She was sending all the wrong signals, quite possibly right down to the very gown she wore, yet she seemed unable to resist.

Eliza surveyed her image in the long mirror. She smoothed the silk of her blue skirts, debating yet again what to wear. Was the gown too sophisticated for the country? She eyed the other gown on the bed, a mignonette-green India muslin. It was far simpler, perhaps too simple for supper with a marquess regardless of where they dined. Eliza bit her lip in contemplation. Better to overdress than underdress. She would stay with the blue silk, but no jewels, just her pearls, and she'd wear her hair up in a modest style, devoid of curls and ornate braids.

No sooner had Eliza made her decision than the sound of carriage wheels crunched on the drive. She peered out of the window and froze in feminine panic. Lynford was here with an open carriage! Heavens, she wasn't quite ready. Eliza dabbed a quick spot of perfume on her wrists and snatched up her shawl from the bed. Was that everything? Oh, her bracelet! She took it from the vanity and headed down the stairs, trying to fasten it as she went, but the dratted clasp wouldn't catch.

'Let me help with that.' Eaton met her at the bottom of the stairs, grinning at her efforts, his fingers nimble at her wrist as they worked the stubborn catch, her pulse fluttering at the contact. He was once more turned out in evening attire, his unruly hair combed in stark contrast to the windblown man who'd ridden into the courtyard of her mine today. He smelled of his woodsy toilette and clean linen, a scent that was just as intoxicating tonight as the smell of the outdoors on him had been today. Maybe it was the duality he presented that was intoxicating—a man of elegance and refinement by evening, a country squire by day. Or perhaps it wasn't his looks that made him intoxicating, but his manner; his competence, his confidence, the way he took charge whether it was finding her a home or managing the tiny clasp of her bracelet. She had to be careful. That competence was something she could not indulge for long. She had her own competence to look after and exercise.

'There, now you're ready.' He released her hand and offered her his arm. 'Your carriage awaits, madame.'

'As does my escort, it appears. I wasn't expecting you or a carriage.' She was glad now that she'd chosen the blue silk. 'This is greatly appreciated, but I could have walked up. It's so much work to harness the horses just to go to the main house.' She didn't want him to think she had to be pampered.

He handed her into the carriage and took the rear-facing seat across from her. 'All true. However, we are not going to the house. We are going to the orangery and, with the weather being so fine, I thought we might enjoy a drive before supper.' He reached beneath his seat and pulled out a hamper. 'I have champagne, still chilled. I recall how much you enjoyed it at the reception. If you could help with the glasses, I might endeavour to pour.' He freed the cork with a loud pop, the sound and subsequent fountain of foam causing her to gasp and twitch her skirts out of the way with a laugh.

The first attempt at pouring was met with a spill of

champagne on the carriage floor and laughing instructions from Eaton. 'Hold the glass still.'

'I am!' she protested as the carriage hit a rut in the
road and more champagne sloshed in sacrifice to his
efforts.

'Steady now,' Eaton cautioned, this time managing
to get enough champagne in each glass for drinking.
He set the bottle aside. 'Now we can toast. Here's to a
day that will end better than it started.'

She held his eyes as she drank, trying to divine what
he meant. Did the toast hint at a forthcoming proposition? Or was he merely toasting the truth? Her need
earlier today had been assuaged. She hoped for the latter, but felt compelled to mitigate cause for the former.
She did not want to have to refuse him point-blank
later tonight. Perhaps she could insinuate as much.
She raised her glass for a toast of her own. 'Here's to
a friend indeed.' It was well done. She was certain he
heard her subtle message. If seduction was on his mind,
he'd been warned not to pursue it.

His eyes glinted with their dark spark over the rim
of his champagne flute, a knowing smile playing on
those sensual lips as his low voice rumbled enticingly,
'I'm always glad to be of service, Eliza.'

Eliza. There it was again. She'd never thought of her
name as sexy before. Eliza was a plain name, but not
on his lips. On his lips, it might be the most beautiful
name in the world. Damn him. With one word, he'd
destroyed her efforts and ridden roughshod over her
warning. If there was a proposition, he would make
her refuse it bluntly at the critical moment.

'More champagne?' he offered, holding up the half-empty bottle. 'The road is smooth through here, I should be able to manage pouring another glass, if you can manage keeping it still,' he teased. They poured with more success this time, Eliza catching sight of the label.

'Veuve Clicquot?' It was French and expensive. No wonder it tasted divine.

'You know it?' Lynford smiled, pouring the remnants into his glass.

'Only by name,' Eliza admitted. 'My husband was wealthy, but he was also frugal.' They'd had luxuries aplenty, but not champagne unless they were hosting an important party.

'It's a special day and I thought it called for a special champagne. We are celebrating our students' arrival for the first term and your first night in the dower house.'

'Oh!' Eliza gasped regretfully as memory flooded her. 'You had students today and I called you away.' She felt awful that he'd spent so much time with her, as if he'd had nothing better to do. He must have gone back to the school after he'd left her.

Lynford laughed, setting her at ease. 'I was expendable, I assure you. Kitto had it all under control.' He gave her a mockingly serious look. 'You would not have liked it, too much chaos with all the boys running willy-nilly up and down the stairs.' But *he'd* liked it, Eliza thought. She saw it in his eyes and heard it in his tone. The day had pleased him, as well it should have.

'You've done a remarkable thing with that school,' she complimented. The sun was starting to set, turning the sky blossom pink. It was her favourite time of day, the magical hour between day and dusk when she liked to imagine the world was at peace, slowing down from whatever had caused it to race during the day. She felt that peace now in the carriage with Lynford, a comfortable silence settling between them as they drove through the grounds of Falmage Hill, sipping their champagne as the sun dipped.

Lynford offered to open a second bottle, but she declined with a smile. 'I chose the champagne for another reason, too,' he said, tucking the bottle back beneath the seat. 'Veuve Clicquot is named for the widow who ran the vineyard. You remind me of her. She was twenty-seven when she took over the family empire. And, like you, she was successful, too.' He held her gaze and a bolt of heat went through her at the intensity of his attention. 'You impress me, Eliza. I am so very glad you didn't turn out to be an old woman.'

A bolder woman might return the compliment and say she was glad he'd turned out not to be an older man. But that would invite an intimacy she did not want. She offered a tremulous smile instead, uncertain how to respond. Once again he had caught her off guard. No one had ever flirted with her using her own accomplishments as compliments. Goodness knew there were few men who approved of those accomplishments. Usually, they were seen as failings to be held against her. 'What I've done is nothing more than the tasks laid before me. It's a little like giving a stranger a home, isn't it? I did them because I could.'

'*Touché.*' He raised his glass in salute and drained

the last of it as the carriage rolled to a halt. 'Here we are, the orangery, my pride and joy.' He hopped down and offered her his hand. 'This way, Eliza, dinner is served.'

Chapter Seven

That was an understatement, Eliza thought, taking her seat at a crystal-and-candle-laden table in the orangery. Dinner wasn't served, it was *presented* on white china plates, arranged in elegant perfection with carefully drizzled sauces and an array of colours—pink salmon, orange carrots, green herbs—all set against a backdrop of exquisite beauty. The orangery itself was breathtaking with the remainder of the setting sunlight coming through the glass, turning the table crystal to diamonds. Potted palms lined a path through the building along with fruit trees sporting oranges and lemons that perfumed the air with citrusy scents. The sound of trickling water came from deeper in the room and somewhere birds chirped.

'This is like a tropical paradise.' Eliza looked about her, unwilling to hide her appreciation. 'It's a little world all of its own.'

'We can walk through it after dinner,' Lynford offered, popping the cork off a bottle of chilled white wine. He poured a small amount into her glass. 'This will bring out the flavour of the salmon.' They'd been served a single plate containing a little of each food item and the servants had withdrawn, leaving them alone in the candlelit paradise.

It was a different way to eat, Eliza recognised immediately. She approved. There were no courses, no stuffing of oneself, no drinking to excess. There was savouring and sipping. This meal was art and science all in one, pairing tastes with one another to maximise both the fish and the wine. Each bite was a revelation, as was the man across the table from her. 'This is the most delicious meal I think I've ever eaten.' Eliza took another slow, deliberate bite of her fish. 'I would not have guessed you to be a gourmet.' The Marquess of Lynford was a big man, the kind of man she associated with a hearty appetite, who preferred puddings and roasts in copious quantities and was more interested in quantity than quality. 'I've found Cornishmen tend to prefer the solid foods of the countryside,' she tried to put it delicately.

Lynford laughed at the comment. 'You're not incorrect. There is much diversity, however, to be found in the countryside. Some Cornishmen are just more inventive than others.' He gestured to the salmon. 'These are from Bodmin Moor. A smart man can fish the upland rivers until December. A smarter man knows fish is healthier, too, than a heavy beef diet. It keeps the gout away.' He poured her a little more wine. 'I am interested in the science of food—not only the different tastes and flavours we can create, but how we can use food to eat well and live well. I've worked with the cook at the school to design a diet for the boys in the hopes they will learn the value of healthy eating along with their studies.'

'Are orange trees part of that?' Eliza sipped her wine, finding the conversation fascinating. Or was it the conversationalist? It was heady, sitting with him, exchanging ideas. There were layers to this man, unsuspected depths and she was filled with the urge to peel each of them back, like one of his oranges, until she reached his core. What would she find at the heart of the Marquess of Lynford?

'Orange trees are essential. Citrus fruits are excellent for keeping scurvy away. They are also extremely difficult to grow in the wild given the English weather. So, I grow them here. The school will be well provided for.'

'That's ingenious,' Eliza complimented, truly impressed with his foresight and his creativity. 'Whatever gave you that idea?'

'Not a what, a who.' Lynford smiled, his gaze taking on a nostalgic cast. 'A mentor, a friend, suggested it. He has—*had*—spectacular greenhouses at his estate.'

'Had?' Eliza asked softly, picking up the past tense reference. She sensed a change in his mood. The nostalgia was tinged with sadness.

'He died this past summer. Richard Penlerick, the Duke of Newlyn. He was a strong supporter of the school and the things I want to do there.' Lynford's dark eyes were shadowed but frank. 'I miss him very much. He was like an uncle to me. His son and I are close friends.'

Newlyn. Of course. The newspaper in Truro had covered it. The Cornish Duke had died tragically, if she recalled. A sudden death, unexpected. She reached out a hand and covered Eaton's where it lay on the table. 'I am genuinely sorry.'

Lynford nodded slowly, accepting her sympathy. The candlelight played across his face, catching sorrow, resentment, lingering anger and something more: bone-deep grief. She knew a little something about that. She'd felt that way for months after Huntingdon had died. 'I don't know what is worse,' she offered. 'To have time to prepare and know the end is coming, or to face it suddenly without warning.' She paused. They did not know each well. Perhaps it was wrong to think she could offer counsel, but she forged ahead, preferring to err on the side of empathy. There'd been no one to grieve with her, to help ease her pain when she'd lost Huntingdon. She would not leave someone else to face that grief alone if she could help it.

There was a certain intimacy between them, the orangery having shrunk to the circle of light surrounding them as she spoke. 'The day Huntingdon died was a normal day, just like any other. He had breakfast. He reminded me we had guests coming for dinner that night. Then he walked out of the door and didn't come back. He had no idea and neither did I that it would all be over in a few hours.'

Eaton's eyes glittered like polished obsidian. 'You loved him? You had a good marriage?'

She smiled fondly. 'Yes, he was a decent man and I knew going into it he would not outlast me, that I would be the one left behind. I just didn't think it would be that day. I suppose one never does.'

Eaton picked up her hand and threaded his fingers through hers, watching the candlelight bathe the bracelet at her wrist. 'Left behind. You've captured it precisely. That is exactly how I feel. He left me. He left Vennor, his son. He left all of us and we didn't even get to say goodbye. It wasn't just goodbye that went unsaid. It was all the other things. The loving words, the gratitude, the acknowledgement of how much his kindnesses, his very life, mattered.' He shook his head. 'Does the hurt, the emptiness, ever go away?'

'No, but it does change.' Eliza's voice was just above a whisper. 'You start to carry them with you instead of your sorrow.'

They were both whispering now. 'And the anger? Does it change, too? I've been angry for months. I wanted his life to matter. I wanted his death to matter. He deserved better than a blade in the dark, killed by a common criminal for no reason.' She felt his fingers tighten on hers. 'I want there to be a reason,' he admitted before pulling back with a rueful smile. 'My apologies. I didn't mean for the evening to take such a turn. I don't normally invite people to dinner and then lay myself bare to them.' He gave a short laugh and wiped his palms on his breeches. 'Thank you for listening. I haven't talked about Richard Penlerick since I came home. Perhaps I needed to.'

'Perhaps there was no one to talk to. I think it matters who you tell. These things…' Eliza waved an ephemeral hand '…cannot be told to just anyone.' She was touched he'd chosen her.

'I'm glad it was you.' Lynford pushed back from the table with a burst of energy, wanting to leave the recent conversation and its emotions behind. 'Are you ready for the tour? I think the orangery is ready for us.'

Beyond him, the path through the orangery had been lit. Eliza had been so intent on him she'd not noticed the servants discreetly placing the lanterns to guide their way. 'This place must be a wondrous refuge in the winter.' Eliza took his arm, looking about her as they strolled.

'It is. I spend a lot of time here, though not in the summer. With all the glass, it gets too warm.' He pointed out the palms with coconuts hidden under their large, leafy fronds, the orange trees with their waxy leaves and citrus treasures, the potted lemon trees that had come all the way from Italy. There were flowers, too, poinsettias from the Caribbean and rare varieties of orchids from Asia.

'I hope to bring the boys from the school here for lessons.' Lynford stopped to study the leaves of a lemon tree. 'I want them to learn science by visiting the ocean, by fishing in the rivers, by tromping through the woods and respecting the natural science around them in their own region.'

He smiled at her and she was nearly undone. 'You've not only designed a diet for them, you've designed a curriculum as well.' Lynford hadn't just built a school, he'd built a world. An entire lifestyle had been subtly woven into the fabric of the conservatory. It shamed her little vision of miners' schools. She had not dreamed big enough.

'I didn't do it alone. Kitto and I worked on the curriculum together. I think it's rather novel. It's hands-on learning, much like music instruction is. We thought, why not extend that idea to other subjects like science and history? They can learn history by visiting old ruins and follies, by re-enacting key battles. They can't learn everything that way, but a good portion of what they need to know can be taught with far more activity than it traditionally is.' He warmed to the subject as they walked. 'When I was growing up, the lessons I liked best and remembered the most were the ones where my tutors set aside the books and showed me. In the summers, I grew a garden and, as I tended it, my tutor talked about soil and the importance of crop rotation, how to calculate crop yield.' He paused here and grinned at her and she could see the boy he'd been in that teasing smile. 'That lesson was a good one. It combined mathematics *and* science.'

'It certainly sounds more exciting than my lessons when I was young. I am already wondering if I can adapt these ideas for the miners' children.' They were accustomed to plenty of activity during the day and definitely not used to sitting for long periods of time. For them, traditional school would be a challenge. 'Is that why you wanted to establish a school? To try out your ideas?' It had intrigued her from the beginning, when she'd first been approached in January to support the conservatory. Why would a man of his standing want to found a school? Self-importance? Legacy? But the urgency behind the school, the determination to open it this autumn, didn't support that theory.

Lynford laughed. 'Oh, you don't want to know.'

'Now I *especially* want to know,' Eliza cajoled. He almost seemed embarrassed and that was interesting when he was usually the epitome of confidence.

'All right, but it has to be a secret.' He gave her a conspiratorial wink, his eyes dancing. 'I had a friend who suggested it in order to convince Cador Kitto to stay in the area on a more permanent basis. I wanted my friend to be happy, so I set up the school.' He looked sheepish with the confession. 'You'll be disappointed now, knowing that it wasn't entirely altruistic, not originally.'

'Just for the good of a friend. Must be a very good friend,' Eliza pressed. Her curiosity wanted details.

'An old friend, down on their luck,' Lynford offered.

'A woman, perhaps?' He was being cryptic, a sure sign a woman was involved and Eliza felt confident she knew who, but perhaps not why. 'Rosenwyn Treleven, maybe?'

Lynford looked surprised. 'Why would you think that?'

'You mentioned she and Mr Kitto were newly married.' She bit her lip, trying to hide a smile at her discovery. Another layer peeled back. Lynford was a secret romantic. She didn't need a great imagination to see how this story went: Rosenwyn and Cade Kitto falling in love, but Kitto needing to leave Porth Karrek for the pursuit of his work, a lifestyle not suited to the gently bred Rosenwyn. In order to help his friend, Lynford had supported her idea of a school. It was overwhelming, really. A whole school given in order to see his friend wed. 'I think that is the very grandest of gestures,' Eliza assured him.

'It was the least I could do for her. She'd been jilted in love before. I didn't want to see her hurt again.' It was a difficult admission for him to make. Eliza heard it in his tone. Another layer fell. Lynford was a humble man at his core. He didn't like attention being called to his good deeds.

They passed a worktable with tools and a book lay open beside a microscope. 'I apologise, I haven't picked up after myself,' Lynford excused the mess. 'I've been researching the healing properties of orchids. Ancient Chinese herbalists believed the orchid could heal disease. I've also been extracting vanilla from the orchids for cooking.'

'You're a gourmet, a botanist, a scientist.' Eliza studied him. She'd not been prepared to find so much underneath. 'The Marquess of Lynford is a Renaissance man.'

'Hardly. I am just me. Eaton. I do wish you'd use my name as I asked you to last night.' He steered them around a corner. 'Ah, here we are, the fountain and the aviary.' They'd reached the centre of the orangery, the source of the trickling water and the chirping birds. Birds hung in large, elaborate cages while others flew about unfettered, decorating the space with their bright colours. Eliza sat at the edge of the fountain, her skirts spread about her, watching in amazement as he held up a finger and a small green-and-yellow bird landed. Lynford—*Eaton*—dug in his evening-coat pocket and retrieved some seed. He let it eat, smoothing the bird's feathers with a gentle hand.

'This is a parakeet. Would you like to hold him? He's quite tame. Stick out your finger like a bar. He'll hop on,' Eaton instructed.

Thinking of him as Eaton was a dangerous step to take. It fostered a sense of intimacy as real as the intimacy they'd shared at the table, only this first-name intimacy was more portable. It would not be left behind with the dishes. It would go with them wherever they went.

The parakeet hopped onto her finger and Eliza gasped, delighted. 'I've never done anything like this,' she said. Eliza almost blurted out how much Sophie would love to see the birds, but her daughter was not a topic of casual conversation. Sophie belonged to her private world, the world she entrusted to few.

'You're a natural. He likes you,' Eaton assured her.

She looked about at the birds in cages. 'I wonder if they get jealous of the parakeets flying free?' As beautiful as the orangery was, she didn't like the idea of that beauty being at the expense of caged animals.

'Those birds can't fly.' Eaton followed her gaze. 'They all have various injuries. I brought them home from wherever I found them and nursed them as best I could.' He took the parakeet from her and set it to flying with its friends; Eliza felt her heart lurch in an unfamiliar way. Here was a man who was kind to animals, who built a school for a friend so she could marry the man she loved, who gave a stranger a home just because she asked for one, who mourned the loss of a dear friend. He was a rarity, like the orchids along the pathway.

'I fear too much of tonight has been about me. I didn't mean to monopolise the conversation.' Eaton reached overhead and plucked an orange. 'Dessert?'

She nodded. 'I was the one who asked the questions. You needn't feel guilty. You're an interesting man.' She could listen to him talk for hours.

'Well, you're an interesting woman and I'm wasting my opportunity to learn more about you by talking about myself.' He began to peel the fruit. 'I should have asked how the house is? If you have everything you need?' He passed her a section of the orange. 'I should also have had the decency to ask what has caused the change in your plans and whether I can do anything to assist? I hope it's nothing too serious?'

That depended on how seriously one took potential mutiny. Eliza took a bite of the succulent orange, buying time to gather her wits. Too often tonight she'd allowed herself to forget about business, to focus instead on being with him and the joy of simply being with someone who wasn't interested in her mines or her money. But his questions brought back reality and with it a reminder about how careful she needed to be.

'Just some unexpected mine business. We're timbering a new tunnel and I need to be on hand more than I'd anticipated.' She could see the answer disappointed him in its brevity, but she could not clarify further.

'Let me know if there's anything I can do.' He offered her another section of the orange with a smile, but she could see her lack of trust had insulted him.

'Thank you, but it's something I need to take care of alone.' A man like the Marquess, born to power, would never understand that she had to work twice as hard, had to be twice as strong as any man, that any weakness was enough to have her leadership called into question.

'Do you always handle everything alone?'

'Yes.' She met his gaze unabashedly. 'I've learned the hard way what happens to a woman when she doesn't.'

His eyes were on her, contemplating, his voice quiet and serious. 'Tell me, what happens to a woman who accepts help from a friend?'

'She becomes the target of society gossip. The worst of her character is assumed and the worst of her friend's character is assumed as well. Society does not tolerate men and women being friends.' It had started innocently enough with Miles Detford. She'd been establishing her control over the shareholders in that first year, unsure how to proceed on a matter. She'd gone to Detford for advice. She been naive in those early days. She'd not thought how others might look at those efforts with less friendly eyes. 'There were rumours that I was weak, unable to assume control of my husband's company. And that the gentleman in question was after my money, swindling me with kindness. I've never believed it. But I've made sure such a situation doesn't occur again.'

'Is this a cautionary tale for me?'

'No, it's for me. So that I remember what happens when I let down my guard.' Their eyes held for a moment before she rose. 'I ought to go. It's getting late and I've taken so much of your time today. Thank you for the evening.' If she left now, she might escape without offending him further, or without making herself vulnerable. She'd let down her guard too often tonight. There'd been only the one casualty for the indulgence—far better odds than she deserved.

'I'll see you out.' Eaton rose with her, but there was a stiffness in their politeness now—gone was the laughter in the carriage over spilled champagne, and the easy flow of conversation at dinner.

'My carriage will take you back to the dower house.' She understood the hidden message. He wasn't accompanying her, *unless* she asked. He was giving her every subtle assurance that he would not impose on her further in any way tonight. Eliza found the assurance disappointing and impressive. There wouldn't be any kisses tonight. He handed her into the carriage and stepped back. 'Goodnight, Eliza. Thank you for a lovely evening.' He motioned to the driver and the carriage set off, leaving him behind.

She ought to be glad of that. She also ought to be glad that he understood her need for formality and distance, that this was strictly a business arrangement, that she saw him as a business acquaintance only. Except she didn't. She saw him as a problem, a very attractive one. She'd only known him the sum of two days and three encounters. Already it was incredibly easy to let him shoulder her concerns and solve her problems. She could get used to that without even realising she was doing it. She preferred to keep her independence fully intact because she knew how this would end.

She had learned her lessons well and she would not repeat her mistakes with Eaton Falmage. She would not let these friendly encounters get out of hand or signal that she might be interested in something…more. She was worldlier now. She knew how her association with any man would look to others. She knew exactly what she risked in marriage to any man who might offer. And she knew how these stories ended in the real world.

Chapter Eight

The night had gone differently from what Eaton had anticipated. What had started as dinner and a chance to explore the connection between them had quite unexpectedly deepened into something more. Eaton made the long walk to the main house under the stars, hands in his pockets. It was chilly in the evening now, autumn had definitely arrived and he was without both his greatcoat and his carriage, having not brought one and having given the other to Eliza.

He'd not meant to talk of Richard Penlerick and yet once he'd started he hadn't been able to stop himself. Tonight had been about more than a physical connection between them. They'd both experienced great loss. Her words tonight had been a balm to him in a way the platitudes of others who'd not experienced such loss could not be. He was touched as well by what she'd shared, cognisant of the honour she'd done him by offering her own story in proof of her understanding. Yet there were other things she had not been willing to share, like the business that kept her in Porth Karrek. For all her openness about the loss of her husband, she'd withheld other things.

Eaton kicked at a pile of early fallen leaves. The restlessness that had tugged at him that afternoon was riding him hard now. It would be nice to enjoy autumn with Eliza Blaxland. They could pick apples, stroll the Trevaylor Woods, check on the boys at the school to see how the new curriculum was working. Perhaps they could work on her schools together. Perhaps he could persuade her that the first school should be right here at Wheal Karrek. Eliza would be a welcome distraction; an intelligent, discreet woman who could discuss the world and ideas with him. She would need persuading, though. Despite her abrupt dismissal tonight, she *did* respond to him. His attentions were not unwanted but he would need to take things slowly. She was not a merry widow but a very circumspect one, a woman who took her virtue seriously. He could respect that.

The sound of a dog howling in the distance brought a smile to his lips. Baldor, his hound, was out night hunting, restless like his master. Eaton whistled. The two of them could prowl the grounds together. He whistled again and Baldor bounded to his side, ready for an evening romp in the woods. A walk beneath the autumn moon would be just the thing to clear his thoughts, beginning with images of Eliza Blaxland as she'd been tonight—laughing in the carriage with him, her face inquisitive and glowing by the candlelight of their dinner, her exclamation of delight over the parakeet landing on her finger, her sincerity as they'd talked of Richard.

Tonight, he'd had a glimpse of the Eliza Blaxland who existed beneath her façade. But that glimpse had been fleeting. She'd remembered all too soon she had something to hide. That mystery would have to wait until tomorrow. He had business in Penzance that would keep him away most of the day, but he would look in on her later in the afternoon, perhaps invite her to another dinner where he could try once more to unravel her secrets.

The day had not gone as Eliza would have preferred. She'd wanted answers and she had none. She'd spent the day at the mine office going over books and peering out of the window at every noise, hoping to see Miles Detford ride in. But there'd been no news, not even a note. She hoped she hadn't erred in sending for him, that he wasn't raising the alarm among the shareholders. She was relying on his friendship to keep her circumspect message private between them. But Miles had not come.

There were plenty of grounds on which to excuse his negligence. It was entirely possible he was off to Scotland, shooting grouse. The message might not even have reached him. He might be delayed by other matters. Still, Miles's absence niggled at her against the backdrop of another who had far less reason to come to her aid and yet had arrived immediately.

Her mind whispered the comparison: *Eaton Falmage came and he owes you nothing, not even friend-*

ship. Eaton had responded to her note with his presence, with the offer of a home. She'd asked for nothing more than some answers from Miles.

Then again, perhaps Eaton Falmage had made the offer in hopes of getting something in return. He'd been disappointed in her last night. Would he still come if she summoned him today, or was he already regretting his generosity? She knew how these trades worked. She'd refused Detford's honourable overtures of marriage when society had confused their friendship for something more intimate. In retrospect, though, society wasn't the only one who'd imagined intimacy where she'd been blind. Detford had wanted more than friendship. There'd been a few kisses stolen in a moment of loneliness, of weakness, kisses that had meant more to him, signalled more to him, than she'd intended in her early grief. She wouldn't make that mistake again. It was why she'd left Lynford last night. To have stayed any longer in the orangery would have resulted in more kisses, more steps along a path she couldn't travel, no matter how handsome the companion.

Eliza looked at the wall clock and shut the ledgers with a resounding thump. Half past three. These were thoughts that made it impossible to work. She'd daydreamed the better part of the last half hour away and to no purpose. She was destined to be alone for Sophie's sake and for her own security. She'd decided this years ago. It was useless to persist in wasting time on such folly. It was time to go home. Sophie would be arriving and she wanted to be there. The day would be infinitely better once her daughter had arrived. Five days away from Sophie seemed like an eternity. She was never truly alone when they were together.

Eliza stopped at Chegwin's mercantile on Budoc Lane to purchase a kite and a doll for Sophie. She would leave the toys on Sophie's bed as a surprise. They could have a picnic tomorrow at the beach if the weather held. Her head was full of plans. This would be a holiday for the two of them. She would carve out time for fun even though she had business to look after. She was always so busy in Truro with the banks and the mines. A holiday would do them both good and the fresh air had much to recommend it.

Halfway down the drive to the dower house, she noticed the activity in the drive, an unfamiliar coach outside the house, servants bustling about hauling trunks inside. A tall, slim, young woman whom Eliza recognised as Miss Gilchrist—Sophie's governess—stood amid the chaos, looking about helplessly as progress was made without her. Eliza's mood lifted with realisation. Sophie was here! They must have arrived early. She spotted her daughter's dark curls bobbing in and out of the servants. 'Mama!' Sophie rushed towards her.

Eliza took her skirts in one hand and began to run. It was an awkward run, burdened as she was with a kite and a doll, but it served to close the distance and within moments Sophie was in her arms, her packages forgotten. 'Oh, sweet girl, you're here! How I've missed you!' Eliza held her tight. This was everything, her whole world right here in her arms.

'I've missed you, too, Mama, but we've had such grand adventures, Miss Gilchrist and I. The wheel on the coach broke just as we were almost here and Miss Gilchrist didn't know what to do. The driver said we should walk back to the last town,' Sophie rambled enthusiastically, 'but Miss Gilchrist said that was impossible because you were expecting us tonight and you'd worry if we didn't arrive. Then a man came by on a great big chestnut horse…'

Sophie paused for a breath, then continued in a rush to make up for lost time.

'We told him who we were and he brought us here. He said he was a friend of yours. He sent his coach back for our things and for Miss Gilchrist, who was too scared to get on the horse. But I wasn't too scared. I climbed right up and he held on to me tight so I didn't fall.'

A hundred thoughts hit her at once. Her precious child had willingly gone off with a stranger just because he said he knew her and Miss Gilchrist had *allowed* it. She ought to sack the woman for such a poor decision. Sophie was the Blaxland heiress. When she came of age, she'd be worth a fortune. In the right hands, or in this case the wrong ones, Sophie would be a powerful weapon to wield against her. Yet beneath Eliza's fears there was gratefulness, too. What a kindness the man had done them. 'Is your rescuer still here?' She searched Sophie's sweet face to assure herself Sophie had come to no harm. They would have to discuss the demerits of going off with strangers later.

'He's inside, giving orders. He's very good at that.

Almost as good as you, Mama,' Sophie averred, obviously impressed. 'But he smiles when he tells people what to do.'

A man was inside her house? Giving orders? That seemed a bit much. She needed to offer her gratitude and send him on his way. Eliza rose, remembering her dropped packages. 'I brought you presents. Why don't you go inside and unwrap them while I make my thanks?'

'There he is, Mama!' Sophie pointed at the archway of the arcade where a tall, dark-haired man emerged from the house, recognisable for his confidence as much as his greatcoat. *Eaton Falmage.* Eliza's heart skipped as he waved and strode towards them. He knew, then. Her secret. One of them, at least, was out. Would he be angry she hadn't told him?

'I see you've called for reinforcements. Have you tired of my company already?' He was all easy laughter and grins. 'I met this fine young lady on the road on my way home from Penzance. She was stranded.' He gave Sophie a wink and then fixed Eliza with his merry stare. 'You can imagine my surprise when she told me she was yours. For a moment I didn't believe her. How could that be possible? I thought. In none of our conversations had the mention of children ever come up.' He was teasing her and scolding her all at once. His gaze turned serious. 'But then I decided it must be true. After all, there are other things you haven't told me as well.' Such as her mine business. Or the fact that she was the *second* Mrs Blaxland.

'You must forgive me, I'm a very private person.'

She rested a hand on Sophie's shoulder. 'I do thank you for your timely intervention and your efforts. Once again, I am in your debt.'

Eaton shook his head. 'I am not keeping score, Mrs Blaxland.'

'Aren't you?' she replied coolly, a little frisson of awareness passing between them.

'A man of honour doesn't leave a young girl and her governess stranded on the road, score or not,' Eaton scolded and she demurred. She'd not meant to slander his honour. What was wrong with her? Had her life really become nothing more than tally marks in ledgers? A keeping of score between her friends and her enemies?

Miss Gilchrist bustled up, having recovered her senses, ready to take charge of Sophie. 'Shall we go to our rooms and see to the unpacking, Miss Sophie?' She ushered Sophie away, the girl chattering excitedly about seeing the house.

'Does she never stop talking?' Eaton asked with a laugh. It wasn't meanly said. 'I find it a marvel she has so much to say.' He slanted her a sideways glance. 'Unlike her mother, apparently. Why didn't you tell me, Eliza?'

'Would it have mattered? Would you not have offered the house?' Eliza answered swiftly.

'Of course it would have mattered. I would have offered *more*. There are toys in the nursery at Falmage Hill just gathering dust. I'll have someone clean them up and send them down. There are picture books, a boat, toy soldiers, my sisters' tea sets and dolls.'

'Your sisters?' Eliza interrupted, intrigued.

'Four of them, all younger than me, and a younger brother, too.' Eaton shook his head. 'They were the bane of my existence growing up, but now that my sisters are all married and live away with my darling nieces and nephews, I love them far more than I ever did when we were all together.' He chuckled. 'They don't come here any more. Falmage Hill is too far away and there are too many of them. It's quite the mobilisation. It's much easier for me to travel to them.'

'You miss them.' Eliza heard the wistfulness in his voice. He was always so confident, always in charge, always knew what to do. It was hard to imagine there were any voids in his life, any gaps he struggled to fill.

'I suppose I do, in my own way.' He grinned, but Eliza wasn't fooled. He'd grinned to hide the hurt. 'I'll tell Cook to send extra cake. Sophie told me her favourite dessert is chocolate cake, but that any cake will do in a pinch. Very practical, your daughter is, very sensible when it comes to desserts.'

'Perhaps Cook should send food for three.' The spontaneity of the offer surprised even her. The words were out before she could take them back. She was toying with temptation now, creating more time in his intoxicating presence, and she was being bold. Perhaps too bold. He might read an invitation in it. Eliza hastily backtracked, offering him a way out. 'That is, if you're not previously engaged or if Sophie hasn't already talked your ears off.'

Eaton continued grinning. 'Supper for three it is. I can't think of anywhere I'd rather be. I shall see you at seven o'clock.'

Chapter Nine

As dinners went, it certainly couldn't compete with the crystal and candlelight of the orangery. The food was plain, more appropriate for younger tastes than the sophisticated palate Eaton had presented her with the previous evening. Yet the meal had a dangerous charm of its own that Eliza was quick to recognise: the pseudo-image of a family gathered for an evening meal, simple foods and fresh cider in place of chilled champagne, a chatty young girl whose exuberant conversation carried an energy of its own. She was delighted in everything: the new house, her room, the gifts, her rescue—which had resulted in a ride on the 'most splendid horse in the world'. She was especially delighted in the chocolate cake, which, despite its promise, saw Sophie asleep at the table before it was even served.

'I suppose that's all the more reason to eat dessert first.' Eaton laughed softly in the candlelight of the dining room. 'We'll wrap up a piece for her to have tomorrow.'

We. How easy it was for this man to insinuate himself into their lives. She needed to put a stop to it before it went any further. Her debt to him was growing, as was her appreciation. 'I'm sorry,' Eliza apologised, 'I need to put her to bed.' She always put Sophie to bed, even though Miss Gilchrist was on hand. Eliza liked the ritual of bedtime, of closing the day together. 'There's brandy in the parlour, if you care to wait?' It felt awkward to act the hostess, as if Eaton was a guest in the house when he owned it and could do as he pleased. He *knew* there was brandy in the parlour. He'd instructed it to be put there.

'Let me help.' Eaton rose and lifted Sophie, who didn't stir at being hoisted away from her longed-for chocolate cake. 'She's done admirably for such an eventful day. Apparently, she's inherited her mother's tenacity.'

Eliza picked up a lamp and led the way upstairs, trying not to let her heart run away with her mind at the sight of Eaton Falmage's broad shoulder hosting Sophie's dark head. She told herself it was merely the paternal image of a man with a child that tugged at her, not the sight of that *particular* man. She might feel that way about any man offering a glimpse of his softer side. 'If you just lay her on the bed, I can tuck her in,' Eliza offered. Once the Marquess had left, she prepared her for bed, smoothed back Sophie's dark hair and kissed her forehead, arranging the blankets around her. 'Goodnight, my dear. Sleep well, we have more adventures planned for tomorrow.'

Downstairs, dishes had already been cleared by the efficient staff and a low fire in the parlour beckoned invitingly. One might find the scene cosy if one wasn't on edge. She hadn't been alone with a man in such an intimate, domestic setting for years. 'Will you sit with me while I have some brandy?' Eaton asked. How could she refuse after all he'd done today? It was a simple enough request, the only danger in it came from herself and the constructs she put on it.

Eliza took a seat while Eaton poured. 'Would you like a drink as well?'

'No, I don't drink spirits, but thank you,' she declined, hands folded tightly in her lap. Prolonging the evening like this was a poor idea. Such a setting begged for intimacies, for sharing things that should be kept private. She was merely passing through.

'You only drink champagne? You have exalted tastes, Eliza. I'd best remember that,' Eaton teased congenially, settling in the wing-backed chair across from her. How did he do that? How did he make it so easy to be with him? To laugh? To banter? One would have thought they were old friends instead of new acquaintances.

He sipped his brandy. 'Did you have a productive day at the mines?' he asked as if they were a married couple discussing their day. They'd be a very different sort of married couple. Wives didn't run mines. Cits didn't marry future dukes and *she* wouldn't marry anyone. Ever.

On those grounds, the fantasy wasn't only different, it was dangerous. Eaton didn't even have to try to seduce her, if that was his intention. She was seducing herself, seeing all sorts of domestic fantasies on her own: a family assembled at the dinner table, a conversation that veered and swerved with Sophie's enthusiasm, jumping from topic to topic, tucking Sophie in when the enthusiasm was spent. But it was a fantasy only, nice in theory, impractical in reality. She wasn't looking for a man to fill that role and she would not trade all she'd fought for simply to have a marriage. It wouldn't be fair to her daughter or to herself to have fought so hard for everything to simply give it over to a husband. 'The new tunnel is proceeding.' Her answer was succinct and she quickly turned the conversation to him. 'And your day? What were you doing in Penzance?'

'I was looking in on one of the school's donors, Mrs Penhaligon, the other widow. She's been very much alone since her husband died and she moved away from Porth Karrek, even though it's only a few miles.' Not just the other widow. The other *woman*. Eliza recognised the name now from that first conversation at the school when she'd made her surprise visit.

'You make a habit of collecting widows, it seems,' Eliza replied more sharply than she intended. Surely she wasn't jealous? She didn't even know this woman. Was she young? Old? Pretty? Did Eaton take her for carriage rides and pour champagne for her as well? They were unworthy thoughts when she'd just reminded herself there could be no pursuit here.

'I needed the name of a piano tuner.' Eaton eyed her suspiciously as if he sensed the envy beneath her sharpness. Too late she remembered Mrs Penhaligon was the donor of the prized Sébastien Érard. Eaton gave her a reprieve, turning the topic. 'Now, what adventures do you have in mind for tomorrow? The weather will be fine. Might I suggest a picnic at the beach? I can bring the carriage at noon. There's a cove at Karrek Sands with arguably the best beach in Cornwall. Sophie will love it. She can fly her new kite.'

He was going to come with them.

It was the last thing she needed. But also the first. Eliza didn't know how to make the arrangements for a picnic other than to burden the servants with the task, which she was loath to do since they weren't hers. His presence would be a great help. 'I've taken enough of your time,' she began to refuse. She really couldn't impose further, couldn't lead him on. She knew the rules of engagement. Most of all, she shouldn't lead herself on, pretending something was possible. How ironic that after all this time worrying about protecting herself from the external threat of men, the real threat to her own freedom seemed to come from her and her own longings.

Eliza rose. She needed to be clear with him now before this relationship of sorts spiralled out of control.

'It's no imposition on me.' Eaton rose with her, understanding her signal to depart.

'Perhaps it is to me,' Eliza said firmly, meeting his gaze. 'It occurs to me that you must really want something to go to these lengths for me. I will not kiss you for your efforts.'

Eaton's dark gaze became inscrutable, an indecipherable smile playing on his lips, part wry humour, part offended honour. 'I should hope not, Eliza, since such a trade would imply I am a man who has to buy a woman's affections and that you are a woman who would sell them. I think neither implication paints either one of us in a particularly good light.' He inclined his head, short and curt. 'Goodnight.' She had meant to put him off and it seemed she'd succeeded. If she didn't care for the terseness in his tone, she only had herself to blame.

Eliza wasn't alone. Eaton absently stroked Baldor's head as the two of them lounged by the fire in the library, Baldor standing at majestic attention beside his chair. 'She has a child,' Eaton said out loud to the dog. He'd not known about Sophie any more than he'd known about Blaxland's second marriage. Perhaps Eliza had got her love of privacy from Blaxland.

Eaton stretched his legs, resting his boots on the fireplace fender. Was Sophie all she was protecting with her privacy or was there something more? There'd been mixed emotions on her face when she'd seen him this afternoon. She reminded him of paintings of the Madonna, on her knees, clutching her child, her eyes closed in a moment of private joy at the reunion, yet when she'd opened them and seen him, there'd been a fleeting look of fear before she'd recognised him. She'd been expecting a stranger and the notion of a stranger had given her a degree of fright. Perhaps that was just maternal instinct. His own sisters were like that, panicking when a child disappeared into the woods for too long.

Eaton closed his eyes, reliving the pleasantness of the evening. He'd not had such a night for ages; no stiff evening wear, no need to be conscious of every word, only honest conversation and laughter. There'd been plenty of that. Sophie told funny stories—at least they were funny when told through a child's eyes. There'd been no terror for Sophie in being stranded on the road, only adventure and excitement. Eaton envied her that precious innocence. Eliza would guard it well if that look on her face today was any indication. She was a fierce mother. Fierce in love, fierce in protection.

His thoughts lingered on the word: *mother.* Eliza was a mother. He understood now why she felt compelled to resist the pull between them. A mother must always think of her children. Her reputation was their reputation. But she was also a woman, a young woman, with a young woman's desires and fantasies. He'd felt those fantasies stir in her when they'd kissed. She was a woman full of passions, not only for her child, but for living and for loving. Yet she was choosing to stifle the latter in order to protect the former. What a very difficult decision to make—to give up adventure and passion in its various forms for the sake of others. Unless, of course, she didn't know what she was missing.

Eaton's eyes opened slowly at the thought. He could help her there. If there was anyone who knew the value of adventure, it was him. But to what end? To coax her into a short-lived affair? He would be discreet, of course. No one outside the two of them needed to know. He could preserve her reputation and in exchange he could have a lover. He could even pretend to have a family. That was dangerous ground, to co-opt Eliza's child as his own even for a short time. In his opinion, it was the epitome of selfishness. No one should suffer from his affliction but himself. He'd not missed the instant admiration in Sophie's eyes this afternoon when he'd taken her up on his horse. Children often attached easily and quickly. Eliza might not be hurt when the affair ended, but Sophie would be. She wouldn't understand this thing they played at wasn't meant to last.

He was not an unkind man, nor a terribly selfish one. Did he dare pursue Eliza Blaxland now that a child was involved? 'And yet how can I not?' Eaton said to Baldor, who only perked up an ear. 'How can I let her go when I sense that she needs me?' Eliza Blaxland had secrets to keep and dragons to slay. She was in desperate need of a knight in shining armour even if an affair was out of the question, even if she didn't realise it. The strong ones never did. It was that very strength he admired most about her. He wanted her to keep that strength. It was the core of her. Eliza would have his sword, whether she wanted it or not. The trick would be in convincing her to accept it. A picnic tomorrow would be an ideal place to start. Perhaps once she accepted his help, more could follow.

It was not a good morning, despite the beautiful autumn weather outdoors. Miles Detford stared pensively at the papers spread out before him on the table before eyeing the other men with him. 'What we dare borders on treachery. To be caught would be tantamount to fraud,' he warned, but his words lacked conviction. There were benefits to the proposal as well, benefits that were worth the risk. He'd waited a long time for success.

'Do you think she'll accept our offer?' asked silver-templed Gismond Brenley, his gaze sharp. 'You know her best, after all, Detford.' There was a derisive undertone to Brenley's comment, a reminder that they'd tried and failed five years ago to take Eliza Blaxland out of the equation of mine ownership through a sentimental offer of marriage. Brenley held that failure over his head like the Sword of Damocles.

Miles shrugged to indicate indecision. 'She certainly should. The terms are generous. We are offering to buy out her shares in the mines at considerable profit to her. She can live in comfort without worry. But she's been offered such benefits before. She can take the money and invest it in some other venture if that's of interest to her.'

'Perhaps money will appeal to her more than a husband,' Brenley needled.

Isley Thorp, slender and sallow-faced, sitting on Detford's right, looked over the tops of his spectacles. 'Considerable profit under *today's* terms,' he reminded the group. 'If she sold today, the money would look generous. But against the future profits once that tunnel is complete, our offer looks paltry.' This was where they trod the grey area of defrauding. One could easily argue they knew it was a poor offer against the expected returns on the new tunnel.

Brenley pursed his mouth. 'Mining is a risk. The manager at the mine, Cardy, says there's a goodly amount of copper in that tunnel waiting to be plucked out. But there's a chance he's wrong. It's our bank accounts that take that gamble. We can't promise what we'll find there. She can't hold us accountable for future success if she sells out before then.' That would be their defence in court if it ever came to that. 'Any woman would be pleased with such an offer. She has a young child. Surely she can spend her time better raising her instead of running between her mines and meeting with shareholders.'

Miles raised smooth blond brows. 'When has Eliza Blaxland ever behaved like any other woman? It's unnatural how she acts, managing business, money and ourselves as if we're children unable to make decisions without her. If she doesn't take this offer, we'll be tied to her apron strings for life. How do the other shareholders feel?'

The third man, Isley Thorp, who'd been silent up until now, shook his head. 'Some are with us. But others are ambivalent. They say she's made us money, she's done a fine job of modernising. Why should she be ousted?'

'Not ousted, *persuaded*,' Brenley corrected impatiently. 'We're not forcing anyone out. We're simply putting an option to her out of consideration for her and her daughter.'

Thorp nodded. 'It sounds legitimate when you put

it that way. Perhaps you should be the one who presents the idea to her?'

Yes, Miles thought. Perhaps it was time Brenley stuck his neck out for this venture instead of making plans for others to carry out. But Miles shook his head. He wanted his revenge, his pride restored. No one had made him look as foolish as Eliza Blaxland had. 'No, that's my job. But not just yet. We'll let her stew for a bit in her own worries. We'll let her wonder why I've delayed answering her summons. The more unaware we can catch her, the more desperate she'll be. The shareholders' meeting is in just a few weeks at Porth Karrek.'

The meeting was being held there to celebrate the new tunnel. Miles exchanged a meaningful glance with Brenley. In this, they agreed. The meeting would be the ideal ground on which to launch their campaign against Eliza Blaxland, the woman who had refused him, who had made him look like a laughingstock when he'd gone to her with a decent offer of marriage. He would not let her play him again. He would go to her in the guise of a friend and she would not realise it was otherwise until it was too late.

Thorp spoke up. 'What if you fail to convince her as you've failed in the past? Are we willing to take more severe measures?'

Miles reached for the papers and rolled them up. Thorp was an icy businessman. He knew what Thorp meant by other measures: violence, kidnapping, murder. 'We certainly won't rule anything out, but let's hope for once that Eliza Blaxland will see sense, for all our sakes.'

Chapter Ten

The cove at Karrek Sands was everything Eaton had promised and more; the picnic was a lavish but simple outing. Servants had gone ahead to set up a canopy and chairs and to unpack hampers of food so that all was ready when they arrived. Yet the preparations did not hinder the authenticity of the picnic. This was not a formal occasion. Sophie had brought her kite and immediately set about getting it aloft. Eliza watched her barefoot daughter from the shade of the canopy, envious of her licence to play in the sand and to tempt the waves sans socks and shoes.

Beside her, Eaton began to tug at his boots. 'Well? Aren't you going to take your shoes off, too?' He cast her a boyish glance as he divested himself of his footwear, revealing a long, narrow foot with a freckle in its centre. 'What? Have you never seen a man's foot before?' he teased before she could look away. 'This might be the last of the good weather; it's certainly the last of the *warm* weather. It would be a shame to waste it.'

Eaton winked and rolled up his trouser legs, showing off well-muscled calves. 'Come on, Eliza, no one will see. We've the entire beach to ourselves, all the privacy you could want.' He shucked off his coat and waistcoat, looking much as he had the first time she saw him, *en déshabillé*, moving furniture at the school. He rose and waved to Sophie, who was calling to him to come fly the kite. He gave her a smile that bordered on wicked. 'Come and play, I dare you,' he said, and then he was off, trotting to the water's edge to fly the kite.

Eliza smiled to herself as she removed shoes and socks and even her jacket. It would indeed be a shame to waste the opportunity to frolic on the beach, especially after all the effort Eaton had taken to ensure the beach was entirely theirs. Marquesses could do such things. Karrek Sands was theirs for the afternoon. Nothing could touch them here—not the mines, not her worries over the ledgers, not even propriety's whisperings that she should not bare her ankles in public or be interacting privately with a man. The beach was both public and private. It was also paradise and it was hers for the day—a precious day to enjoy her daughter. Sophie was nine and nearing that bridge between girlhood and womanhood. How much longer would she be allowed to wander shorelines barefoot before society deemed it unladylike? Her dear girl was growing up too fast.

Eliza tied up her skirts and went to join them. There

was a good breeze blowing and the kite was flying high. 'Look, Mama, we've used almost all of the string! I've never got a kite up so high before,' Sophie exclaimed.

'You're a natural flier,' Eaton complimented. 'Why don't we try some tricks?' His hair was mussed and his calves were speckled with sticky sand, proof he'd been running in the water, no doubt saving the kite from a soaking before Sophie had become a natural. Eaton stood behind Sophie, an easy hand on her shoulder, ready to intervene if needed. A gust of wind took the kite and it dived, dipping dangerously towards the waves. 'Oh, no!' Sophie exclaimed in panicked worry.

'Steady, Sophie.' Eaton's voice was calm. Instead of taking the spool and fixing the situation for her, he coached her in even tones. 'Reel in the string, just a little, don't tug, that will only make the kite jerk more and then it can't stabilise. There, see, you've done it. The kite has settled and you can let out the string. Well done, Sophie. Now, are we ready for some tricks?'

They were enjoying each other. How exciting it must be for Sophie to have the attention of an adult other than herself. Eliza busied herself gathering seashells, wanting to be close, but not wanting to intrude overmuch on the interlude. She surreptitiously watched Eaton show Sophie how to make the kite soar like a bird, swooping and diving in the sky before turning the kite back over to her. Sophie was clapping her hands and saying something to Eaton that Eliza couldn't hear. It must have pleased him. He smiled at Sophie and bent down to say something in return.

This was yet another sight to warm her. How different he was from Huntingdon. Huntingdon had been an old parent, too set in his ways to visit the nursery and play with a toddler. He'd adored his daughter, but he'd been unable to be the sort of father a child dreams of—a father who runs along the beach with them, a father who takes them for horseback rides and carries them to bed as if they were featherweights.

Eaton would be a spectacular father.

It was an unsettling and inappropriate thought. Eliza looked away from the kite flying. She could not give flight to that sort of fantasy. It was best to quell it before it got out of hand and the best way to do that was to think about reality. Argument one: a day with a child did not prove a man was good father material. It merely showed that he had a capacity for kindness. Argument two: Eaton Falmage had no intention of taking on another man's child. It wasn't what heirs to a dukedom did. Dukes' heirs made their own families. Argument three: she wasn't looking for a father for Sophie or a husband for herself. She'd made that decision years ago. She'd best get her emotions under control and rein in these fantastical constructions. She'd made her situation clear to Eaton last night. Today, he was merely being kind. He knew there was no hope in pursuing her. She was complicated.

Eliza allowed herself to glance at the duo again. Eaton smiled, this time for her. He strode towards her, collapsing beside her in the sand. 'She's having a good time.' He propped himself up on an elbow. 'Your daughter is wonderful. You've raised her well.'

'Thank you.' Eliza found herself blushing. 'I worry for her, being an only child. I was an only child and it's a lonely way to grow up. I would have preferred she had a brother or sister, at least one.' She drew an abstract figure in the sand, uncomfortable with the confession. It brought the conversation too close to other truths. She had not meant to say so much. She hazarded a glance at Eaton and offered a tremulous smile.

Eaton's dark gaze clouded, his brows knit as a shadow scuttled across his features. Perhaps talk of children unsettled him. It unsettled many bachelors. 'You could marry again. You're still young. You have much to offer.' A quiet intimacy settled between them at the suggestion. A new awareness of him unfurled in her belly, warm and inviting. She must resist.

'No.' Her answer was firm but barely audible over the waves. 'I've become too set in my ways these last five years. A husband would not find me biddable.' She shook her head with finality. 'I refused the last man who proposed.'

'Why?' Eaton did not allow her to dismiss the topic.

'I had nothing to give up when I married Huntingdon. But I have much to lose in a marriage now and I've seen what a woman gives up when she marries. It cost my mother everything. She turned her life over to her husband, who was only moderately good with money, and then to her husband's brother when her husband died. My well-meaning uncle was even worse with money than my father. By the time I was fourteen I knew with surety I'd do whatever it took to avoid my mother's fate. I started learning about the family business.'

'And then you married a man twice your age and more.'

'I was *not* after his money,' Eliza snapped.

'I did not mean to suggest that you were. I was merely curious as to what impelled you to marry as you did,' Eaton answered in sharp offence.

They were teetering on the brink of a quarrel. She would not be judged by anyone, certainly not by a marquess who'd had his perfect life handed to him, no matter how humble he seemed. 'Huntingdon Blaxland came to my uncle and proposed the match. And I took the offer. He was a good man and my choices were limited.' Not that it was any of Eaton's business. If she was upset over these disclosures, it was her own fault for having shared them.

Eliza blew out a breath, gathering her composure. She should not be discussing these things with a man she barely knew. She groped for a better topic of conversation, something lighter. 'Sophie will be spoiled after today. She'll expect to come to the beach every day.'

'Perhaps she should.' Eaton's smile returned, the shadow had passed. 'I think fresh air and exercise cannot be overestimated for children. You know what they say about all work and no play.' Eaton gave her a thoughtful look. 'It seems her home in Truro is a quiet place.'

Eliza looked down at her hands, wondering what Sophie had told him. 'We don't go out much. I have the mines to look after and before that we were in mourning and she was very young.' Sometimes she felt they'd never truly come out of mourning. It had been a convenient shield to hide behind, a legitimate reason to take herself out of the public eye. She went to business meetings and charity meetings, but she seldom went out at night to Truro's social gatherings. The few times she had gone out, Miles had been beside her and that had proved disastrous. Afterwards, it had seemed easier and safer to use mourning as an excuse not to engage.

'You're not in mourning any longer,' Eaton pointed out. 'Pardon my saying so, but it's been five years.' His gaze held hers and she knew he was doing the sums. Sophie would have been four, she wouldn't recall her father at all. He was thinking she didn't need to hold on to mourning for Sophie's sake. 'It must be lonely, living a secluded life with just Sophie for company.' His gaze studied her, unnerving her with the intensity of his dark eyes. 'Oftentimes people who choose seclusion see it as a form of protection.'

'And sometimes they simply value their privacy,' Eliza answered swiftly before she could take advantage of the opening and spill her troubles. How tempting it was, with nothing around them but sea and sand, to lay her problems on his shoulders.

'Should that cease to be the case, Eliza, I hope you would tell me.' Eaton pushed up from the sand with a burst of energy. 'Shall we eat? I have it on good authority Sophie is starving. I had the chocolate cake from last night packed and there might even be a few late-season strawberries.' He grinned at her and gave her his hand, banishing the seriousness of the prior moment; perhaps he also realised that a line had been crossed and a retreat into friendly acquaintanceship was necessary.

Lunch was an animated affair with Sophie talking of kites and seashells between bites of sandwiches and swallows of cider. As they relaxed on pillows beneath the canopy, Eaton fished through the bucket of shells. He held one up and shook it. 'Put that to your ear, Sophie, and tell me what you hear.'

Sophie did and her face lit up. 'I can hear the ocean!' She shook it again. 'Is the ocean in there?'

'No.' Eaton shook his head and took the shell, holding it on the flat of his palm. 'Do you see how the shell is curved? Air gets trapped in there and it makes a roaring, rushing sound when it bounces around inside the shell.' He looked over their heads and caught her gaze. 'Ambient noise is what it's called.'

'Let's try another!' Sophie was already digging through the pail, eager to test the hypothesis. This was an example of his curriculum, Eliza realised, the one he'd designed for Cador Kitto's conservatory. Learning by doing, by touching. How splendid it was to watch Sophie's face light up as she tried out the new word.

'Am…bi…ent…'

Eaton sorted through the bucket and pulled out one of the larger shells. 'Do you think you can spare these, Sophie?' He rose and went to his long-abandoned coat and fished in the pockets, discarding all sorts of bits until he drew out a length of twine and a penknife.

Eliza laughed. 'You have the pockets of a schoolboy. Are you sure there are no toads in there?'

Eaton gave her a wink. 'No toads, but plenty of useful items. Just watch.' He sat down beside Sophie and took the shell in hand, stringing it on a length of twine before tying it about Sophie's neck. 'There, a sea talisman for you. Now you can keep the ocean with you wherever you go, even when you're in Truro and miles away.' For a moment, the reminder lingered that this would all end. Then, Eaton leapt to his feet. 'Now, who wants to go exploring? There's an old smuggler's cave down the beach. Let's find it and see if there's any treasure left. You go on ahead, Sophie, and clear the way, while your mama and I follow.'

'You are as indefatigable she is. Do you never slow down?' Eliza laughed as they strolled at the edge of the beach, waves teasing their toes.

'Never. There's too much to do, too much to enjoy.' Eaton grinned and steered her out of the way of a large wave that threatened their feet.

It was her turn to probe as he'd done earlier on the beach. 'If we don't slow down, we often lose our chance to think, or perhaps that's the very reason we don't slow down. We don't want to think.' A whirlwind could be as effective a place to hide as the solitude he accused her of keeping. 'What's your reason?'

Eaton chuckled. 'What would I hide from, Eliza? I have everything I could want. Money, status, the power to do good in this world.' He bent down to pick up a pebble and skipped it out over the waves, perhaps to give himself something to do. He couldn't be still even in the moment. It made her wonder if she'd hit upon something after all. What could he possibly have to hide? What didn't he want to tell her?

'What will you do now that the school is underway? Are there other projects looming on your agenda?' She'd not meant to discuss the business of the mining schools today, but the opening was ideal.

Eaton shrugged and skipped another pebble. 'I'll plan my trip to Italy. I was supposed to go last spring, but then the school came along.' He smiled. 'I'll visit my sisters for the winter holidays, maybe spend a little time in London to make up for not being there this Season. I have experiments to conduct in the orangery. Perhaps Sophie can be my assistant. She has an agile mind.'

'You needn't feel you have to entertain her, or me,' Eliza quickly absolved him. 'I have work at the mine and a shareholders' meeting coming up and she has Miss Gilchrist to see to her.' Although Miss Gilchrist's lessons would hardly compare to the excitement of learning about ambient sound on the beach with Eaton or the physics of flying a kite. He might say he wasn't keeping score, but she was, and the ledger between them was becoming woefully unbalanced.

Eaton leaned close, whispering at her ear, 'Have you ever considered that maybe you're the one doing me the favour? That it's not the other way around, after all?'

'I fear we are a distraction, not a favour,' Eliza chided softly. She was not wrong. Eaton Falmage was a busy man for whom children were a passing fancy, not a priority. He had other things to consider: trips to Italy, London Seasons. His life was a collection of whirlwinds of which she and Sophie were merely one. Within a month they'd be forgotten.

They reached the cave. Sophie was already inside and Eaton had to duck to get through the entrance. 'I used to explore in here with my friends,' he told her. 'We once spent all summer looking for hidden treasure. We even had a map.'

Sophie's eyes went wide. 'Did you find anything?' she asked and Eliza found herself holding her breath along with Sophie, waiting for his answer.

'No, we never did.' He knelt down to Sophie's level and said seriously, 'But you know what that means.'

'That there isn't any treasure?' Sophie replied, disappointed.

'It means the treasure is still there. Waiting. Maybe for *you* to find it. Off you go, don't leave any rock unturned, no crevice unexplored.'

Sophie ran off and Eaton turned to Eliza, catching her frown. 'You disapprove? Or is it that you don't believe in treasure?'

'You're getting her hopes up. She'll be disappointed when she doesn't find it,' Eliza scolded softly.

'Disappointment isn't all bad,' Eaton replied, unconcerned. 'It's adds a certain flavour to life, as you well know. Certainly you're the better for your challenges, wouldn't you agree?'

It was hard to disagree with him at the moment. In the confines of the cavern, Eliza was acutely aware they were very much alone. In the cave, Eaton came fully into his height and breadth. His physique was not made for confined spaces. 'Do you speak from experience? You hardly seem the sort to have had disappointments,' she queried, slightly breathless. In such a space, it would be easy to be intimidated by him, or to think him invincible. She was not. She was enormously attracted to him. He filled the space entirely and her senses with it, reminding her, as he had in the garden, as he did *every time* she saw him, that she was more than a mine owner and a mother.

'Maybe I have found treasure, despite my earlier disappointments, after all, Eliza,' he whispered her name. 'These last two days have been extraordinary.' He leaned an arm against the rocky wall, bracketing her with his body. 'Maybe treasure doesn't come in an iron chest.'

'No, maybe it doesn't,' she answered, her breath catching, her imagination running wild. Maybe it came in the form of kisses stolen in a golden moment on a sun-kissed day. Her lips parted just a fraction in invitation and he took it without hesitation, his mouth commanding hers with a kiss, his body strong against her, and she gave over to it, surrendering herself to his mouth. How wondrous to lose herself just for a moment, to be swept away by another's touch, not to be an island unto herself.

There was a scream of glee somewhere beyond them, recalling them to reality. Eaton stepped back, but his eyes were hot even as his mouth curled in a smile. 'Sophie's found something,' he said softly with a laugh, but he took her hand, apparently as unwilling as she to break contact entirely. 'Shall we go and see? Then we'll have to head back. The tide will be in soon.'

Sophie didn't find any treasure, but she had found a starfish Eaton helped her throw back into the sea.

They headed back to the picnic area, their linked hands surreptitiously hidden in the folds of her skirts. It was a simple intimacy, one she should discourage, but it was less dangerous than a kiss. Perhaps that was why she allowed it. Perhaps there were other reasons, too. Perhaps she was lonely, starved for adult-human contact, although it did her no credit to admit it. It made her seem desperate, something she didn't like appearing even to herself. That was a craving she'd have to bottle. It had no place in her life now. She slipped her hand free.

'Where shall we go tomorrow?' Eaton asked as they gathered discarded socks and shoes.

'I have to work.' Eliza made her excuses before her willpower waned. Another day with Eaton was an intoxicating prospect.

'Not *all* day, certainly?' Eaton pressed irresistibly.

'No, not all day, but it's not just that.' She drew him aside with a meaningful glance and lowered her voice. 'One day is understandable, perhaps, if anyone saw us today. But a second day? I am a private woman by choice, Eaton, and by necessity. A woman in a man's company does not pass unnoticed, especially when that man is a marquess.' She arched a brow. 'Do you think because I am a widow that I am above censure?' It was precisely what he thought, she could tell from the rebuttal that died on his lips. The widows he knew were the former wives of aristocrats, who could afford, perhaps even welcomed, a little scandal to spice up their lives. 'What do you suppose happens to me as the head of the mining company if scandal is attached to my name?' She put the question to him point-blank. He did not run in her circles. She did not expect him to understand the knife edge she walked, but she could expect him to respect it. 'One false step and all I've worked for is forfeit.'

For a moment, she thought she'd convinced him, but his next words surprised her utterly. 'Then we'll go to the Trevaylor Woods. No one will see us and I can ensure complete privacy.' He was caressing her with his voice, low and seductive beneath the rhythm of the waves. 'Never say never, Eliza.'

Intuition told her this was the pivotal moment that would put her on a path down which she should not journey. She needed to proceed with business as usual. That meant no attachments. She needed to say no, but she didn't.

Chapter Eleven

Eliza hadn't said no. Eaton preferred to view that as a victory, despite having had to cajole an acceptance out of her.

He swung up on Titan. The day had been a heady one. It would be too easy to get caught up in the euphoria of it. A good canter over to the school to check in with Cade would help clear his head. Eaton kicked Titan into motion. He could appreciate a virtuous woman, but he couldn't resist her, although he probably should. There had been small victories today. Eliza had spoken of her marriage and he'd had a glimpse into her world. Into her.

One false step, one whiff of scandal.

Such a statement was not hyperbole to her. She knew it first-hand and, if he wanted to pursue a deeper relationship with her, the trick would be in convincing her to try again, that he could be trusted with discretion.

I'm a private person by necessity.

Detford had lacked that discretion and she was paying for it, forced to use the concept of privacy as a synonym for remaining apart, he thought. She was *alone* by necessity. Not unlike himself. He knew how hard it was to live that way. It gave them something terrible in common and it prompted the question: Could two people, destined to be alone, be together? Could two adverse situations result in a more optimistic outcome like multiplying negative integers to get a positive? It was a dangerous equation to consider.

Eaton gave Caesar his head on the long flat stretch before the school, letting the wind in his face obliterate any further thought. To travel down that particular road carried certain perils he did not wish to revisit.

At the school, he tossed his reins to a groom and went inside, listening unobtrusively at the open doors to the last lessons of the day in progress. He stopped at one door and smiled as bits of music filtered into the hall. Richard Penlerick would have been pleased.

He strode to the headmaster's office, poured a drink and settled in to wait for Cade. The dream was coming to life around him. Other dreams were coming to life as well, far less innocuous dreams—dreams of Eliza Blaxland and her darling Sophie, a family in need of completion. A Tantalus dream. That was what it was. Everything about today had whispered the old temptation. A widow with a child. A woman in need of a husband, a child in need of a father. On the surface, it could be the perfect arrangement. But beneath the surface, it wasn't. It was fraught with limitations and compromises.

Eaton took a long swallow of the brandy, letting it go down slow with his thoughts. Eliza Blaxland was not a widow looking for a husband. She'd made that extremely clear on the beach. She did not believe she could afford to remarry. She was unwilling to surrender her independence. It was for the best. He wasn't looking to marry her even if she were hunting a husband or a surrogate father. Marriage to him would be a death sentence for her dreams.

He took another long swallow, finishing the drink. He certainly couldn't marry her after her confession today that she wanted more children, that she regretted Sophie was an only child. Marrying him would mean trading her independence and getting nothing in return. The old pain rose again. Today had presented him with a mixture of emotions, from the excitement of pursuing an attractive woman, to the bittersweet glimpses of what could never be. Sophie was an energetic child with a keen mind. He'd loved creating adventures for her, watching her eyes light up, and yet that very response was a painful reminder of all he could never have.

Cade Kitto opened the door and entered, glancing at the clock. 'You're early. I apologise for the wait.'

'I needed a moment with my thoughts.' And now it was time to put those thoughts away. There were things he could not affect. He would never father a child. Medicine and science couldn't change that. But he could make life better for other children. He could love his nieces and nephews. He could create opportunities for students at his school and perhaps even help Eliza create opportunities for miners' children. He needed to focus his energies on what he *could* achieve. He knew from experience it was the best antidote to his own loss. And he'd spare some of that energy for planning an excursion to the Trevaylor Woods. It occurred to him, as Cade settled in to discuss the first week of school, that a search for antidotes was something else he and Eliza Blaxland had in common. They both dedicated significant effort to helping others in order to ease the emptiness in themselves—or perhaps to ignore that emptiness altogether.

The Woods. The sea caves on the beaches. A visit to the conservatory for a private recital from the upper-level students. Eaton had filled her days with excursions. This was all new territory for her—someone making plans for her, someone putting her first. Business as unusual had become business as usual, much to Eliza's tenuous delight. Eaton had been as good as his word; the outings were discreet. He'd ridden rough-shod over her insistence that she and Sophie didn't need to be entertained. 'I'm not interested in need,' Eaton would say when she protested. 'Perhaps I *want* to entertain you and Sophie.'

Who was she to resist the smiles of her daughter and the compelling grin of Eaton Falmage? And so the days established their own pattern. In the mornings she worked at the mine office while Sophie did her lessons. In the afternoons, Eaton planned adventures: autumn hikes in the Trevaylor Woods to collect colourful leaves and mushrooms, with Baldor sniffing at their heels; salmon fishing in the rivers; a carriage drive with the top down to old promontory forts. The list seemed inexhaustible, like the man himself. What drove him? Surely it wasn't simply the delight of her company. 'We'll save the adventures closer to home for when the weather turns,' he'd tell them whenever she protested at the distance and effort each outing took, fearing it took too much advantage of him.

Today, the adventure was the ruins of Bosrigan Fort, one of the many cliff 'castles' built along the coast. In truth, it was more of a wall or enclosure than a castle, but it provided adventure for Sophie. On the cliffs the wind was colder, the sky more grey, a reminder that autumn had arrived in full and time was passing. She'd been at the dower house for three weeks. The shareholders' meeting was in five days and she was dreading it. There'd been no word from Miles, which had inevitably led to her thinking he would arrive any day, only to have those hopes dashed each evening. She was entirely alone in her efforts.

'If the weather was better, we could walk from Bosrigan to the hotel at Gurnard's Head for tea.' Eaton helped Sophie and Eliza down from the carriage. 'I think today, though, we should take the carriage to the hotel when we're finished here. We'll walk another time.'

Eliza smiled distractedly. 'Be careful, Eaton, you are building dangerous assumptions with your excursions and future promises.' Eaton was always making plans for another time. Perhaps he did it unconsciously, a man used to leading, used to taking charge for others. But perhaps he did it for other reasons as well. In the weeks she'd known him, he seemed to be a man in constant need of activity. She understood the reason for it. He was grieving the loss of his friend, but he couldn't hide from it interminably. 'We will go home one day. Sophie will be disappointed,' Eliza cautioned. People without children seldom understood how carefully they had to guard their words, how they had to refrain from making promises that couldn't be kept.

'Sophie won't be the only one. *I* will be disappointed. What about you? Will you be happy to go home?' Eaton asked, in all seriousness. They came to a jagged section where rubble had accumulated. Eaton offered her his arm and she took it without thought. Touching him had become too easy these days, just like the outings, but no less devastating for its repetition. He'd fit into her life effortlessly.

'I will miss this, too,' she replied honestly. Truro would be drab compared to the brilliance of the last weeks. But the brilliance was due to the temporary nature of their association and it would soon be tarnished if they continued at length. It couldn't be sustained over the long term. 'I must thank you for your discretion and your regard for our privacy.'

'It's been a pleasure to spend time with you.' There was a caress in his words. 'Do you know when you might leave? I should not like to drive down to the dower house and simply discover you've gone,' he joked.

'The shareholders' meeting is in a few days. I suppose we'll leave shortly after that business is settled.'

'There is no rush.' Eaton smiled. 'Stay as long as you like.'

There was every rush, Eliza thought as he went to help Sophie scramble up to a lookout point. The longer she stayed, the harder it would be to resist the very natural temptation of giving in to him. He had not pressed the issue of kisses since the beach, but it was there in his eyes when he looked at her, it was in every attention he showed her. He was interested in her, in sharing more than conversations and outings. So was she, truth be told. She had a healthy curiosity about what it might be like to be with a young man, a man who held her in great regard, who wanted her for *herself.* The heir to a dukedom would not find her money alluring, nor would he find her child, her background, or her age an asset.

Of course, he needn't care on either account. An affair would be easy for him. He could love her and leave her when he chose. It would not be so easy for her or for Sophie. They would live with the memory of him for the rest of their lives. And yet, the longer she was with him, the more Eliza began to think it might have been worth it if there was only herself to think of, only herself to protect from the inevitable loss of him.

Already, it might be too late. Sophie adored him. Not just for the outings he planned, but for himself. Evening had become Eliza's favourite time of day. Eaton played cards with them after dinner, or Sophie would play the spinet in the parlour—sometimes he would read with them. Lately, he'd taken to reading excerpts of *The Odyssey* out loud by the fire. He was being reckless with them, leading them on, although perhaps unintentionally. She ought to be angry with him, but she was too addicted to the individual moments to relish ruining the larger picture.

Eliza looked out over the water. She didn't want to hurt Eaton. The longer they were together, the more she sensed he *needed* them. It was a realisation that had come upon her early in their stay. She was not naive. Eaton was grieving his friend. He was a man who thrived on projects to fill voids. She and Sophie were his current project. No wonder he wasn't in a hurry to see them leave. What would he do next? Was he merely hoping they would fill the gap until Christmas when he could visit his sisters? Perhaps he was attuned to her loneliness because he was lonely, too. The man who claimed to have everything had nothing with which to fill his time, to fill his heart. *Perhaps you're the one doing me a favour,* he'd said. Perhaps she was, but at what cost?

'The view is breathtaking, is it not?' Eaton was behind her, the bulk of him blocking the wind, the heat of him triggering an intense awareness of his body's proximity to hers. 'I feel very small when I'm up here. It's a great reminder of my place in the grand scheme of things to see the sky above me, the crashing sea below and to know that I can do little to affect either. It's quite humbling, yet sometimes it spurs me on to do more, to be more.'

How was it possible for this man to be more than he already was? She turned and looked up at him, studying his face, a new awareness taking hold—not a physical awareness but an emotional one. She was learning to read him, learning to know him and his life, the events that had shaped him. 'You're thinking about Richard Penlerick,' she said softly.

'Yes,' he confessed with a small smile as if he was pleased she understood this facet of his life, of his mind. 'I was thinking, too, how very finite life is, how every moment, every choice, counts.' His voice was low and intimate. It made her pulse race and her body warm. His words touched her, but here on the cliffs she wanted more than his words.

'I want to wrap you in my arms, Eliza. What would you think of that? Is it too familiar?' Ah, so he felt it, too, this need to connect physically, to have something tangible from this meeting of their minds.

'Hold me, then, just for a moment,' she whispered. Surely she could afford this one lapse? He did not hesitate. His arms were about her, gathering her in, her head against the strength of his chest, the breadth of his shoulders sheltering her. It felt good to be held, to be surrounded by someone else's power as the wind blew.

Out of necessity to be heard, his head bent to hers as he spoke, the wind wreaking havoc with his dark curls. 'It's only that I'm feeling my humanity, my smallness. Up here those things have a different meaning. The cliffs, the waves, the clouds, the wind, are all far more powerful than me. I cannot change them for all the money and land I own.' It was honesty that prompted his words, not vulnerability, not weakness, and she responded in kind.

'I've fought for every place I've occupied, knowing

full well I could lose it. When I married Huntingdon I knew I would have him for a short time only and afterwards the mines were a fight. No one wanted me to have them. Everyone encouraged me to give them up. Even now, I must constantly prove myself.' It was a lonely, wearying task she could never put down. But perhaps just for this moment she could indulge.

She breathed him in, her head pressed to the lapels of his coat, the scent of him, all man and wind, in her nostrils. She closed her eyes, wanting to hold on to this moment: the sound of the waves below, the feel of his arms about her, as if he could keep out the world and all of its threats. If only that were true. But to even test that hypothesis, first she'd have to tell him her secrets, she'd have to give up a piece of her control, she'd have to risk letting him in, letting him see her vulnerability. She drew a breath, her decision made. She only had five days left before the meeting and she had no answers. She needed to reach out. 'Eaton,' she said, letting her eyes open, letting them rest on his face, 'I want to ask your advice on something.'

'Yes, of course. We can talk now or perhaps later at the tea room at Gurnard's Head.' He was all immediate concern, but there was something else in his dark eyes, perhaps joy that she had decided to trust him at last.

'After dinner will be fine.' She didn't want to talk about it in public where she might be overheard.

He nodded with a private smile. 'After dinner it shall be.' When he held her hand on the way back to the carriage, she didn't resist the gesture. A line had been crossed and this time there would be no going back.

But it seemed there would be a detour. They never made it to the Gurnard's Head Hotel tea room. In fact, they didn't even make it back to the carriage before Eaton's tiger ran up to them with some news. 'My lord, it appears we have a visitor.'

Eliza looked beyond the boy's shoulder, hesitating involuntarily. There, standing beside the carriage, not a golden hair out of place even in the breeze, was Miles Detford, here at last, and most inconveniently so. There was none of the relief she'd originally anticipated his arrival would bring. Eliza dropped Eaton's hand, but it was an effort she feared came too late. From the look in Miles's eye, the damage was already done. How long had he been standing there and just what had he seen? Had he seen her one moment of weakness, when she'd given in to the strength of Eaton's arms? Was he going to hold that moment against her despite her years of strength and self-denial?

The visitor was unwanted. Eaton sensed it in Eliza's hesitation. She didn't want the man here any more than Eaton did. Damn the man for interrupting the outing now, when Eliza had been in his arms, when she'd finally let down her guard long enough to confide in him, not only the request to talk but that precious bit of information she'd imparted.

'I've fought for every place I've ever occupied, knowing full well I could lose it...'

It was the second insight he'd had this afternoon of what lay behind the impenetrable façade of Eliza Blaxland's smooth features. For just a moment on the cliffs she'd been vulnerable and that was as intoxicating as her strength. *To be needed by her*, the woman who needed no one.

Eaton strode forward, putting himself between Eliza and the intruder. 'Lord Lynford at your service, how can I be of assistance?' He would make it clear that this man would answer to him should Eliza so desire.

'I have business with Mrs Blaxland.' The man gave him a hard stare, the strength of his gaze was perhaps the most impressive thing about him besides his tailoring. All else was quite ordinary, from his middling height to his middling build. Here was a man who wanted to appear more than he was.

'I hope it is not an emergency? Although I fear it cannot be otherwise since you've chosen to seek us out instead of awaiting our return.' Eaton's polite tone was cold.

The man's gaze shifted over his shoulder, heralding Eliza's approach. Miles Detford would be awful at cards; his face gave away everything. 'Ah, my dear, there you are! I have answered your summons just as you requested.'

Summons? Eliza had sent for this man and then hesitated upon his arrival? Eaton had barely posed the question to himself when Eliza snapped, 'You are three weeks late.'

'Not without reason, my dear. I bring news from the shareholders that I am eager to discuss at once.' Something flickered in Eliza's eyes. Concern? Interest? Interested concern? Eaton intervened before curiosity could get the better of Eliza. He recognised a flanking movement when he saw one even if she did not. This man, this medium-sized, interloping, upstart thought to separate Eliza from the herd.

'We shall meet you at the dower house, then, sir.' Eaton held out his hand to help Eliza into the carriage and then he reached for Sophie, making it clear the carriage was full. *He* was driving home with Eliza, not this man who invoked hesitation and called her 'my dear' every chance he got.

'Who is he?' Eaton asked the moment the carriage was underway. A suspicion had blossomed at the familiarity between them. This was the friend she'd mentioned that night in the orangery. The man she'd mentioned on the beach, who had proposed and been refused.

'Miles Detford is a shareholder and the primary administrator of the Porth Karrek mine,' Eliza answered, but Eaton had already lost her. The open woman at the fort was gone, her thoughts racing ahead to the conversation to come with this Miles Detford, this man she'd sent for, her brain already wondering what news he might have brought.

'Do all the shareholders call you "my dear"?' Eaton was terse. He was not keen on men who made a habit of so fluidly mixing business with pleasure, perhaps with the deliberate intent of confusing the line between both.

Eliza's eyes flashed. Good. She understood exactly what he was asking. 'He's a shareholder and a friend. He's been a support since Huntingdon died.' It was telling that Eliza would defend him. How much of a friend was he? Eaton refrained from asking. To insinuate there'd been more than friendship was to do her a disservice, but that did not quiet the little green monster in him, or the doubt that began to mewl alongside. Was this why she resisted the spark between them? Because she had a lover back in Truro and it was this Miles Detford? He could not believe it of her, not after her protestations of privacy and the need to remain alone. Or was it that he didn't *want* to believe it of her?

When they arrived at the dower house, he helped her down and took his leave with a final question in his eyes. *Did* she want him to leave her with this man? He would not abandon her. 'I think I must see him, Eaton.' It was a softly whispered reminder that she had a life beyond the dower house, a life he still knew precious little about. The intruder was very physical evidence that she had a life elsewhere and some day soon she'd rejoin it.

He let her go. He had no choice. 'Come to me later. I'll be in the orangery if you still want to talk things through, or even if you don't want to talk.' He whispered the invitation as she moved away. *Even if you want me just to hold you like I did on the cliffs.* That had been a moment of heaven, the two of them against the wind. He would reclaim that moment if he could. Not just for himself, but for her. Miles Detford might call her his dear, but she did not welcome his attentions in that fashion, Eaton would bet his last guinea on it. He waited until Eliza and Sophie were inside, the door closed behind them, before he gave the signal to drive away. He would go to the orangery where he could be alone with his dog and his thoughts. And he would wait.

Chapter Twelve

'What were you thinking, Eliza?' Detford sputtered incredulously as he paced the front parlour in overt agitation.

Now that they were alone, he let loose his emotions, his polished veneer slipping. Sophie was upstairs with Miss Gilchrist having a bath and Eaton had decorously taken his leave at the front door, but not before slanting her a querying look that asked questions: Who was Miles Detford? Was he more than a business partner? But mostly, there'd been concern in Eaton's gaze, his dark eyes asking silently, *Should I leave you alone with this man, this intruder who has pre-empted our talk*?

But she could not afford to think of Eaton's dark eyes now, or the way his arms had felt about her. Miles was in the middle of a tirade and she needed her wits about her to keep him in check. 'For heaven's sake, Eliza, you were out there alone with him.'

'Sophie was with us. What is the crime, Miles?' Eliza snapped impatiently. If there was any crime committed, it was his. He'd kept her waiting for three weeks. She'd summoned him to help resolve a problem and he'd taken his time to make his way here. Now he had the audacity to act as if he had some claim on her.

Miles Detford stopped pacing and speared her with a stare. 'You know very well what the crime is. He's heir to a dukedom and you are a widow who can choose to be available to him without the benefit of marriage.' He folded his arms across his chest and she was struck by the dissimilarity between him and Eaton. Miles was a mediocre man in all ways: neither tall nor short, neither thin or large. His features were refined and finished, bland in their smoothness. He was nowhere near as rugged or as interesting as Eaton. Eaton looked like Cornwall. Miles looked like London. He thought like London, too, with his quick, wicked insinuations. He raised a blond brow and asked point-blank, '*Are* you available to him, Eliza?'

'Hush! Do you want the servants to hear you!' Eliza scolded. How dare he suggest such slander. She ought to tell him the truth, that absolutely no, she was not 'available' to Eaton, but that would only affirm for Miles that he had the right to lecture her on behaviour, that she answered to him, which *she* most assuredly did not. He answered to her. She controlled the mines. He was her employee, nothing more. 'Envy is unbecoming on you, Miles. Is that it? May no one have me because you cannot?'

Anger flared in Miles Detford's pale blue eyes, so very light where Eaton's were dark. Once, she might have found those eyes attractive, once she might have compared them to sea glass, but whatever nascent attraction had existed was long ago extinguished. Miles Detford might be a friend, but he could never be more. He sat beside her on the sofa, his anger banked now, his tone softer. 'It is your reputation I'm concerned about, Eliza, and the mines. This is not a good time for a dalliance. Too much hangs in the balance.'

'I don't think it's as dire as all that. I merely requested you to come and look over a few things for me as the shareholder primarily responsible for this mine. I have some questions about the tunnel,' Eliza chided him. He was for ever making mountains out of molehills and, while she appreciated his ability to think critically about situations, it was wearisome to have everything presented as a crisis. He glanced away briefly, and there was the slightest hesitation; but it was enough to put her on alert.

'There is something else?' she prompted coolly. 'Perhaps a reason why you delayed in coming?'

'You know I would have come immediately if there hadn't been a good reason to wait. I have news, something I hope you'll be happy to hear.'

'Good news, then?' Eliza probed. He seemed too tentative for it to truly be good news.

'I think it can be, my dear, but I need you to listen with an open mind.' He reached for her hand and she frowned at the familiarity, but did not withdraw. One could never have too many friends and she'd made her position with Miles clear. Surely there was no harm in allowing this simple touch and it would perhaps reassure him that nothing existed between her and Eaton, especially when there was something more important to consider. 'The shareholders want to put a proposal to you at the upcoming meeting,' Miles said. 'They want to make a generous offer to buy out your shares. Isn't that wonderful? You will be as wealthy as you are now without all the effort. You needn't be Atlas any more and carry the world on your shoulders. You can get on with your life.'

Get on with her life? This *was* her life. Every choice she'd made since the day Huntingdon died had been for this. But there was another implication, too, and that was the one that took her like a blow to the stomach. Miles thought the idea sounded splendid. He *wanted* her to take the offer. At the moment, she couldn't decide which news was more earth-shattering: that the board had concocted a secret deal to buy her out or that Miles Detford, someone she'd counted as a friend, thought the action ought to be allowed, accepted even, as a boon. She was betrayed on all fronts.

Eliza did draw her hand away, then, spearing Miles with the daggers of her gaze. 'The mines are my life. Why would anyone think I'd *want* to be bought out? Or that I would give up control of Sophie's inheritance?' She rose from the sofa, agitated. 'This is *not* generosity, this is a hard shove off a very high cliff. *They* are pushing me aside.' Her stomach was roiling. This was evil wrapped in a very pretty package. What was the cause of this? Had she not made the mines successful? Had she not lined the shareholders' pockets with profit every quarter?

Eliza racked her mind, searching for a reason, and

settled on one. 'This is about the tunnel. I thought we'd resolved that. We decided not to dig out under the ocean.' She'd thought a lot of things had been settled, though. Apparently not. The shareholders had been plotting against her behind false pretences of acceptance. For how long? How long had they faced her with smiles at the board meetings and nodded their heads while they whispered behind her back?

She faced Miles. 'Surely not everyone agrees with the decision to dig under the ocean? It's not safe for the workers and it's not safe for the investors. Who knows what we'll find out there? Maybe nothing that justifies the risk. One accident will be all it takes for poor men to lose their lives and rich men to lose their money. Are we all not rich enough as it is? Why do we need to grasp for more wealth and for such stakes?'

'Is anyone ever rich enough?' Miles countered with a patronising chuckle, sidestepping the real issue. Did he think she wouldn't notice? Did he think that she was so easily distracted? 'Perhaps this is exactly the reason you should take the offer and step away. I laud your concerns, Eliza, but money isn't made by playing it safe. I understand, though, that risk is not in your nature. You aren't made for it. No woman is.'

That had her bristling. 'You think a woman won't take a risk? You think it is my gender that makes me cautious as opposed to my good sense?' She whirled on him, making him the target of her anger, her disgust at the board's betrayal. Better to be angry than to be shocked. Shock made one weak, anger could make one strong, at least temporarily, and she needed to be strong now.

'It's not *my* opinion that matters, Eliza, but the board's. I am your friend. It's my job to help you see things as others see them. You have to understand what the board sees. They see steady profits, not rising profits—'

'At a time when smaller mines are shutting down!' she interrupted fiercely.

'At a time, my dear, when you are asking them to put funds into new safety equipment and schools for miners' children. There is no profit in those things. The board thinks it is too much coddling while we're not making enough of the mines' natural resources.'

'*People* are our natural resource,' she argued. 'They are not disposable.'

'That's where you're wrong, my dear. They *are* disposable. I know you don't like to hear it, but there it is. There are plenty of miners looking for work and willing to claim a pitch beneath the ocean. I wouldn't worry my pretty little head about it, if I were you.'

If he called her 'my dear' one more time, she'd scream or worse.

'I suppose I am disposable, too?' She saw what this was. A power grab, a chance for greedy men to seize more wealth at the expense of others. 'It would be a mistake to think so. I will fight this.'

'Then take my advice. Stay away from the Marquess. The last thing you need is for the board to hear you're having an affair.'

'Is that a threat?' She faced Miles squarely. 'Who

would tell them such a thing? Would you? Otherwise where else would they learn of it?'

Miles looked wounded. 'Eliza, be fair. I wouldn't need to say a thing. You know how it will look to the shareholders. You're living on his property, you were out gallivanting with him *en famille*. Dear heavens, it's like Prinny and Mrs Fitzherbert all over again.'

Her eyes narrowed; she did not miss the insult in his exasperation. 'I should slap you for that. You've no cause to assume anything of the sort.' But she knew what Miles did not, that her association with Lynford had progressed far beyond a trip to Bosrigan Fort. There'd been numerous outings, all discreet, all designed so that no one might see them together. She knew that Eaton dined in her home almost nightly, that he carried her child up to bed, that he'd kissed her *twice* now, he'd wooed her in his orangery with parakeets and champagne. Miles didn't know the half of it. Perhaps she needed to stop denying that other half existed, the half where her pulse raced when Eaton touched her, where she coveted each hot glance he sent her way and craved each kiss as if it were the treasure Eaton alluded to.

'If you want my counsel, Eliza, it is this: take the money, step away from the mines and you can tup whomever you like. No one will care. This offer is freedom, the one thing you crave above all else. I wish you could see it that way, my dear.'

My dear. It was the last straw. 'Get out.' She would not stand here and be condescended to, lectured, berated for sins she had not committed, not after all she'd endured. Miles's elegant brows knit in perplexity. 'Did you not understand me, Miles? Or is it that you can't believe I'd actually throw you out?'

Miles straightened and picked up his hat from the table with unhurried gestures that patronised her further. 'What I understand is that you're upset. We will talk again later when you've had time to think. We need to discuss the tunnel further.' Not any more, not after today's revelations, not when she was so suddenly aware that even Miles's loyalty might be questionable. If he was truly loyal to her, he would understand this was not an offer she could accept.

'It's nothing. I can sort it out myself,' Eliza lied. She wanted him gone before she broke down, before she showed how much his news had shaken her.

She saw him to the door and shut it firmly behind him. Miles might claim to be her friend, but he was a man easily swayed by the mind of the crowd. After all, he'd proposed to her out of social pressure to scotch mere rumours of their association. How long would he stand beside her now if he thought her decision a poor one? Especially if others were willing to line his pockets? She'd like to think better of him, but she could not. To award him attributes he didn't possess would be naive and it would make her vulnerable if she was wrong.

Eliza leaned against the door, exhausted. When would it end? When would she be left in peace to run her mines and live her life? She'd held up the world for so long. She was tired, but she could not relent. She climbed the stairs and checked on Sophie. She was asleep with a smile on her face. Perhaps her sweet girl was dreaming of their magical day. Eliza was envious. Her dreams would not be as sweet. But they were a far-off consideration. Her mind was still churning from Miles's visit. Eliza returned downstairs, occupying herself with a tour of the house, checking doors and windows, although the servants had already done it. There was little for her to do and she was restless. She needed exercise, something to ease her mind over the news and something to provide objectivity. Perhaps a walk?

Eliza took her shawl from a peg by the door and wrapped it about her shoulders. A moonlit walk would do her good. An emotional response to this latest gambit from her shareholders would not solve anything. She needed to be rational and she needed to be grateful to Miles, who'd told her the news. Friends risked much when they had to impart difficult news. The shareholders had meant to take her unawares by presenting the offer at the meeting and forcing her to a spontaneous response. But Miles, for all his differing views, had bought her time to think, time to marshal her troops even when she disagreed with him. Wasn't that the hallmark of a true friend? She had not treated him well for it.

The moon was bright and she walked without fear or thought of distance. After all, she was on Eaton's land and as long as she kept the main house visible to her right, she wouldn't get lost. She thought over the offer as she walked. Perhaps she *should* sell her shares? She could purchase an estate like this one, where Sophie could run and play all day and she'd never have to worry about leaving for a meeting. No, Eliza knew she'd be bored within a month. What would she do with herself all day without the mines to run? There wasn't just the activity to think of, there was the legacy as well. The shareholders would run Blaxland Mining into the ground if she stepped away. They'd pursue profit at any price.

The orangery loomed before her, the moonlight reflecting off the glass. Her feet had led her here even if her thoughts had not, at least not her conscious thoughts. Perhaps her subconscious? Perhaps she'd wanted to see Eaton all along, wanted to borrow his strength for a moment as she had on the cliffs that afternoon. Was it really so wrong to want to lay down the burden for a moment? Especially when one had been invited to do that very thing?

Come to me later...if you still want to talk, or even if you don't...

Eaton was not pressing her, he was giving her space and choices, two things Miles Detford was not keen to offer. Right now, those things looked like heaven. Or hell. Her hand stalled on the orangery door as her conscience whispered its final admonition.

Step in there and you will be tempted. The hour is late, you are tired, and he is persuasive. Who is the real devil, Eliza? Detford with his truth or Eaton Falmage with his fantasies?

Eliza turned the knob of the orangery door. To hell with it, then. Tonight she needed Eaton in his garden.

Chapter Thirteen

Baldor's ears pricked up and the big dog rose to his feet from beside the worktable. Eaton set down his tools, a satisfied smile taking his mouth. Eliza was coming. He could hear her on the path winding through the orangery, swishing skirts, staccato steps. She had not entered the orangery timidly despite the darkness, nor was she picking her way through. She was coming at full speed, straight and direct...*to him*. He wondered which Eliza had come to him tonight: the determined woman who'd ambushed him in his own school, or the woman he'd held in his arms on the cliffs today, the woman who was both strong *and* vulnerable. He was ready for either woman. He'd come to care for both. Goodness knew he'd waited longer for Eliza Blaxland than he'd waited for any woman. Not that three weeks was any great length to wait in general, but for a man who was used to having his every wish carried out instantaneously, used to having his pick of lovers, being in hard pursuit with no surety of success was something of a novelty—a very trying novelty. And yet these three weeks with Eliza and Sophie had been the best three weeks he could recall in his adult life.

'Eaton, thank goodness you're here.' Eliza emerged breathless and relieved, her mask of indomitability slightly askew.

'I told you I would be.' He motioned for Baldor to lie down. He studied her, following her restless per-ambulation about the atrium with his eyes. She was agitated, her colour high—perhaps from the evening walk or perhaps from some inner excitement? 'Have you come to talk, Eliza?'

She turned from the fountain, the distress on her face unmistakable. Eaton's gut clenched in primal protectiveness. Whatever Detford had said or done to cause that distress, the man would pay for it. 'The shareholders want to push me out.' The next moment, she broke, her voice trembling, her strength leaving her. 'I know I said I needed to do this on my own, but I need help.' She took a shaky breath. 'Eaton, they want to take the mines. They want to take everything. I'm not enough for them.'

Everything. His mind focused on that word. He knew what it meant to lose something so monumental that it felt like everything. He saw in an instant what 'everything' was to her: pride, hard work and long hours of toil to maintain her independence. All those things could be swept away in one act: his ability to have a family, to perpetuate the line of Bude, his pur-pose in the world. How long had he berated himself? What if he'd not sneaked off to Kilkhampton for the horse show? A single poor choice in a life full of good decisions had cost him. Oh, yes, he knew exactly how Eliza felt.

Eaton was beside her, guiding her to the bench at the fountain's edge, firm hands over hers where they lay clenched in her lap. He lent her the strength of his touch as he listened. The shareholders wanted to buy her out. Did Detford not understand this woman at all? Did Detford not see all it would cost her to take such an offer? That money could only cover so much. There was no price that could be put on her pride. 'How long until you have to decide?' Eaton asked calmly when she finished.

'It's five days until the shareholders' meeting.' Eliza shook her head, 'But I don't think I will have a choice. They will expect me to take the offer. I do not think they will take no for an answer.' She drew a shaky breath, emotion catching her again. 'How could they do this to me, after five years, after letting me think everything was all right, that they respected me?'

'I wasn't enough for them,' she'd said and now Eaton saw that the disappointment that overwhelmed her stemmed from more than the offer itself. This was about how it had been planned behind her back. This was a betrayal. Women saw the world so much differently to men. For them the world was built on a series of relationships. The relationships she'd counted on had been false. No wonder she felt alone.

'Eliza, I am sorry.' He stroked the back of her hand with his thumb, a soothing motion, as he thought. 'But surely you don't mean to take this lying down? What if you buy *them* out? Make a counter-offer and then find new shareholders who support your vision and admire your leadership.'

'If I were a man, such a thing might work. But if I were a man, this would never have been an issue to begin with. Besides, where would I find such investors, even if I could afford to buy everyone's shares? I could not sustain the business on my own for long.' Already, he could see her agile mind running the sums it would take and measuring them against the capital she had to hand. That meant there was a spark of hope and Eaton would take that spark over the desolation he'd seen in her eyes.

'What if I could find investors?' He was already thinking of Cassian and Inigo, and Inigo would have financial connections to others with capital. 'I will write in the morning.' Inigo and Cassian were in Truro for the autumn, just a half day's ride away. Arrangements could be made quickly. If the shareholders were counting on the isolation of Cornwall to work against her, the bastards would be unpleasantly surprised. They thought to hold her hostage to their offer, thinking they were all she had.

'Would you even need to buy out everyone?' Eaton began to hypothesise. 'Maybe these malcontents don't speak for everyone?'

'It's hard to say, perhaps not for a few.' She withdrew her hands from his and Eaton tensed. There was more. She was withholding something else. 'They may not wish to sell their shares to me, or they may drive the price up to a point where I cannot afford to purchase their shares. Those who are most interested in buying me out feel there is lucrative expansion for the Porth Karrek mine under the sea.'

She explained the recent quarrel over the tunnel with an apologetic nod. 'So you see, Eaton, I don't know that you can just throw money at the problem and make it go away. This can't be one of your projects.'

Those were fighting words, or they would be if Eaton didn't see what she was doing. She was pushing him away, pushing aside help because she thought it made her vulnerable, made her beholden to others.

'Eliza, my men won't fail you. These are good men with deep pockets.'

'And *you'd* be there to ensure their compliance. Not me. Why should I trade one board of shareholders—men I've known through my husband for years and by rights should have been able to trust—for a board of shareholders who are strangers to me? Men who owe their loyalty first to you, a marquess. How could I ever compete with that?' She sighed. 'Your offer is generous, Eaton, but it would cost me everything I'm trying to protect. It wouldn't be mine any more. It would be yours. Your men, your money, your plans.'

'The mines would be yours, you would still sit at the head of the board,' Eaton argued. 'I don't want to take anything from you, Eliza. I want to help you keep what is yours.'

'You want to slay my dragons.' She was quick to go on the defensive, or perhaps Detford had already put her there as the 'friend' bearing bad news. Did she not see Detford for the snake he was? Eaton had seen the man for all of a few minutes and had his measure completely. He was not to be trusted.

'What's wrong with that? Surely it has not escaped your attention that I care for you.' It was the first time either of them had given voice to their feelings and it ignited a powder keg.

'Everything is wrong with that! My mother lost all she had when she allowed a man to act on her behalf,' Eliza cried.

'I am not that man and you are certainly not your mother. You cannot compare the two situations,' Eaton argued, attempting to do battle with her ghosts and her dragons.

'But you *are a* man. People will not see your interference as chivalrous. How long do you think it would be before everyone concluded I was your mistress? A kept woman, propped up by your money and your friends? My reputation would be in tatters.'

Eaton gave a wry chuckle. Detford was a serpent indeed. Something else had happened in that awful conversation. 'It seems your "friend" has been poisoning the well. Is that what he said? Did he warn you away from me for the sake of your reputation? Convenient for him, don't you think? To isolate you, to cut you off from help, very powerful help, I might add. I doubt he and his friends have a marquess in their pockets. Perhaps he aspires to be more than your friend, Eliza?'

'Perhaps once, but not any longer. I disabused him of such thoughts years ago.' Eliza dismissed the notion, but Eaton did not. Did she really think she was so easily forgotten? His suspicions had been right. Detford was the man in Truro who had been the focus of the rumours. A man who had been after her money, if the gossips could be believed. Perhaps they should be believed. Eaton had suspicions anew.

'What did he do to earn such a rejection, Eliza?'

'Nothing more than offer an honourable proposal of marriage after Truro society made inappropriate observations about us. I've learned to be more discreet since then.' Did she really not see the man for the worm he was? Detford should have been more discreet years ago. Eaton would have liked to have wrung the man's neck for such behaviour. Detford should have known what it would look like to others even if Eliza hadn't. In the aftermath, she had not learned to be more discreet, she'd learned to be more alone, convinced that her freedom must always come at the price of intimacy. Detford was a cunning devil, ruining her for other men.

'You should not discount Detford so easily. I saw the way he looked at you today at Bosrigan.' Eaton brought a hand to her cheek. He knew the way *he* looked at her, how she brightened a room simply by being in it, how she captivated him. He was not willing to give her up. He imagined Detford wasn't either, although he suspected Detford's protective-friend act was fuelled by more than romantic notions. He stroked her cheek, his eyes holding hers. 'You are the sort of woman who drives a man insane, Eliza, the sort of woman a man sees at a dinner table and he wants to undo her—not just her clothes, but her secrets, too.'

'And you, Eaton? Is that what you want?' Her eyes searched his, wary and cautious, yet desire was there, too. She had come here tonight for more than talk of mines. She was on the precipice of surrender and so was he. He wanted her with an intensity that surpassed longing, but he could not take her lightly and he could not fail her in his answer to her question.

'I want to do neither, Eliza. I have no desire to undo you, to claim you, to remake you in my image. I want you just the way you are, the determined, stubborn, private, whole of you.' He took her mouth then, his hands cradling her neck, framing her face as his mouth testified to his want, his need. Once begun, he would give her no quarter, no permission to hide from her desire. He merely needed a sign from her that she had accepted his earlier invitation in full. He did not want her in his bed because she was mad at Detford or because she was desperate and upset. Those things might have been reason enough in the beginning when pursuing her had been a distraction. But she had not been a game to him for a very long time now. Before this went any further, he had to know. 'Eliza,' he whispered her name against her lips, 'what changed your mind?'

Her hands were in his hair, her gaze locked on his. 'I don't want to be alone any more. I used to think being alone was the price for my freedom, but I saw today that my sacrifice didn't matter.'

'Is that what this is about, Eliza?' His voice was hoarse, a sign of how tight the leash was he kept himself on for her sake. She would hate herself in the morning if that was what this was, but by the saints it was hard to do the right thing just now. 'Do you want me, Eliza?' Eaton breathed, his voice a low, seductive husk at her neck, his mouth at her throat as she arched against him.

'You know I do.' Her own voice was smoky with desire.

'But do *you* know it? I want to hear you say it. Say you want me. I won't tolerate regrets in the morning.' She understood. He was gifting this to her, wanting her to grant herself permission for claiming pleasure after years of denial.

Her hands were moving through the tangles of his hair, her mouth pressing kisses to his face. 'I want *you*. Only you.'

'Then come with me.'

This was what she'd come here for. Deep at the core of her, she'd known the moment she entered the orangery this was how the evening would end. She'd come here wanting more than to talk with him. She'd wanted to be in Eaton's arms, wanted his mouth on her mouth, his hands in her hair when he kissed her. She fairly trembled with anticipation as Eaton led her to a small antechamber hidden behind the foliage of the aviary. It was a sparse room furnished neatly with the necessities—a bed, a battered trunk at its foot, a table—but she spared little time for the details. Her attention was for the man who'd brought her. Tonight, she would not be alone. It could not be more than that; the world wasn't made for such things to last. This one night would be temporary succour. She would take tonight and hold it against all the nights to come. She would not make excuses for this. In the morning, she would not claim seduction or false promises.

She wrapped her arms about his neck. She let her mouth answer his, let her body answer his, let her hips press against his. She would give no man dominion over her, but she would partner one, be the equal of one. He was dancing with her now, a slow sensual waltz of bodies against one another, his lips lingering on hers as they reached the bed.

His eyes were hot on hers as he whispered the solemn admonition, 'Watch me, Eliza.' He stepped back to pull off his boots and to tug his shirt over his head, revealing his body to her in the lamplight, as glorious in its nakedness as it had been dressed.

Yes, she would watch him. Eliza sat down hard on the bed's edge, every fibre of her being alive with hungry anticipation. He was riveting, all ridges and planes, with the chest of an outdoorsman who strode through woods and sands, with arms that hefted sleeping children upstairs with ease. Stark virility was etched in every hard line of him, particularly the two muscled lines that flanked his flat abdomen and disappeared into the waistband of his trousers with tempting invitation for her hands to follow. She bit her lip. Oh, to touch him, to trace those lines to their wicked destination.

'Do I please you, Eliza?' His dark eyes glittered, all too aware, no doubt, of the effect he had on her.

'I am drowning in how pleasing you are.' She swallowed, her mouth dry. She'd known from the first how out of her depth she was with this man and tonight only confirmed it. None of her experience with intimacy had prepared her for this moment. Lack of preparation did not make her shy, though; it only made her hungrier.

'Would you like to join me?' he drawled in low tones. 'I can play lady's maid, if you wish.'

'If you wish.' He wanted to undress her? The very notion made her heart pound with anticipation. She went to him, giving him her back. How long had she dreamed of such intimate play with a man, fantasised about it alone in her bed?

'I wish, very much.' His voice was a raw, heated whisper at her ear sending a trill of hot desire down her spine. 'You smell divine, like a summer's day, Eliza. It was one of the first things I noticed about you when you walked into the school.' She blushed in the lamplight at the compliment, overcome that he'd noticed such a minute detail about her from the start. While she'd been intent on calling him to account, he'd been intent on her perfume. Of course he had. He was a physical man in all ways.

His hands made short work of her lacing and he pushed her gown from her shoulders, letting it slide to her feet. Her stays followed as his mouth pressed kisses to the bare skin of her shoulders, her neck, her back. He reached for the hem of her chemise and her hand captured his in rote reflex, despite the fantasy. 'Wait.'

'Have you never been naked before a man, Eliza?' Eaton whispered at her ear. 'We shall be naked together, nothing between us, skin to skin.' His words nearly undid her. It was all the coaxing she needed. This was how she imagined lovers talked. Husbands and wives most assuredly did not speak to one another this way. Huntingdon had not. Eaton's hands cupped her breasts, drawing her against him, back to chest, the heat of his body warming her, calming her even as the hardness of him aroused her and the issue of the chemise was put on short hiatus.

'Shall I go first, Eliza? Shall you help me with my trousers?' he murmured, turning her in his arms. 'Slide them off, Eliza, free me.'

It was wondrous to undress him, to drink him in with her eyes, to touch him with her hands, to know he wanted her hands on him. Pushing the fabric away, his manhood rose strong and thick from a nest of dark hair, proud like its master. She circled him with her hand, delighting in the adamantine hardness of him. He had strength, even here at his core there was no weakness to him. He would need no efforts from her to ready himself. The thought shamed her. Tonight was not for comparisons or for remembrances. It was for fantasies.

Eaton's hand tipped her chin upwards, forcing her to meet his gaze. 'Does something displease you?'

'No, how could it? You are beautiful. Too beautiful. I hardly dare believe you're real.' Would he hear the unspoken comparison? That she had known a good man, but not a beautiful man. Her husband had been decades beyond the virility of a man in his prime. There'd been little hardness to his body.

'You are beautiful, too.' His hands were at the hem of her chemise once more. 'Allow me to show you.' He kissed her then, a deep, slow, abiding claim as he lifted the chemise from her and tossed it away. 'Come to bed with me. Let me chase away your ghosts.'

Eliza wound her arms about his neck. 'And let me chase away yours, too,' she whispered. How had she not seen it until now? It wasn't all her needing him. They needed each other.

Chapter Fourteen

Only his reverence for her kept Eaton's want in check.
She stole his breath and very nearly his control, but
this was too important to rush in the first flush of lusty
pleasure, no matter how hungry they might be for one
another. And she was ravenous, eager, and, despite
the moment's hesitation with the chemise, she was determined to be the master of her own pleasure at last.
Her late husband might have loved her, he might have
given her a comfortable marriage and even comfortable companionship, but he'd not given her passion,
had not made her pulse race and her breath catch. He'd
not lain with her naked, had not worshipped her in the
lamplight of an orangery.

Eaton levered himself over her, his arms taking
his weight, his eyes meeting hers, offering promises of pleasure, offering encouragement. *Follow me
down pleasure's path*, his body whispered to hers. He
moved against her, her own hips rising to meet him.
He gathered her close, making love with his mouth
at her mouth, at the base of her neck where her pulse

beat fast, at her breasts where his mouth suckled and his tongue caressed, at her navel where he tickled her skin with a feathering breath until her body arched in to him, a little moan escaping her pretty mouth.

From the intimate seat of her navel, Eaton hazarded a glance up the seductive line of her body with a wicked smile, thrilling in her response. She was bold in bed just as she was bold in life, a woman who knew what she wanted. 'Ah, just wait, my love. There is more, there is better than this.' His own voice was husky with anticipation. His hands bracketed the slim curve of her hips, his mouth moved down to the feminine juncture of her thighs, his body heady with the feel of her, the scent of her, his own arousal growing in response to hers, need driving him as hard as it drove her.

He teased her with his tongue at her seam, at her tiny, hidden nub, licking her, tasting her, until she cried out above him. Her hands wound tight in the depth of his hair as she rose to him, against him, her thighs tightening as if she would hold him there for eternity, reluctant to let him go, even as she trembled with the first shudders of burgeoning pleasure. His own breath was coming fast now from the excitement of his efforts. Had the giving of such delight ever been so fulfilling, so overwhelming? He lifted his head, panting hard, to watch climax sweep her, to let himself be undone. She was eroticism personified in her release, her hair flowing across the pillow, her long neck arched, her face thrown to the ceiling, eyes closed in rapture as the moment took her. Had anything, anyone, ever looked as beautiful as she did right now? Or as vulnerable?

In this moment, she was entirely without artifice and without armour. Something primal surged in him, the urge to claim this woman, to possess her, to protect her in all her guises. No other man should see her thus.

Pleasure ebbed, her eyes opened, meeting his, reflecting wonder and astonishment. Gone was the emerald-sharp hardness that so often resided in her gaze. 'Your eyes remind me of green Cornish sea glass,' he whispered, kissing her navel. He would get her a ring of that colour, perhaps a necklace, so that she might never forget such pleasure or the man who'd given it to her.

She stroked his head, her fingers combing through his curls, her tone coy. 'You have been selfless. You have not had your pleasure yet, my lord.'

He laughed against her belly, his grin wide as he smiled up at her. 'Oh, but I have. There is great pleasure for a man in seeing a woman enjoy his gifts so thoroughly.' Would she understand this was pleasure for them both? That he exalted in the giving of pleasure as much as she exalted in receiving it? He crawled up the length of her until they lay skin to skin. He pressed a kiss to the indentation of her shoulder, another to her neck, to the lobe of her ear; he could worship her all night. 'Besides, who says we're done yet?'

She met his whisper with a private, knowing gaze, as she reached for him, her hand wrapping possessively around him. 'Not me.'

'Have mercy,' Eaton breathed as she dragged her thumbnail over the tender head of his shaft.

'No,' she whispered, 'I think not.'

Eaton let her have her way—he was human after all and he adored an assertive lover. He loved the slide of her silken hair, the press of her mouth as she took her turn, sliding down the length of his body, exploring the ridges and crevices of him until her mouth took over for her hand at the hot throbbing core of him. She glanced at him once, her eyes burning, melted, lava-hot sea glass, as she tossed the long skein of her hair over one shoulder and went down to meet him, to take him.

Her teeth grazed his tender tip and he let out a wolf-ish groan at the contact, an intoxicating mix, part plea-sure, part pain. 'Vixen!' He ground out the word in a hoarse rasp as she licked the length of him and his blood surged, his release looming. Heady as her efforts were, he did not want to spill like this. He wanted to take her, wanted to be inside her, joined together in mutual pleasure.

Eaton shifted, disengaging her. She threw him an enquiring look and that nearly undid him. He reached for her, drawing her up his length, holding her against him until he could roll her beneath him. 'I cannot wait for you any longer,' he rasped, desire once again his master. She'd roused him to untold heights. He took her then, in a swift thrust that had her arching and moan-ing beneath him; a good choice for them both, then. She'd been ready, too. Her legs were locked about him, holding him tight, close, her hips rising to meet his as they joined in the pulsing rhythm of mating.

This was life, this was pleasure and it was coursing through her unabated. Eliza strained towards Eaton, her body pressing hard against him as if it could melt into his, as if they could be closer, joined more intimately than they already were. All she had to do was look into Eaton's face, his eyes obsidian dark; feel the tension of his arms as they bracketed her head, taking his weight, to know pleasure's wave was cresting. They'd be in it together this time when it came. It was the most exquisite sensation she'd ever felt, novel and yet innate, bone deep in its thrill, and it was coming again, more intense than it had been before.

'Keep your eyes open, Eliza, look at me when you come,' Eaton groaned, thrusting once more, eyes locking with hers, holding her accountable, before the wildness was upon them, covering them, claiming them, hearts racing, blood pounding with life, as if in that completion she knew the answers of the universe. Later there would be practical measures to take to ensure there were no consequences, but for now, she would revel in the ephemeral bliss of the moment.

It was another level of decadence to lie quietly in Eaton's arms, her head against his shoulder, her hand on his chest, as the night with its single lamp cushioned them. She would have liked to have stayed in that limbo for ever, ignoring everything except the pleasure, but her mind was not made that way. As pleasure ebbed, reality began to reassert itself.

'You are thinking.' Eaton's voice was a seductive murmur in the darkness, part question, part accusation.

She looked up at him. It was time to set the pleasure aside and define terms. She'd had her moment of respite. Now she had to think about the consequences.

'This was extraordinary but it cannot happen again.' They could not be discovered.

'Why not?' Eaton nuzzled her ear.

'If the shareholders think I have indulged in an affair…'

Eaton reached for her hair, letting it spill through his fingers. 'Life is too short, and your passion is too splendid to be hidden away because some unimaginative men say it should be. If what you've told me is true, they want to break you in every way possible, Eliza. Don't let them.'

She fell back on the pillow, his words slamming into her with the weight of a newly revealed truth. The shareholders wanted to take her husband's legacy, wanted to take the mines from her—more than that, they wanted to take her soul. In fact, they'd been in the process of stealing that since day one. Only she'd not understood it that way. They'd tried to make a man of her by forcing her to adhere to the codes of a man's world and, when that had failed, when she'd still been very much a woman facing them at the boardroom table—a woman who would not be brought to marry one of them—they'd forced her into a half life where she could look like a woman, but she'd be pilloried for acting like one. And now they'd tired of even that.

She sighed. 'What shall I do, Eaton? Can I ever win?' She was so very weary of it all. She could not fight on enemy soil any longer, pretending she was gaining ground only to have it pulled out from under her. She'd never win. Perhaps she should walk away, after all? But the idea of giving up soured her stomach.

Eaton rolled to his side, facing her. '*You* do nothing. *We* fight back. You are right. As long as they are in power, you are in enemy territory. Replace them. Build your empire from a position of strength. Let me mount an army for you.'

'Have you forgotten what it will cost me?' Her eyes lingered on his beautiful face. 'And you,' she added. 'If you come to my aid, people will talk of us both.'

'Everyone talks about dukes.' Eaton was unfazed. She needed him to take this seriously, but all Eaton did was flash her a wicked smile and tackle her in a tangle of sheets and limbs until she was beneath him once more, her heart pounding as he looked down at her, all naked, powerful male, eyes full of wanting and play. 'Didn't anyone ever tell you not to discuss business in bed? There are punishments for that, you know.'

She laughed—how could she not? He was irresistible like this. 'What might those be? I think you'll have to show me.'

He nipped at her earlobe with a wolfish chuckle that had her forgetting about blackmail and ledgers. 'Damn right I will. Up with you, I have a horse that needs riding.'

Eliza let out an undignified squeal as she saddled up, taking him astride. 'You will exhaust me, sir,' she warned coyly, lifting herself up over his manhood, already hard and wanting her.

'No business in bed,' he answered firmly, his hands at her hips as she brushed the entrance of her core over the tip of his shaft. He moaned, the cords in his neck tightening. She took mercy on him then, sliding down his slick length and riding him to a short, explosive end that left her exhausted indeed. She didn't remember rolling off him, only slumping down on his chest, his satisfied length still tucked securely inside her.

He was gone from the bed when she woke, the grey morning peeping through the long window. She groaned, panic fuelling her into a full state of alertness. She'd not meant to sleep so long. She'd meant to be home before daybreak. She didn't want Sophie to wake without her.

'Good morning.' Eaton's familiar tones, still husky from the night, drawled from the other side of the room. She rolled over, following the sound of his voice, her effort rewarded by the sight of him, trousered but shirtless, sitting behind the little table as if it were a duke's desk, writing materials set before him. A dark curl fell across his face as he looked up. 'Sleep well?'

'You know I did, and too long,' she scolded him. 'You should have woken me.'

'It's still early,' he assured her as if he knew what prompted her thoughts. 'We'll have you back in time.' He nodded to the carafe at the corner of the table. 'There's coffee.'

'What are you doing?' Eliza sat up and began to make a plait of her hair, anxiety causing her fingers to fumble. He was working. She feared she knew on what. She had not given permission.

'I'm writing to a friend, Inigo Vellanoweth. He's in banking. He'll know men who are interested in investing.' Eaton smiled benignly as if he hadn't just upended her world. 'After you have Sophie up, I'll meet you at the mines. We can look over the books together and decide which shareholders to buy out.'

'Why are you doing this?' Eliza asked cautiously. 'I thought we'd decided last night…' Plans for outings had become plans for her businesses. This was what she'd feared. A man sticking his oar into her ventures, trying to sail her ship for her. It was not unlike Detford's efforts five years prior to save her from society's backlash. *But this man was different.* Was he? Perhaps because he was more powerful, more tenacious than Miles. That should frighten her, not reassure her.

Eaton fixed her with a dark stare, the imperious one, the one he'd used on Miles at Bosrigan to remind the interloper who was in charge. 'Last night, *we* decided we were going to fight back.'

She threw off the covers and gathered her clothes. 'The only person I want to fight at the moment is you.' She dressed in hasty motions, emotion overcoming her. 'I knew this would happen. The moment I gave in I knew you would try something like this, try to manage me and the mines. I can do this on my own. I *have* been doing this on my own.'

'And that's precisely *why* you came to me.' He left the desk and strode towards her in quick paces that matched the staccato curtness of his words. She stepped backwards instinctively but found nothing except the wall. 'You were doing it alone and you wisely realised you needn't. Only now, in the morning light, you're doubting that decision.' He rose and came to her, stopping her hands and taking over the laces. 'I am not one of your shareholders looking to usurp you. And I am not Miles Detford looking for marriage. It's high time you stop treating me as such.' He was scolding her and there was anger in his words. He did not like being classified with Detford and the mutinous shareholders. 'After all I've done, after all I've shown you, Eliza, do you truly still doubt my character? I can't believe you do.' His voice softened, the scold over. 'You *can* trust me, Eliza, you know it in your bones. You would not have come last night otherwise.'

Eliza swallowed. She *had* come to him because she had nowhere else to turn; because her own resources wouldn't be enough; because Miles Detford, the one friend she'd thought she had, would not help her in refusing the offer; because she was empty, her emotional and mental reserves sapped. She'd come to him because being alone was no longer alternative enough. Now it was time to own up to it. She lifted her chin and squared her shoulders. 'Of course. I'll meet you at Wheal Karrek after I check on Sophie.'

Chapter Fifteen

Eliza was late. Eaton gave the wall clock one more glance and decided to start without her while he had the element of surprise on his side. It had worked well so far. The manager at Wheal Karrek had been so flummoxed to have him on site he'd shown him to Eliza's office, unlocked the door and left him there unattended. Eliza should probably have a word with the man about such trusting behaviour, but for now, it suited Eaton's purposes.

He had the office to himself and her ledgers. He might as well start while he waited for Eliza to arrive. She'd wanted to stop by the house first to check on Sophie and change her clothes. There was no question of showing up at the office dressed in the same attire she'd worn the previous day. But even given that delay, she was running late. He was unbothered by it. His sisters were consistently late, trying to marshal their broods. Besides, it would give him time to appreciate Eliza in an entirely different context.

He toured the perimeter of the space, stopping at the window. This austere, grey office was her domain, when she was here. How often had she visited the mine and he'd been unaware she was near? It was hard to imagine she had been here all along and he hadn't known. It was like Plato's old argument on the subjective nature of reality: things did not become real until they were known to exist, regardless of whether they'd been there all along, just waiting to be discovered. The office was sparse, a testimony to many things other than the fact that she was not always here, that she had other holdings. Truro was the centre of her empire, close to banking interests and only a few hours away from any of her holdings. Perhaps her office in Truro was more forthcoming in its decor?

Or perhaps not, given what he knew of Eliza. Austerity was a type of privacy and she valued hers above all things. This office was giving away no secrets. There were no pictures of Sophie here to invite a visitor's comment as she made small talk with a guest. There were no crystal decanters from which to pour a celebratory drink, no carpet on the floor to brighten the space, no artwork on the walls, just a plain clock. Eaton thought of the headmaster's office at the conservatory with its Thomas Witty carpet, mahogany furnishings, the elegant sideboard with its assorted decanters and the art chosen for its adherence to the theme of music. The space had been designed to inspire conversation and confidence, to persuade donors to support the institution and parents to enrol their children in a fine school where they were surrounded by the trappings of wealth.

That was not the case here. This space was not designed to entertain or persuade. Visitors would not be inclined to stay long given that the room held the minimum of furniture: a desk, two chairs and bookshelves that contained only ledgers and legal paperwork. It was a boring room. There wasn't a braided rug set before the fireplace. He doubted even Baldor would find the space comfortable. Eaton tried to imagine her in the office, behind the desk, listening to reports, giving orders, her chestnut hair and green eyes the only sparks of colour in room. She would draw all eyes as she'd drawn his.

Eaton selected a shareholders' journal from the shelf and settled in the chair near the fire. Perhaps it was best she wasn't here. He was already having difficulty thinking about work instead of her. It would be deuced difficult to concentrate on the books with her providing a very physical reminder of what they'd shared last night. She dominated his thoughts. He knew with certainty that one night with Eliza wasn't going to be nearly enough for him.

She was a confident lover who made him feel like a partner, like something more than the embodiment of a title and a bank account, or a demigod to be assuaged in order to request something from him. Sometimes he felt like Scheherazade's genie in the lamp, granting wishes for others, but never for himself. That was the curse of the genie. Unlimited power to be used in the service of others. The school was for Cornwall, for

Cade and for Rosenwyn, the ducal estates supported the local economies of their regions, providing jobs and crops, homes and business for tenants and villagers. But Eliza was for him. What he had done for her was for him as well. He'd wanted to help. He'd not been obliged. Eliza was a woman he admired and whose admiration he wanted. And therein lay the danger.

He wanted more than her admiration. Eaton looked up from the journal and expelled a slow breath, letting the knowledge settle on him. He was falling for Eliza Blaxland and he was falling hard. This relationship was not a game and it hadn't been for a long time. Maybe never. She'd been clear from the start she did not play the merry widow. It heightened the importance and the honour she'd done him by coming last night.

She'd not taken last night lightly. What had it meant to her? What were her expectations? She was not looking to marry. She was not looking for an affair that might bring scandal either, which left Eaton adrift for an answer. Perhaps the better question was, what were his expectations? What did he want? But the answer to that would be very different than the answer to what could he have. The way he felt right now, he didn't want it to end. He liked who he was when he was with her and with Sophie. Perhaps because they had no inkling what it meant to be him—a man who could give no woman a future. They only knew he liked to fly kites and hunt for sea-cave treasures. He was at his best with them and he'd not been at his best for a long time.

Was that true? It was quite the epiphany and it set him back. How long was it since he'd been truly, deeply *happy*? Perhaps it wasn't that he was *unhappy*. He laughed with his friends, he had compassion for others. He knew he wasn't the sort to let disappointment shape him into a grumpy, reclusive hermit who groused at the world. But he hadn't realised his happiness hadn't gone bone deep, that his happiness hadn't been *joy*. Not until now. Not until Eliza.

There was joy and peace with Eliza. With Eliza he was content sitting before the fire at the dower house in the evening, strolling in the orangery and playing with the parakeets, or walking the surf line of the beach. He didn't *need* to be rushing from project to project or worrying about what came next when life slowed down and he had to face the void. Eliza was no longer another project, something to begin and end. *Eliza filled the void.* The realisation was followed by another just as stunning. He didn't want Eliza to go back to Truro.

He wanted her to stay. But he couldn't have that. To stay meant to offer marriage. She was not looking for marriage and she would not want the marriage he could give her. There was nothing inside that offer for her. He could not give her children, the one thing she felt she'd had to give up for the sake of her independence, and the only thing that might compel her to rethink her position on marriage. A certain inevitability settled on him. At some point, he would have to give Eliza up. But not today. Today, she was still his and there were still things he could give her. It would have to be enough.

Eaton returned his attention to the journal and set to work in earnest. He noted the different percentages owned by which shareholders. He began to work combinations that afforded Eliza the most leverage for the least amount of money. Before long, he had an arrangement that would suit her purposes. When she arrived, Eliza would be pleased. If they could convince these shareholders to sell, she would have a modicum of power against the mutineers. She should be pleased.

He hadn't waited for her! To say she was displeased was an absolute understatement. Eliza huffed up the stairs to the office, steaming with anger. This was precisely why she should not have got involved with him! What had Eaton been thinking? She threw open the office door—no need for a key apparently when Gillie Cardy was letting in everyone who waved a title around. She'd have words with him later, once she'd had words with Eaton—Eaton, who was lounging decadently in the room's one chair, long, booted legs propped on the fender of the fireplace, a ledger in his lap confirming his worst sin while he managed to look desirable in the world's most uninspiring room. It was not a space designed for desire and yet he'd succeeded wildly in transforming it with his presence. 'You! You started without me!'

'And finished, although I much prefer when we finish together.' He was all smug insouciance against her rage. Did he not understand what he'd done?

She marched over to him and grabbed the ledger off his lap. 'No! You do not get to be in a good mood after you've violated my privacy. What did you think you were doing? This is *my* office. You've flustered poor Gillie Cardy to no end. He had no idea to expect you.'

Eaton gave a hearty laugh. 'I was taking a leaf from your book, Eliza—the power of a surprise visit. Cardy was not ready for my unexpected arrival and I used it to my advantage. You're right, it does create a certain momentum. Instead of waiting for you and letting the day slip by, I found the answer.' He was unfazed by her scold, another reason she should not have indulged. She had no power with him. He ran roughshod over her usual strategies and then followed them up with an irresistible grin. 'It's a little different when the shoe's on the other foot, isn't it, Eliza?'

'You should have waited, as a courtesy,' Eliza snapped. This was not a game. Her future as the leader of the mining corporation was at stake.

Eaton glanced at the clock. 'So that it could have taken us four hours to discover what I did in two? Perhaps I was mistaken, but I thought time was of the essence with the shareholders' meeting looming in a few days? I thought the plan was to buy out the necessary shareholders by then.'

'It is,' Eliza acceded, untying the ribbons of her hat and hanging it on a peg. But she didn't have to like it. She was still uncomfortable with the idea that the plan was Eaton's, that the resources she'd be using to repopulate her board were Eaton's. Yet the decision to follow the plan had been hers. She should not take her frustration out on Eaton. 'What did you find?' After the morning she'd had, it was time to get down to business.

'In a moment.' Eaton went to the desk and lifted the room's second chair out from behind it. 'First, come sit and tell me why you were late.' He placed the chair by the fire, angling it to meet his satisfaction. 'I'm afraid a chair is the most comfort I can offer. This office is *most* incommodious. I do recommend stocking it with decanters at the very least and think about redecorating.'

There he went again, being charming, all the while he was stealing control away from her. 'No decanters. They'll just fall off the shelves and smash when we blast.' She'd known indulging with him would be hazardous, but she'd misjudged the depth of the danger and of her liking. She didn't want him to be charming, or considerate. Why couldn't he be an arrogant bully she could despise?

'I'll add it to the list of problems to solve.' Eaton grinned. 'Now, about your morning? Is Sophie well?'

'No, as a matter of fact, Sophie ate something disagreeable at supper.' A supper she'd not overseen because she'd been too busy arguing with Detford. Sophie had been asleep by the time Detford had left. 'She woke up sick this morning.' Which was something else she'd almost missed because she'd been in bed with her lover. She'd been home barely five minutes before Sophie had woken up retching and needing her. Eliza shook her head, trying to dispel her remorse. 'I should have been there.'

'You mean, you should not have been with me,' Eaton corrected.

'Yes, but I was with you and now things are just as bad as I knew they'd be.' She leaned forward, dropping her voice to a hiss. 'Detford is downstairs. Gillie Cardy told him you'd been here since nine. He knows you're up here *alone*, with carte blanche access to the office records.' She would look like the whore Detford had implied yesterday. Miles would think Eaton was her lover and *now* he'd be right. If Miles told anyone, she'd look immoral and weak. Would Miles expose her like that or was he still her friend? She fixed Eaton with a stare. 'This is exactly the kind of opening the shareholders needed and I've handed it to them on a silver platter.'

Eaton disagreed. 'Yes, I do know what this means. Those who plot against you will be very concerned about their duplicity when they realise a peer of the realm has taken an interest in their industry. Would you like to see the list? These are your best options for a buyout. If they sell, you can increase your majority in the company by fifteen per cent. Brenley's bunch can't muster more than forty per cent if anything comes to a vote. Even if Detford's five per cent sides with them, you'd still have a margin.'

The whirring of her mind halted at his words. 'Say that again?' Had she heard him correctly?

Eaton grinned. 'I said, Eliza, you can make yourself fireproof. But you'll have to act fast.' *You.* Eaton was empowering her, not taking anything away from her. It might have been his suggestion, but she had to enact it and the shares would be hers. Eliza smiled. It felt as if a weight had been lifted from her, her doubts evaporating in the wake of success. They had found a way through. She was on the offensive now.

Eliza Blaxland wasn't going to go down without a fight. Miles eyed the group assembled over ale, crumpling Eliza's note in his hand. 'She's refused our offer. Well, we expected as much. She's never been the most biddable of women.' Miles's dissatisfaction was palpable as he addressed the group. His interviews with Eliza had been disappointing. He'd hoped she would have found the offer more appealing. 'We never expected Bude's heir was in her pocket,' he said, trying to rationalise the refusal.

'More like he's in her bed,' Gismond Brenley supplied derisively. 'Looks like someone beat you to the finish line, Detford.'

'Hardly matters where he is, only that he's involved now and that makes him part of our problem,' Miles replied, redirecting their attentions back to the subject at hand. They could not blame Lynford's presence on him. 'We have three days until the shareholders' meeting. We have to make sure we have a case against her if she means to refuse our generous offer. If she won't step down for a nice offer, we have to force her out.' He liked the idea of force. He was done playing nice with Eliza Blaxland. It was time she learned her place.

'Lynford *is* the case against her,' Isley Thorp put in with a sly grin. 'If we put it about that she's his mistress, her reputation is in question. We can't have an immoral woman running the corporation.'

'It depends on how the rest of the board sees it.' Detford shook his head. Under regular circumstances, the current board would find such behaviour inexcusable. But if the board was under Lynford's thumb, it would hardly matter if Eliza walked down the street naked. Miles waited until he had everyone's attention. 'There's something else.' He pushed forward a letter. 'I got this from one of the minor shareholders last night. She's made an offer to buy his shares, at profit. I am assuming she sent similar letters to others.' If she were successful, this would ruin everything. It would give her majority control against their coalition.

Gismond Brenley seemed unconcerned. 'They won't sell. There's the money to be made from extending the tunnel once the widow is removed. Profits will go sky-high, then. Surely these shareholders know that. Besides, she'd need to garner more than someone's three per cent. She'd need to buy all the three per centers. Odds are, not all of them will sell out.'

Miles wasn't as confident. He'd seen how resolute she'd been when he'd put the offer to her. 'Maybe. Or, perhaps those three per centers don't want the risk of an accident. Everyone knows nothing ever goes smoothly in mining. But that isn't the point. She's building a new group of shareholders, people who are willing to champion her, to leave her in power. Gentlemen, she's replacing us and it takes no imagination to know who is behind this.'

Miles met each man's gaze directly. There was a fortune in copper beneath the sea if they could just reach it. But they had to go through her.

Brenley thought for a moment. 'Then we have to get to her. She would never let a man control what she's worked for. We need to convince her that Lynford will take control away from her no matter what he's promised thus far.'

'And if that doesn't work?' Miles pressed. 'We may

need to remove her in a more permanent way.' A certain excitement roused in him at the prospect. Eliza Blaxland had crossed him too many times. Of course those methods were dangerous. There was too much money at stake for people to ignore her death. When those people included the Marquess of Lynford and the Duke of Bude, there would most definitely be an inquest. Yet, if it came to that, he would find a way to ensure the cards went his way. To be denied now, and by a woman who thought herself the equal of a man, would be an enormous loss of financial opportunity and pride. This was war. All was fair and the endgame was near. Eliza Blaxland would get a final chance to accept the offer at the board meeting and then she would get what was coming to her.

Chapter Sixteen

The game had started without her. Eliza drew a deep breath to steady her nerves and her anger before entering the upper room at the Ship Inn on Budoc Lane. She could hear voices within that confirmed what the innkeeper had reported: the shareholders were already assembled and had been for half an hour. How dare they begin the meeting before she arrived! She was the chairman, the head of the company. She would remind them nothing they did without her presence had meaning.

Eliza smoothed her skirts and squared her shoulders. She'd dressed to command today in a tailored ensemble of heather grey, the coat cut with military lines and trimmed in black velvet, a white stock peeking up at the collar. There would be no disputing that she was the one in charge. She ran through her mental list of resources, reminding herself what her goals were here today: to emerge with her leadership of the mines intact.

Eliza turned the knob and entered, gratified when the conversation faltered, when all eyes turned to her, some of those eyes looking guilty. Good. Six of those men had happily taken her money last night when she'd bought their shares in the company. Her chair at the head of the table was empty. Also good. They hadn't replaced her yet. To the right of her chair sat Miles Detford. Today, the sight of him didn't fill her with the usual comfort. But he was still her friend, still her ally, she told herself. He'd brought bad news, he'd counselled her to take an offer she didn't agree with— that didn't make him less of a friend. Perhaps it made him more of one.

'Now that I am here, we can begin.' Eliza strolled to her chair and consulted the watch pin she wore; ten minutes until the hour. 'That is, if no one disapproves of starting early? We did agree to meet at eleven.' She surveyed the room with a cool gaze before sitting. 'I do appreciate how very…*prompt* everyone is.' She took her seat. 'I officially call the quarterly meeting of the Blaxland Mining Corporation to order.' Miles Detford read the minutes and Eliza pasted on a cool smile as though nothing was out of the ordinary. They would see that their contretemps had not shaken her.

'A report from the treasurer is now in order. Mr Thorp?' Eliza called on the sallow-faced man, wondering if she'd imagined his Adam's apple bobbing nervously. She looked around the table when he finished. 'Are there questions for Mr Stinson on our expenses?' The question was met with silence. She stared at Isley Thorp, at Jerome Blackmore, at Sir Gismond Brenley.

Who was the betrayer? 'No questions?' She kept her voice frosty, her gaze returning to Thorp. 'I find that hard to believe when the lumber order for the Wheal Karrek tunnel was twice what it should have been. It is not our practice to deliberately over-order.'

'What are you suggesting, Mrs Blaxland?' Gismond Brenley patronised in a bored tone as if there was no need to be concerned.

She met him with a steely gaze, her own tone matching him in condescension. 'I am suggesting that someone countermanded our decision not to tunnel under the ocean. Why else would we purchase twice the required lumber? If that is not the case, I would think you'd be more concerned since it's your money that's been spent unnecessarily.' How horribly telling that he wasn't aghast. In fact, *none* of them was aghast, although a few of them exchanged looks. She did not give away her dismay. 'Very well, let the minutes show that no one was bothered by the expenditures.' She'd put them on notice, she'd gone on record in the minutes for having addressed the issue head-on. It would be harder to accuse her now of being inept, of having not been aware of what was happening in her own company. 'Now, on to old business, the Porth Karrek tunnel and the schools.'

'Ahem, Mrs Blaxland, I would like to table old business until we've discussed a proposal.' The interruption came from Gismond Brenley. 'I think it will affect how the discussion of the tunnel and the schools goes, which is why I'd like to have it introduced first.'

Eliza braced herself. So the ringleader was Brenley. She was not surprised. He was the most august of the shareholders. Under friendlier circumstances, he would have been her right hand just as he'd been her husband's. But he'd never been in support of her, having always fancied himself the heir apparent to the mining corporation. 'Mrs Blaxland, in honour of your fifth year as the head of the company, and in recognition of your extraordinary efforts, we have an offer to put to you to help relieve the strain you've endured. With the advent of the new tunnel, the corporation is entering a new era and it occurred to us that it is an opportune time for new leadership, a chance for you to step away and enjoy your life with your daughter.'

On her right, Miles murmured, 'These are good terms.'

Eliza suspected the murmur was for show. But whose show? For her benefit or for the board's? Would a polite refusal be enough? 'Thank you, gentlemen. I am sure the offer is made with my benefit in mind, however, I have no intention of stepping away from the mines at this time. It is an exciting period and, precisely for that reason, I will remain at the helm for the foreseeable future.' Eliza smiled her rejection. There was uncomfortable silence. No one spoke. For a moment, she thought she might have won, that all that had been required was a firm hand. Surely it couldn't be that easy. She waited for the count of five.

Brenley's eyes grew hard. 'It may not be up to you. The board believes it is time for you to step down. We want to go forward with the underwater tunnel. We feel financial resources are better spent on the pursuit of ore than establishing schools. We didn't want to do this as a vote, but we will if we must.'

'We definitely must. I want to see my betrayers, those who have plotted behind my back to bring about this moment,' Eliza snapped. 'The vote will be done by a show of hands and votes will be counted based on the allotted shares each member holds in the company.' There were no grounds for argument there; it was how votes had always been counted. 'Those in favour of new leadership?' Thorp, Blackmore, Brenley—the usual coalition—raised their hands along with Stinson. 'That's forty per cent, Brenley.' Eliza smiled coolly as she informed him, 'That is not a majority.'

'But Havens, Eldridge, Saxon, Halliday, Mycroft and Kincaid haven't voted,' Brenley replied.

'Nor will they. As of this morning, they are no longer shareholders in the corporation. They have sold their shares to me. That gives me a majority in the company.'

'Detford, you haven't voted.' Brenley skewered him with a prompting gaze.

'I only hold five per cent of the shares, so it wouldn't matter which way I decide,' Miles prevaricated. He smiled at her as if his abstention was some sort of victory for her. Was it? Was abstention a way of siding with her? She could hear Eaton's warning in her head. Detford was not to be trusted.

'So, we are to be a board of five, then?' Brenley challenged.

'Perhaps, or maybe I will sell my shares at some point. Not today, though, and not to you, although if you are jealous of your friends' profits made in selling to me, I am happy to purchase your shares at the same rate, as well as anyone else's here at the table.' That included Detford, who'd not declared his side, more was the pity, but that was not the main concern today.

'Replacing us will strain your resources.' Brenley glared. 'We are not so easily bought as these other piddling stakeholders.' No, they wouldn't be. Their shares would be expensive, but she did not flinch.

'I am offering to treat you equitably, as I have treated your colleagues, even though you secretly plotted a mutiny behind my back after I have spent years making you money.' Eliza rose from the table. 'As the single majority stockholder, I declare that the underwater tunnel will cease once it reaches the ocean and the schools will go forward as planned. This meeting is adjourned.'

She made it to the door of the Ship Inn before Miles reached her. He placed a hand on her arm as she stepped outside. 'Eliza, what do you think you're doing? Did Lynford put you up to this?'

'I put myself up to it, Miles. Since when does a man put me up to anything?' All she wanted right now was to be with Sophie, with Eaton.

'I've never known you to be reckless. Do you think you can simply buy them out and your problems will be solved?' Detford kept pace with her as she marched up Budoc Lane. 'Brenley's right, you can't buy out the rest of us without breaking your bank to do it. You'd have to sell those shares immediately.' It was as if a light came on in Detford's mind. 'Lynford has investors lined up, doesn't he? Don't be a fool, Eliza. He's setting up to take over the corporation. How long do you think you'd remain in charge?'

'As long as I like,' Eliza all but snapped. She was done discussing business.

'As his whore? Or will he seduce it out of you?' Miles snarled. 'You know that's what everyone will say. They'll say Lynford is propping you up because it humours him to let his mistress run mines. What do you think they're saying upstairs right now? It's already started, Eliza. They will come after you and this time they won't play by the rules. You should have pacified Brenley's coalition when you had the chance.'

She reached her carriage. 'Thank you for the advice, Miles.' She got in and pointedly shut the door behind her, leaving Miles alone on the street. She had much to think about. She'd poked a sleeping dragon and now it was awake and roaring. The meeting had gone as expected. She had what she wanted. But the fight had just begun. By tomorrow, the rumours would start. She had one last day of peace and she would spend it with Sophie and Eaton.

Eliza leaned back against the leather seat and shut her eyes. Eaton. She should not want him. He would be the undoing of her, perhaps not in the way Miles predicted, but there were other ways to steal her control and undermine the life she'd built. There was no future with him. They both knew it and yet they both continued to pretend it didn't matter. But it did. When it ended, she would be disappointed. Eliza sighed. Already she knew that word was too mild to encompass what she would feel. Intentionally or not, Eaton had given her a glimpse of heaven, a glimpse of herself, how she might have been if only things had been different.

'Mama! Mama! Come see the parakeets!' They were the sweetest words in the world to Eliza as Sophie tugged on her hand the moment she stepped inside the orangery.

Eaton emerged behind Sophie, jacket off, sleeves rolled up, a wide, open smile on his face. He'd been enjoying himself. 'You're just in time.' His gaze was intent, lingering on her, looking for signs there'd been trouble. 'We're going to feed the birds.' She smiled, offering reassurance that all had gone as well as could be expected. There'd be time to talk later. Eliza allowed Sophie to drag her off to the aviary, the tension of the meeting rolling off her with each step. Moments like this were what mattered. This was what she was fighting for, to protect Sophie's inheritance.

'Did the gambit work?' Eaton asked once Sophie was busy with the parakeets.

'Yes, the coalition was exposed and they were reminded I retain control of the board for now. But Brenley made threats.' She paused. 'Nothing we did not anticipate, but I'd hoped it would not come to that. He will say awful things about me, Eaton.' She watched Sophie hold up a finger for a parakeet to perch on and giggle when it did. She was so sweet, so innocent. 'I would not want her to hear those things said about her mother.'

'It will not come to that.' Eaton's voice was fervent and low. 'Once we have a new board in place, people will see the truth, I will see to it. Your reputation will remain intact.'

'It's not your responsibility, Eaton. It's mine.' Eliza felt the prickles of Miles's warning creep up her spine. No, she would not believe that of him. Doubt would only serve Brenley. What would Eaton do with a mining corporation? He didn't need it. There was no reason for him to take it over. *Any more than there was ever a reason to help her*, her conscience whispered. Why had he bothered at all? What did he gain?

'Your responsibility alone, Eliza?' Eaton queried. 'It doesn't have to be.'

'Yes, it does,' she insisted. What could he want? What could ever come of this association? Everything was so much simpler when she'd just been a patron of his school, a faceless widow who wrote cheques, who didn't know how handsome the Marquess was or how persuasive. This conversation was fast becoming about more than managing the board. This was about managing them—this relationship. Did one night in his bed constitute a relationship, or had that relationship existed long before they'd made love?

'I thought we'd settled the bit about being alone.' Eaton offered her a devastating smile. 'Can we argue about this later? I promised Sophie we'd pick oranges for tea. But I'd like to continue this discussion tonight?' She heard the invitation in that. She ought to decline. Accepting would make it harder to leave.

Just one more night, she promised herself. Then it

would have to be over and she would be alone again. The lines of demarcation were clearer that way. She'd had just the smallest taste of how easily it could all slip away if she indulged herself with him. To blur those lines was to blur her priorities. Eaton could not be one of them, no matter how much she wanted him to be.

Chapter Seventeen

One more night. One more night of torturing himself with a glimpse of what might have been, showing himself what could never be. Eaton would take it, whatever its guise. Sophie finished playing the spinet in the parlour and went up to bed, Eliza with her, while he waited downstairs with a glass of brandy. It was a fatherly, husbandly thing to do. Not for the first time he thought how different things might have been if he had not gone into Kilkhampton that day fourteen years ago. He might never have contracted the measles, might never have been stripped of his ability to reproduce. He wouldn't be faced with losing a woman he loved.

Up until now, the consequences of his infertility had been a theoretical concept. Certainly, he had agonised over what it would mean for his life as he grew older, how it shaped the choices he would make. That theoretical concept had become more real with Richard Penlerick's death and the overt pressure put on Vennor to marry. Now, with Eliza, that reality was complete. There were no more hypothetical dimensions to it. He'd met a woman he loved. A woman he wanted to marry. A woman who wanted children. A woman he couldn't have.

'Are you thinking about Richard Penlerick? You seem sorrowful.' Eliza entered the parlour.

'In part,' he offered. 'I was thinking of you and Sophie and how much like a little family we've become.' He gestured for her to join him on the settee.

'You've been good to her. She likes you.'

Eaton played with the stem of his brandy glass. 'And her mother? Does her mother like me?' Eliza was beautiful in firelight, the flames catching her chestnut hair.

'Her mother is very thankful for your support in this difficult time. You didn't need to give it and I fear your kindness has been repaid by dragging you into the quagmire.' Eliza's hands were tight in her lap. She was nervous. 'I think it might be time to leave. I don't want to be the guest who overstays her welcome.'

'Leave? Now? You can't leave now, not when you've just got control of the board. What about your school?' This was the worst possible time for her to leave— unless this wasn't about business but about *them*. Knowing he had to let her go was one thing. Actually letting her go was another.

'I control the board whether I am here or in Truro. The shareholders don't need me to be here for them to take their places. I won't see them in person until the next quarterly meeting, assuming I survive Brenley's character assassination.' It was coolly said, but for the first time, Eaton saw how worried Eliza was.

'You will survive it,' Eaton assured her. 'Why wouldn't you? Brenley and the others will sell out before long and walk away because they won't be happy once your new board members are in place. You simply have to wait them out, let them save face. You can afford to be a gracious victor.'

'I don't control the community. Even if I win this battle of wills, I wonder if it will be enough? I've wondered all day if I should have taken Brenley's deal. I wonder even now, at the eleventh hour, if I should write to him and accept the offer, as much as it would gall me to do it. Still, it might be better than what is to come.' Better than having her name dragged through the mud if Detford's information was right. Better than having Eaton's name dragged there, too. He deserved more for his assistance than a scandal. She'd been a poor investment to repay him thusly.

She gave him a sad smile. 'Victory at what price, Eaton? At the price of my good name? At the price of a scandal my daughter will hear of?'

'Is that why you're so anxious to be off to Truro? You want to avoid Brenley's next barrage?' Eaton drew her to him, wrapping her in his arms and tucking her head beneath his chin in the hope of giving her comfort. 'There's the principle of the matter, too, Eliza. If you accept Brenley's offer, you would be letting dishonest men win.' Eaton paused, allowing her to digest that piece.

'I can have peace. That is no small thing.' She sighed against his chest. God, he loved having her in his arms.

'But what of the miners? What peace will they have

when Brenley pushes the tunnel out into the ocean at their risk?' He had her there. He could feel her tense in his arms, another reminder of how multifaceted the fight was and how she was the shield maiden for so many. Perhaps it was for that reason her answer surprised him.

'I may reach a point very soon where they will have to fight for themselves. I can't hold up the world for ever.' There was a new weariness in her tone. 'Please don't talk to me about ethics and principles, Eaton. I *know* I should fight for them.' She looked up at him, her green eyes filled with regret. 'But Sophie needs my protection, too. At some point, a parent doesn't have the luxury of fighting for ethics. If I have to choose who to protect, I'll choose Sophie.'

But who protected her? Eliza Blaxland manned the wall of her defences alone. She needed a protector, an ally. He stroked her hair, his thoughts wandering down tangled paths. How could he make this right for her? How could he protect her and Sophie so that Eliza could fight?

'Does my choice disappoint you?' she asked, her eyes searching his face.

'No, it makes you honest.' And smart and brave, all the things he'd come to admire about her, *love* about her. It was not the first time he'd associated that word with Eliza. He loved her strength, her independence, her fierceness, her willingness to sacrifice everything for those she loved, and perhaps that meant he loved not only the characteristics that made her who she was, but he loved *her*, too.

Temptation whispered, *You can protect her. You can marry her, give her the protection of your name and your station. Save her mines, ensure her reputation, be a father to Sophie. Marriage to her gives you everything you've ever wanted.*

But it gave Eliza nothing. She would resist. She'd made her position on marrying clear. He would have to put it to her carefully and at the right moment. This was not that moment. She was too conflicted, too uncertain. His offer would look like charity coming now on the heels of her fear. And he'd have to tell her his secret, something he didn't discuss even with his close friends and family. They knew, of course, but he hadn't been the one to tell them. He had to tell Eliza. She had a right to know what marriage to him would cost her. It would cost her dream. Telling her might very well cost him his. He could lose her over this and that came with fears all its own. But loving Eliza demanded he take the risk. He'd not told a woman about his condition, ever. There'd never been a need to. How did one go about divulging dark truths and shattering dreams and hope to emerge intact? But those were discussions and considerations for another, better, time.

'Don't give in, Eliza,' he whispered. 'It will be all right in the end, I promise.' He would move heaven and earth to make it so. He'd created a school for Cade and Rosenwyn. Surely he could do at least as much for the woman he loved.

She smiled softly, something moving in her eyes. 'I shouldn't let you make impossible promises, but I don't want to think about it any more tonight.'

'What *do* you want?'

'I want to forget everything for just a little while. Do you have a remedy for that?'

Eaton grinned. 'I might. If you'd come with me, there's a place I know.'

She should not use him for escape, but it was hard to remember the reasons why as she reclined on the pillows in the orangery's antechamber, watching him disrobe. This little room had become their refuge, the place where the world could not touch them, where she was entitled to give her fantasy free rein. Eaton strode towards the bed, gloriously nude, all broad shoulders and muscled thighs, like a wild pagan god of old, desire heating his eyes with a fierceness that made her tremble. How phenomenal, how thrilling, that this man wanted her and how wicked that she should want him, too, with the same fierceness. Tonight she needed the pulsing, thrusting pleasure that drove one towards oblivion.

He came to her and she drew him down, bringing his length against her until they were skin to silk, her nightgown already sliding up her thighs, already revealing her eagerness, her desire. She welcomed him. His eyes reflected her own hunger. She was hungry to forget the day, hungry to recapture the passion that had flared to life in this room, hungry to be touched, to be cherished if even for a few moments.

'Tonight you are Breasal, the Celtic High King, come to earth.' She nipped at his earlobe, whispering the fantasy from Cornish folklore. 'You've come to claim a mortal maid for your pleasure.'

He gave a husky laugh, his hand running up her thigh, bending her knee. 'I will hope for better since his kingdom is only visible one night in seven years.' He kissed the inside of her leg, working up her thigh with his lips. 'Perhaps I am the mere mortal and you are the fairy Aeval, come to command my sexual favours.' He kissed the crease of her thigh where it met with the entrance to her private core.

'Hmm. I like that.' She stretched, cat-like, letting the warm thrill of him spread through her. 'I always thought the story of Aeval's midnight court was rather decadent, but secretly inspiring, that a woman might, nay, *should* command her own pleasure. Indeed, even hold a man accountable for it.'

'And did you? Command your own?' Eaton asked, his eyes dangerously feral as he kissed her navel, working his way up her body, heat following in his wake.

'Absolutely, or I would have had none.' She locked gazes with him, answering his look with one of her own just as wild, letting the implication settled on him. Married to Blaxland, she'd been responsible for her own pleasure alone in the dark after he'd claimed his rights. She'd never begrudged him that, but she begrudged knowing that there should be more, that perhaps she was entitled to more.

'And the holding-a-man-accountable part?' He sucked at her breast, drawing out a nipple with his teeth until she gasped.

'Only you.' She smiled wickedly.

He answered with a grin of his own. 'What does my Fairy Queen command of me this night?'

She shifted her hips, widening the span between her legs. 'Your Queen commands that you take her, swift and fast, that you drive her into pleasure's oblivion until the sun rises.' She kissed him hard on the mouth, reckless with desire and need, and he answered with a savage hunger that mirrored her own. She felt him move once and then he thrust deep, a bright spear that splintered her core. Yes, this was exactly what she needed. She gave herself over to it, knowing that oblivion awaited.

But so did the morning. Even Eaton's exquisite lovemaking could not hold back the sun, nor could the pleasure of waking in his arms, her body tucked against his, override the troubles of the day. She was no nearer to any resolution than she had been the prior evening. She and Brenley were still at odds and viciously so. His threats still loomed like ghosts on dawn's horizon waiting to take shape. But larger still was the issue of leaving Eaton. This had to end and she would have to end it. The longer she stayed, the more unfair it was to both of them. There was no expectation of a future, but there were feelings. How did one navigate the end of an affair neither party wanted to end? Last night had solved one need, but created others. If she wasn't careful, she would fall in love with Eaton. Maybe she already had. Maybe that was why she was still here.

Eaton's body stirred behind her, his voice warm at

her ear. 'Have I acquitted myself appropriately, my Queen?'

'Extraordinarily so,' she murmured, wishing to hold on to the night just a moment longer. They'd loved and slept, and loved and slept until they could conquer exhaustion no more as dawn crept up on them and the game had ended, taking oblivion with it. She was the Queen no longer, but a beleaguered businesswoman beset on all sides by those who wished to see her fail. Eaton moved against her and she amended the thought. Perhaps she wasn't beleaguered on all sides. Perhaps she had one ally, one person who wished for her success.

'Perhaps I might acquit myself one more time,' he whispered, his arm tight about her waist, hugging her securely against him. She would be his Aeval one last time.

Eliza moaned, her bottom wiggling against him. Morning pleasure was a habit one could easily get used to, addicted to. To wake like this beside such a man was heavenly indeed. No, not *such a man*. That suggested there were other men who could command such a response from her, that such a response was available on a whim.

No, only Eaton would do. Not Blaxland, not Detford. None of the men who'd tried to woo her had ever succeeded in wringing a response from her even close to this. Nor would any man ever, her conscience counselled. Eaton was one in a million and she knew why. He wanted nothing from her that she did not want for herself. She was safe with him. He did not want to take the mines by manipulation or by matrimony. He slid into her, faster this time, his slow, drowsy seduction increasing its urgency as she gasped, her hands gripping his arm where he held her close as she came apart.

She was reluctant to put the pieces back together. It would require getting out of bed, getting dressed, dealing with Brenley. It would also require putting distance between her and Eaton. That distance had to start today. That was what she'd promised herself and that was what the situation required if she was going to survive the scandal intact. Eliza sighed. She still had to be the one to do this. He could not fight this battle for her, although she knew he would insist otherwise.

'That sigh sounds ominous.' Eaton kissed her shoulder.

'I need to get up. I can't stay in bed all day.' For so many reasons.

'Why not?' Eaton propped his dark head on a hand, looking entirely too seductive by dawn's light.

'Because it solves nothing.' She shifted to the side of the bed and swung her feet over the edge, shivering now that she was away from the heat of his body.

'What can we solve today? We can do nothing more until we hear from Inigo.' She could feel his eyes on her as she moved about the room, gathering up her clothes.

She stopped her gathering and faced him. 'We can't solve the issue with the mining board, but we can solve what lies between us. This has to end. Even without pressure from the board, there's nothing here for us.'

Eaton sat up, hands behind his head, his torso with its dark hair on blatant display, a reminder of what she was giving up—all that masculine virility. He smiled and her heart thudded. 'Nothing here for us? Do you really believe that? I don't. If you do believe there is nothing here, then it seems you and I have very different understandings of what has occurred between us in the past month.'

Eliza set her clothes down, hands on hips. 'All right, you tell me what you think happens next.'

'I think we wait. We wait out Brenley. We wait for news from Inigo. I have no intention of deserting you in the heart of the storm, which is precisely where we are now. I am in no hurry to divest myself of you, Eliza. Yet you seem in quite the hurry to be rid of me. I am wounded.'

'You'll recover,' Eliza said sharply.

'I'm not so sure I will.' The lack of humour in his voice caused her to pause. There was no laughter in his tone; he was in earnest. Eaton crawled out of bed and wrapped a sheet about his waist. 'Let me help you dress. We can take Sophie to the woods today and hunt for another round of truffles. Baldor needs a good run. I'll have a picnic packed.'

'I have business in town, errands,' Eliza protested, but Eaton was adamant on this point.

'Do not go into town today, Eliza. Let Brenley do his worst. Your absence will simply show everyone how little you care for his accusations and how little you are worried.'

She wanted to argue, but his advice made sense. It would be best not to invite comment by going into town. Still, she did not want him making decisions for her. He'd already made so many. She'd known it would happen like this; first the house, then dinner, then the little entertainments with Sophie, all harmless in the beginning. But now, here she was in his bed, allowing him to repopulate the shareholders with his friends, allowing him to decide where she went. 'You have done too much.' It was a warning that he'd exceeded the allotment of favours she'd take from him.

His hands rested at her shoulders and she very much feared there was every chance they'd be back in bed before she got her dress on. 'Eliza, let me in.'

'You cannot fight for me. I've explained.'

'No, I cannot. But we can fight together. I can fight *with* you. You just have to trust me, Eliza.'

Eliza said nothing.

Chapter Eighteen

The end of October was out in full, glorious colour. The golden leaves of the Trevaylor Woods crunched under their boots as they strolled beneath the autumn foliage, the sound serving as a reminder of the silence that had sprung up between them in the orangery. Up ahead, Sophie threw handfuls of leaves into the air, laughing and dodging among the trees, while Baldor wagged his tail and did his best to get in the way. Eliza envied the duo their romp, oblivious to the tension that had risen between her and Eaton. She had said very little to him since they'd left the orangery, focusing an over-bright smile on Sophie and getting ready for the picnic. In short, she was ignoring him. Did he not understand he was asking for the moon? The sooner she and Sophie left the better. This dalliance had gotten out of hand. She'd consented to the experiment, but now it had to end. She would retreat to Truro and clutch her fifty-five per cent majority to her for all it was worth. No matter what Brenley did, she would rise from the ashes.

Eaton stooped to pick up a particularly vibrant red leaf and twirled the stem in his hand, breaking the silence. 'Autumn has always been my favourite season. My father started bringing me truffle hunting when I was Sophie's age. We brought Baldor's grandsire with us. My father's hounds are bred for truffling. They have incredible noses,' he explained, casting her a smile, his dark eyes full of nostalgia. 'I loved those days when it was just the two of us, tramping through the woods. We'd stop by the stream and build a bonfire. That's where he taught me how to roast mushrooms. Sometimes we'd bring eggs and sausages.'

'It sounds delicious. Is that where your love for food comes from? You and your father must be very close.' She returned his smile warily, not wanting to be drawn into the story, this precious glimpse into his childhood.

'We are. In many ways, he is my best friend. He taught me how to be a man, how a man takes care of his family, of friends, of those less fortunate around him. He taught me how to be a duke, when the time comes, although I am in no hurry to lose him. In fact, I can't even imagine it. It will be so much worse than losing Richard Penlerick.' A shadow crossed his face and he looked away from her, clearing his throat against emotion.

'You're very lucky to have a father who cares for you,' Eliza offered, the wistfulness evident in her own voice. 'Sophie was four when Huntingdon died. She barely remembers him at all. I worry for her, growing up with a mother who must also be a father to her.' Eliza stooped to gather up leaves into a bouquet, aware she might have said too much, given the wrong impression. She didn't want Eaton to think she was angling for a proposal despite her previous arguments to the contrary. She didn't want to quarrel with him any more today. She'd rather enjoy this afternoon for what it was—a moment out of time where she could set aside her worries over the board and what came next.

'Do you honestly think being mother and father to Sophie is your only choice? That you absolutely must remain alone for the rest of your life? That there could never be a man worthy of your trust and respectful of your independence? Who could love you just the way you are?' Eaton was studying her. She was aware of his gaze, hot and contemplative. 'Humans are meant to marry, I think. You included.' Eaton handed her a golden fistful of leaves to add to the bouquet.

'And yet you haven't,' Eliza was quick to argue. 'You, who perhaps has more reason than most to marry.'

'I keep finding better things to do.'

'Like taking care of mining heiresses?' she joked, but it was as she'd suspected. She was a project, something to fill the void for this energetic man. She could be nothing more. He was meant for a different type of woman: a younger woman, a more innocent woman, a better-born woman. He was not for her, not in that way.

'I happen to like mining heiresses.' They stopped by a tree and Eaton distractedly chipped off a piece of bark. 'I used to think I wouldn't ever marry.'

She slanted him a questioning look. 'Why not? Surely it is expected of you?'

'No, not of me.' He slouched against the tree trunk, arms crossed, dark eyes serious. 'Can I tell you something, Eliza? Something I wouldn't want anyone else to know.'

He was asking her to keep a secret. A real secret. She'd learned to read him well enough to know this was not flirtation. She straightened, her leaf bouquet forgotten. She reached for his hands and held on. Intuition hinted whatever he wanted to tell her was difficult to speak of. 'You may tell me anything, Eaton.'

He would rather tell her anything but this. But honour demanded it. If he did not tell her, there was no possibility of moving forward. 'When I was fourteen there was a measles epidemic in Kilkhampton, which is not far from our family seat in Bude. I wasn't supposed to be there, but I was young, stupid and overly optimistic about my own immortality as many adolescent boys are. I sneaked away to take in a horse fair on the outskirts of the town. At fourteen I had no notion how illness was spread. I reasoned the fair was far enough from the village and I'd never been sick a day in my life, not the slightest fever ever.

'My luck ran out that day. I caught the measles. I took ill and almost died. We were fortunate. No one else in the family caught it and I lived. Many families around Bude lost loved ones that year.' Eliza nodded. Measles, mumps, any disease of that nature was a mother's nightmare. But her thoughts weren't for mothers in that moment. Her thoughts were for Eaton and where this story was headed and why she might need to know.

'It took most of that summer for me to recover. I've never been so weak. I hope I am never that weak again.' She squeezed his hands, giving him her strength once more the way she had that first night in the orangery when he'd told her about Richard Penlerick. 'I didn't realise it until a few years later, but it left me...unable to father children.'

Her brow knit. She was trying to be delicate and yet it was obvious her disbelief and curiosity were so much stronger. 'But, you don't seem to have any trouble...in the bedroom.'

'Sterility is not impotence. I can sleep with a woman as much as I like, but it will never result in a child.' Eaton gave a dry laugh. 'I know some men who wouldn't mind that sort of problem. I am not one of them.'

'No, you wouldn't be.' He could see the thoughts chasing across her face: how good he was with Sophie, how dedicated he was to the boys at the school. *Please,* he prayed, *don't offer me pity.* He simply wanted her to understand. He didn't need consolation. Eliza did not disappoint. 'How do you know for sure? Is there a test?'

'Just my own and some observations I made. There are other boys in Kilkhampton who caught the measles and have not sired children in their adulthood. I think it's unlikely there are that many barren females in Kilkhampton.' He shook his head. He knew what she was thinking. He'd once thought it, too. 'Eliza, do not give yourself false hope, that perhaps I am wrong, that there's a chance somehow.' This was the hard part, telling her about his experiment. 'I did a test, Eliza. My seed is dead. I put it under my microscope in the orangery and it didn't move. I know microscopic lenses are imperfect and I am no doctor but, taken with the other observations, there is no margin for hope. My father and I consulted a doctor in London and he was of the same opinion. He had made several studies of men who'd contracted measles in their childhood or adolescence. Not everyone was unable to father children, but there were enough to suggest it was a significant possibility.'

He waited for the pity, the platitudes. He waited for her to politely move away from him as if she could catch it. She would leave him now that she knew loving him, being with him, came at such a price. But Eliza did none of those things. Her words were full of gratitude for his honesty. 'Thank you for telling me. You didn't have to.' No, he could have kept the awful secret, could have let her believe their childless union was somehow her fault. It wouldn't have been a hard argument to make. She'd had one child in ten years with Huntingdon. Perhaps it hadn't been his age after all. Society would easily participate in that lie. But Eaton could not do that to her, this woman who wanted a family, who thought he might be able to give her one.

'The school isn't just for Cade and Rosenwyn, is it?' Eliza said softly. 'It's for you, too, to fill a void. All this time, I thought your life was perfect. The boys at the school, they're your children in their own way, aren't they?'

'Much like the miners' children are for you. It seems we must make families where we can find them.' He raised her hands to his lips and kissed each of them. 'You and Sophie have been a family to me in these weeks. I will always be grateful to you for that. Huntingdon Blaxland was a lucky man.'

Eliza laughed. 'He thought so, too, but I always thought I was the lucky one. He gave me Sophie and a second chance.' Baldor bayed in the distance, a reminder that the hound and Sophie had run far ahead of them. Eaton pushed off the tree trunk and they began to walk again.

'He did more than give me financial security. He gave me the ability to make that security for myself. Hunt enjoyed the fact that I took an interest in his mining empire. It entertained him to show me how to calculate tonnage and profit, to take me along when he explored the new shafts and to explain the new technologies that harvested ore faster. For our first anniversary I asked for stock in the company and for each anniversary after that, then as a birthing gift when Sophie was born. I don't know if he ever took me seriously, but it didn't matter. *I* took *me* seriously. In his will, he left me twenty per cent of the stock, but I'd amassed another twenty per cent in gifts during our marriage. I knew I'd outlive Huntingdon. I wanted to be prepared. I wanted to make every moment count.'

The very words of his toast from Richard Penlerick's funeral. Eliza knew the import of that. 'I thought you were extraordinary from the start and I was right. What a surprise it must have been for the likes of Brenley.'

'Oh, yes, you should have seen his face when the will was read. He'd been expecting to be named head of the corporation. He's hated me ever since. Now, he's having his revenge.'

Eliza Blaxland was remarkable for her strength, her tenacity, her foresight. If he'd been uncertain of his love earlier, he was certain of it now. The woman he wanted to spend his life with was walking beside him, but the wanting did not make her any more attainable. 'Eliza, I will keep you safe from Brenley. I will marry you if it comes to that.'

She gave him a kind smile and squeezed his hand. 'Let's hope it doesn't.'

Yes, that was probably the best to hope for. He wouldn't steal her dreams. She'd already had to choose between financial security and a family once. He didn't want her to have to choose again.

Eliza was hungry for proof of Brenley's treachery. Eaton could not keep her away from Porth Karrek another day, so he did the next best thing: he accompanied her when she went to the mine. He stood at her shoulder as she asked Gillie Cardy about progress on the tunnel, making sure that digging hadn't extended beyond *her* specifications. He went below ground with her as she inspected the new timbering in the shaft. He did nothing that would usurp her authority or give the impression that she took direction from him. But very soon he would have to intervene. There was a new tension when she passed the miners—gazes that slid away, or unfriendly bold ones that he was quick to dispel with a glare of his own.

'Sir Brenley and Mr Detford were here yesterday.' Cardy was distant but polite. 'They said we were to push the tunnel further out, after all.'

Eaton watched Eliza for the slightest hint of anger and found it in the narrowing of her eyes. 'They have no authority here, Mr Cardy,' Eliza reminded him in steely tones. 'Detford merely oversees the mine for me and Brenley is not the majority shareholder.'

'It wasn't clear whose orders we should follow, begging your pardon.' Gillie shifted nervously from one foot to the other and Eaton felt sorry for him. Dealing with an angry Eliza was not a comfortable experience. Gillie held out a crumpled handbill. 'Sir Brenley said you would be resigning soon.'

Eliza folded the handbill without a downward glance. 'Sir Brenley is wrong. There is to be no more work on lengthening the tunnel. Wheal Karrek is not extending under the ocean.'

Eliza waited until they were alone in the office before she gave vent to her fury. She pulled off her gloves, one fierce finger at a time, trying to hide her irritation, her hurt, and Eaton ached for her. This was another whole betrayal she had to face—loyal workers backing away from her, unsure who to take orders from—and it was worse than anything Brenley could have printed in his handbill. 'Give me the paper, Eliza.' Eaton took it, his own temper rising as he read. The man deserved to be called out for his vicious lies.

'Is it awful?' Eliza's cool sangfroid did not fool Eaton. He crumpled the paper and threw it into the fire. It was bad enough that Brenley had called her a trollop for her 'immoral' association with the Marquess of Lynford. She didn't need to see what else had been written. Cade Kitto would not be pleased, nor would the parents at the conservatory if word of this reached that far. Eaton doubted it would have teeth in the long run. A man like himself was allowed his peccadilloes, but in the short term the conservatory could founder until this was resolved.

'It is what we expected.' Eaton shrugged. 'Shall I send a man down to gather the pamphlets up and burn them? We could have a bonfire on the beach.'

'Like the king in *Sleeping Beauty*, who burns all the spinning wheels?' Eliza gave a tired sigh. 'The worst has probably already been done. Everyone will have read them by now.' Eaton hoped not. If anything happened to the conservatory, Eliza would blame herself and Eaton didn't want to be in the position of being forced to remove her from the patrons' list. To choose between Cade and Eliza would be an impossible situation.

'Perhaps I'd like to burn them for my sake, then, if not yours.' Eaton smiled his reassurance. 'Inigo arrives today. In the meantime, remember that Brenley's words can't hurt you. You control the company. He can do nothing but rant.'

'And people can do nothing but listen,' Eliza warned. It was hard to be patient. Waiting carried with it its own risks—the school's viability, a scandal that would last longer than it needed to. He wanted to quash it now before it ran rampant, before Eliza could be hurt further. Perhaps he should have framed his offer differently in the Trevaylor Woods. He'd just thrown it out there haphazardly as a contingency. Would it have been better to have asked her seriously then, before she'd seen Brenley's vicious pamphlet calling her a whore? If anything, the situation was more desperate now than it had been yesterday. He didn't want her facing his proposal from a vulnerable position. Perhaps he should ask her tonight after the meeting with Inigo. She would be more desperate still tomorrow, his window of opportunity slipping away exponentially.

Each day that passed weakened his own position. She would not believe he asked out of love instead of duty. And each day his doubt grew. Was proposing to her the right thing or the expeditious thing, a selfish knee-jerk reaction to a problem? It could solve her immediate problems, fulfil his own wants, but it did not change what he could offer her. He wasn't yet convinced either of them could live with that no matter how much his heart wanted it.

Chapter Nineteen

Eliza waited nervously in the grand salon of the school for the arrival of Eaton's friends. Sophie was in her element, thrilled at the chance to play on the Sébastien Érard piano. Eaton sat beside her, reading through documents. They'd decided meeting at the school would draw less attention and provide neutral ground. Anyone might think the arrivals were here as potential new patrons instead of in town to unseat Gismond Brenley.

'They're here, my lord,' Johns announced in hushed tones just after the clock struck four. Classes were done for the day and the boys were outside taking exercise on the back lawn. They would have the place to themselves. 'All four of them. Shall I show them in?'

'Four?' Eliza shot a querying glance at Eaton. 'Did you invite others?' They'd only been expecting two. But Eaton seemed as surprised as she.

'The Duke of Bude and the Duchess are with your friends, my lord,' Johns supplied and Eliza's nerves tensed. Eaton's parents were here! But there was no time to panic. The duchess sailed into the room.

'There you are, my darling.' His mother entered, tall and graceful. Anyone could see that Eaton got his looks from her and his bearing from his father. She crossed the room straight to him, embracing him warmly. 'Inigo tells us there's quite the stir down here.'

His father followed, shaking his hand. Inigo and Cassian clapped him on the back in turn. Cassian shot him a look that said, *I couldn't stop them.*

'We do apologise for surprising you,' his mother offered.

'I'm always happy to see you, Mother. Let me introduce one of the school's leading patrons, Mrs Eliza Blaxland, and her daughter, Miss Sophie.' Eaton ushered Sophie forward, keeping a hand on her shoulder. Sophie wasn't normally a shy girl, but one never knew when faced with so many strangers.

Introductions made, Eaton gestured for Johns to take Sophie to the kitchens for gingerbread and milk and to close the salon doors on the way out.

Eliza found herself with Inigo Vellanoweth on her left, Eaton on her right, and the Duke and Duchess of Bude across from her on a sofa. She was surrounded by powerful men on all sides. A frisson of foreboding ran down her spine. It was as she'd feared when Eaton had originally put his scheme to her. Had she simply traded one board of shareholders for an even more powerful one? How would she ever wrest power from these men if she needed to? She simply wouldn't be able to buy them out as she had some of the previous board. What else could she have done, though? She needed Eaton's friends. The board was still corrupt, it still plotted against her. Without them, she could not unseat her enemies.

Inigo was eager to share his information, 'Brenley has stocks in other mining ventures. He's buying up everything he can get his hands on. My sources tell me he's looking to establish his own cartel. If he succeeds, it will be a virtual monopoly.'

'Then Thorp and Blackmore are in on it, too,' Eliza mused out loud.

'It would seem so,' Inigo affirmed. 'You, Mrs Blaxland, are all that stands in his way.' It was not an enviable position to be in. 'Given what we now know, it's not surprising he made such a generous offer to buy you out, or that he's so angry you've refused.'

Eliza held up the sheaf of documents. 'Then we have to confront him now. We tell him we'll have him brought up on charges of attempted fraud, that he's buying me out because he knows there's more money to be made. My shares will be worth five times this next year. We'll tell Thorp and Blackmore, too, and see if we can't divide and conquer.'

Eaton nodded his approval. 'It looks as though we all have some writing to do. Inigo, you can draft the letters today informing Brenley of what we know about his actions. Eliza, you should send a letter of your own as well, introducing the new shareholders. Inigo tells me he deposited their funds in the bank at Truro where they are awaiting your permission to proceed.'

The sooner the better, Eliza thought. If they could

arrest Brenley and expose his crime, there would be no more threat. If she could get the new shareholders in place quickly, Eaton needn't sacrifice himself for her. The group rose, preparing to go their separate ways, she to the kitchens to retrieve Sophie. Bude smiled at Eaton. 'My son, if I might have a word?' Ah, Eliza thought. Speaking of dividing and conquering.

'I can see you're taken with her and why that might be the case. She's attractive and intelligent. She's certainly in need of protection. Even if we're successful in repopulating her board, her reputation may never recover without the benefit of marriage,' Bude said once the room had emptied.

Eaton blew out a breath. 'I can't give her that.' And the realisation was tearing his heart out. 'I can't do that to her. She wants children.'

'She has one.'

'She wants more. She dreams of a big family, but she insists on not remarrying in order to preserve her autonomy. Even if she were considering marriage, I can't take her hope from her.'

'You've told her?'

'Yes. She knows.' Eaton began to pace. A simple marriage would be the final coup de grâce to cut off the burgeoning scandal before it was out of control.

'Even so, most women would leap at the chance to marry a man of your assets,' his father pressed. 'Perhaps you underestimate her? She comes with her own limitations as well. She's older than you are. She's had her best childbearing years. It may be she won't have any more children regardless.'

Eaton studied his father. 'What are you saying?'

'Ever since we've realised what your illness took from you, you've looked at it as a curse. I know it is a disappointment, not only for yourself, but to your mother and me. Not for the succession, but for yourself. If ever there was a man who should have a family, it's you. You have so much to give in that regard. So, what I say next in no way makes up for what you have lost, but there is a silver lining.

'If you can withstand the gossip, you are able to wed where you wish. You can marry a rich mine-owner's widow if you choose. You needn't consider an alliance, a bloodline or an heir. You need only consider your heart. Do you know how many men with titles can do that? Very few.' His father's encouragement was overwhelming. Always, his parents had supported him in whatever endeavour he undertook. It was a feature that made the Falmage family unique, one that society often misunderstood. But never had Eaton felt his father's love more fully as he felt it in this moment.

'There's the family to consider. It will reflect on all of us,' Eaton replied. He'd never fully explored marrying outside the *ton* for that reason.

'Your sisters are all married and settled. I doubt your decision will affect them much at this point or that their husbands would allow any rumor against them. If you love her, don't let your assumptions about what you can't offer her stand in your way. Put the question to her, let her decide.' His father put a firm hand on his shoulder. 'You looked very natural with her daughter today. It was all I could wish for you.'

'What if she says no?' Eaton toyed with the ink-well. That was his greatest fear. He had to face it now that there was no longer family honour to hide behind. If Eliza said no, he would lose her. There could be no middle ground here.

'Then it's her loss. Eaton, you are worth loving. It's time you started believing it. Whatever her reasons for resisting marriage, she is attracted to you, she cares for you. I watched her at the meeting today, the way she'd look at you, study you, listen to you. Go after her.'

'I want to be sure. I don't want this proposal to be about the current crisis. Perhaps I should wait so that she knows my affections for her are not driven solely by resolving the situation with Brenley. I want her to know my love is constant.' But even he knew the argument was a stalling technique, a reason to delay the question. If he asked, then he would know. All would be resolved one way or the other. Eaton wasn't sure he was keen on such finality. If she refused, for ever was a long time to live with a broken heart. He would do it at dinner tonight. He'd already planned a special supper in the school's garden to take Eliza's mind off the situation. Now, the supper took on an additional import. It might be the most important meal he'd ever eaten.

Chapter Twenty

Saying yes to dinner had been a sound idea in theory, a seemingly natural extension of their day. How many dinners had they shared over the past month? There had been that first dinner, dinners with Sophie at the dower house, picnic suppers in the orangery. Dinners had taken many different shapes over the weeks she'd been in Porth Karrek, but no dinner was like this one.

For starters, this supper was not held in any of their usual places—not the orangery, not the dower house—but at the school, in the gardens where they'd first kissed. Secondly, the garden looked beautiful, far too lovely for a regular meal. The place was lit with paper lanterns strung overhead and candles on the table set for two. Beside the table, two smudge pots burned, creating heat against the autumn night. Eliza stood in the doorway leading to the gardens, taking it all in and wondering what Eaton was up to. What had he and his father spoken of after the meeting?

Eaton approached from behind. He was in dark evening clothes again, his hair combed, his manners impeccable as he placed a gentle hand at her back and kissed the side of her neck. 'You look beautiful, Eliza.' She'd worn a silk gown of peacock blue and taken time with her hair, and she was glad she had. Regardless of what Eaton intended for this supper, she would be leaving soon. There weren't many dinners left between them. 'Come this way, our fairy garden awaits.'

He held her chair and poured champagne. 'What do you think of the garden?'

'It is stunning. This is a lot of effort for a simple supper.' That worried her. What was this dinner really about?

Servants brought dishes and lifted the covers, revealing stuffed game hens and fresh vegetables. 'It's a truffle stuffing,' Eaton explained, offering her a tiny pitcher. 'And this is my very own truffle oil.' He drizzled a small amount over the game hen. 'I thought about having dinner at Falmage Hill. It's time you see the house, but it's been empty too long. It doesn't feel like a home, not right now, not like it used to when I was young. And what I want to discuss, I want to do here where we first met.' He reached for the champagne bottle and refilled her glass.

'Do you mean to seduce me with champagne?' Eliza asked, feeling off balance.

Eaton merely smiled. 'Perhaps, in my own way.' His eyes held hers and Eliza felt a frisson of desire course down her spine. No one would ever look at her the way Eaton did. No one would ever see her the way he did. 'I want to fill Falmage Hill with a family of my own—

with you and Sophie. Brenley cannot defy a duchess. Put Brenley's threat to rest before it truly takes hold. What I am asking you is to let me be a husband to you, Eliza. Let me be a father to Sophie. I cannot give you other children, but I can love you with everything at my disposal: my money, my influence, my name and my heart.' He reached for her hands. 'Marry me, Eliza.'

This was the purpose of tonight; a true proposal, one not as easily brushed off as the one in the woods. He wanted to marry her. He wanted to bind himself to her. She could not allow it. He was doing it for the wrong reasons. She was reeling, her thoughts turning in fragments like Brewster's kaleidoscope. 'You can't marry me. Dukes marry debutantes with immaculate pedigrees.' She was groping for arguments, for ways to protect herself, to protect him. How would she find the strength to resist, to say what she must when he was touching her? Reminding her of how he made her feel—strong, invincible, as if the world and its narrow-mindedness could indeed be overcome, as if she didn't need to fight alone. But the world didn't work that way. *She* couldn't work that way. To accept would cost her too much and him, too, if he stopped to think about it. He wasn't thinking now. He was worried about Brenley and he was reacting in the only way he knew how.

'You aren't meant for me, Eaton.' She locked her gaze on him, forcing him to look at her, as if her gaze alone could make him understand. 'You can't marry me, I'm not duchess material.'

'You will be a splendid duchess.'

She gave him a hard, querying look. 'A mine-owner's widow? Who would accept me? Maybe it doesn't matter here in Cornwall so much, but it will matter in London. I will not be an asset to your ambitions there.'

'Then we won't spend time in London,' Eaton answered easily. Didn't he see it wasn't that simple?

'You can't just say that. You will eventually have obligations in the House of Lords.' Eliza sighed. How did she make Eaton see reason when she didn't even want to? 'You will come to hate me, Eaton. I will be a barrier to the life you have now and the life you were raised to have. I don't belong in your world.' She gave him a soft smile. 'I will miss you, though.' Her heart was breaking. Couldn't he see this wasn't easy? That she hadn't the will for these arguments?

'The life I was raised to was drastically altered when I was a boy. Yes, I will be a duke, I will sit in the House of Lords, God willing, years from now after my father has had a very long life. But I will not be the usual kind of duke, Eliza. I needn't concern myself with heirs. I can marry where I choose and I choose you.'

She was silent. 'You are sacrificing yourself for me. It's too much. I can't allow it.'

'This is about love. I love *you*, Eliza. I would want this even if Brenley didn't threaten.' Eaton gripped her hands. 'What more can I do to show you that I care for you? Why won't you fight, Eliza? Why won't you fight for us?'

'Because there is no us, Eaton. I am just someone you are helping. You are doing this because you don't want to lose to Brenley. You want to protect me. You don't really want to marry me.'

'The hell I don't,' he growled. He pushed a frustrated hand through his hair, his carefully combed waves tousling under his fingers. 'You are exactly what I want.' He paused, eyes narrowing in thought. 'Why don't *you* want to marry *me*? Do you know what I think? I think you're the one who's afraid to lose. You think by marrying me you lose control, you lose the mines, your independence. But that's not how it would be. Eliza, you would be freer, more powerful than you've ever been. The mines would be yours entirely, Sophie's legacy protected always. Your money would be your own. I have no desire for it. Everything you've wanted—safety, security—would be yours. Think of the mining schools we could build. I can't give you children, but we can have a life together based on love and respect.'

It was a potent fantasy. She could have all she wanted. All she had to do was trust him, turn herself over to him in the eyes of the law and the church and hope he would be as good as his word. Nothing would stop him if he wasn't. In many ways he was above the law. Would any of it ever truly be hers again if she consented? He might mean to turn the mines over to her, but it would be his name on the deeds once they married. Should he, at any time, think to revoke her nominative ownership, he could take them from her.

Eaton would never do that.

She knew it in her gut and yet Detford's doubting words haunted her still. Perhaps Eaton did want the mines for himself? What better way to acquire them than to woo them out of her, to make her promises and then not keep them?

He'd offered her the moon and the stars and the planets to boot and she was still going to refuse him. Not just refuse him, but leave him. The game hen lay like a leaden rock in his stomach. Had he misjudged his strategy? He'd thought Eliza would want a balance sheet for a proposal. She'd want to see the assets such an alliance brought her. She'd want to weigh it against the disadvantages, of which there was only one— albeit an enormous one. He'd known she would resist, but he'd never dreamed he would come out on the short end of her analysis. He'd thought he could overcome it.

Eliza moved from her seat, her peacock silk swishing as she crossed the garden. She'd been beautiful tonight at the table. He'd been so hopeful when the evening had begun, but he was less hopeful now. He'd never met a more stubborn, more independent woman than Eliza Blaxland. How awful that the two qualities he admired the most about her were the very ones keeping her from him. 'Marriage is for ever, Eaton. It will last far longer than defeating Brenley.'

'Need I remind you that marriage may be the only way to beat him?' Eaton corrected. She was slipping away. If she wouldn't do this for love, perhaps she'd see the sense in doing it for business, for her own safety. He needed to reason with her, not beg. Eliza responded to strength.

'Eaton, I thank you for the offer. I wish it could be

otherwise, but my definitive answer must be no.' She was quiet and cool, the finality in her tone absolute, and his impatience slipped.

'We are all that stands in his way, Eliza. Brenley will be dangerous if he thinks he's cornered. Why can't you see that?' It was a growl, a yell. He was furious with her for not seeing the obvious and furious with himself for not being able to persuade her, for losing her despite his best efforts.

'Why can't you see that I don't need another Miles Detford? You don't need to sacrifice yourself by rescuing me. If you'll excuse me, I think I'll take my leave.' Eliza's tone was cold, her face blank as she picked up her skirts and walked out of the garden, taking all his hopes with her.

Eaton let her go. She'd all but slapped him in the face with her last remark, equating him with that snake. What was the point in chasing her down now? What would he say when he caught her that he hadn't already said countless times over in so many different ways?

I love you.

He could not change what he could not give her nor could he change what she couldn't give herself. He could not magically give her children. Tonight, he'd pushed her too far and this was the result. He could not erase her need for independence, her perception that marriage was about dependency, not love.

He did not know how long he stared at the doors leading inside, the very last space she'd occupied before she'd disappeared from his sight. It might have been hours or minutes. Time lost all meaning. What he did know was that he would see her everywhere, in everything. Every time he drank champagne he would see her as she was that night in the carriage. Every time he passed a mine, every time he stepped inside his school, his orangery. Every time a parakeet landed on his finger. No place would be safe. This was what happened when you let someone into the private parts of your life, into the corners of your soul.

He knew. This was what it had felt like to lose Richard Penlerick. Only that time, he'd been able to escape to the places that were his and take refuge. He couldn't do that now. Eliza had been his refuge, someone he'd emotionally invested in in the absence of his mentor. He'd not meant to. In the beginning he'd not intended it to be that way. But Eliza wasn't just any woman. She'd demanded more from him than a standard dalliance. Even then, it hadn't been enough. She'd gone anyway and he was left with the torment of knowing she was still in the world. He might see her again by accident on the streets of Truro when he went there on business. He might meet her again at an event for the academy. There would be correspondence from her regarding her patronage. She would be with him in a hundred different ways, but she would always be apart. In this new, post-Eliza world, he could not touch her, could not draw her close for a kiss, could not spend an evening in her parlour, could not walk the beach with her. Tantalus in Hades reaching for his ever-elusive drink would have nothing on him. It was to be expected when one wagered one's soul and lost.

'Are you going to spend the whole night out here?'

Cassian stood in the doorway, blanket in hand. 'I thought you might need this. It's cold out.'

'I hadn't noticed.' He noticed nothing but the pain that had taken up residence in his heart.

'Where's Mrs Blaxland?' Cassian took a seat on the stone bench—Eliza's bench, the place where he'd seen her watching the stars the night of the reception. Good lord, it was starting already.

'She's gone. I let her go.' She would be at the dower house, getting ready for bed. He knew her ritual by heart. She would have tucked Sophie in and read her a story. Sophie would have asked for one more. They would have giggled together and blown out the lamp beside Sophie's bed. He'd loved hearing that sound.

'Did you...ask her?' Cassian was trying to be subtle. It was not his strong suit.

'Yes, damn it.' Eaton's temper flared, sorrow turning to anger. 'I asked her to marry me. I gave her all the reasons, I made all the promises.' He had to stop to keep his voice from breaking. He took a breath. 'And it wasn't enough. I wasn't enough.' He'd never felt more inadequate than he felt now, not even when the doctors had told him he would never sire children, never be able to carry out what was arguably a duke's most important duty.

'That's not true,' Cassian said resolutely. 'You've always been enough for all of us, for your family, for me, for Ven, for Inigo, for the Trelevens, for Cade, for your tenants and for countless other people whose lives you've touched of which you're not even aware.'

'But not her, not the one woman I love, the woman I want to marry. I am not enough for her.'

'That's not true either. She just doesn't see it.' Cassian held his gaze. 'Are you going to let her go? Or are you going to fight for her?'

'I have been fighting for her.'

Cassian clapped him on the knee. 'Then carry on. You've just made a minor miscalculation tonight, soldier. You thought this would be the end of the battle when it was really only the heart of the battle and the outcome could still go either way. You, my friend, need a flanking movement.'

'No,' Eaton countered. 'I need to figure out how to go on without her. She has made her position clear.' There had been life before Eliza, and there would be life after Eliza where nothing would be the same, not even him. He would be a shadow, a ghost of a man who'd once fallen in love.

Chapter Twenty-One

❧

'She means to divide us.' Miles Detford scoffed at the letters lying open on the table. They'd each received one. 'She has no proof. She just wants to scare us.'

'Well, I'm scared,' Isley Thorp replied honestly from his chair in Brenley's study. 'I could go to jail for this. It's your fault, you know.' He glared at Miles. 'You've been paid well for your part in this, as I recall. You had three tasks in all of this: marry the widow, get the tunnel built and take the fall if needed. You could at least manage to succeed at one of them.'

Miles sneered. 'Why are we allowing her to get away with this? We keep talking about drastic measures, but we never take action.'

'We distributed that pamphlet about her immoral character,' Brenley reminded him. 'No one will want to do business with her.'

Thorp laughed derisively. 'A lot of good that did. Now we have the Duke of Bude in town.' It was arguably the worst thing that could have happened, Miles acknowledged. He'd hoped the pamphlet would have caused Lynford to rethink his position as her champion, that Lynford would have chosen to distance himself. He hadn't. He'd closed the distance instead. That was what worried Miles the most.

He, like Brenley, wasn't afraid of the law. Bribes could work wondrous magic. But if they could not get hold of those mines, she would ruin Brenley's monopoly and Miles could not afford that. He would lose a fortune. He'd made promises, taken out loans based on gambling on Brenley's success. If he couldn't pay, very soon his credit would be cut off. Invitations to certain circles would cease, opportunities to invest in lucrative ventures would become non-existent. Lynford would consign him to a slow death in a social hell. He'd worked too hard to get where he was to let that happen.

'Lynford can't support a woman who isn't there to be supported,' Detford growled. Enough with talk. It was time for action. 'She marries *me*, or she…disappears. Perhaps I'll take her down to assess progress on the new tunnel and put the proposal to her there. Anything can happen in a mine. Not everyone who goes in comes out again.'

Brenley nodded. Miles hadn't worried about him liking the idea. Brenley liked anything that meant someone else was willing to do his dirty work, one more person to stand between him and the law. But Brenley wasn't stupid. A dead Eliza had implications, too. 'If she says yes, you'll control the mines, Detford.' He voiced the concern out loud, making it clear he wasn't terribly interested in someone else having all that coveted stock. Miles had to go carefully here. Brenley might be an enemy in the making.

'That is to your advantage. I want what you want,' Miles assured him. It was true, for now. But this was a dog-eat-dog world. How long would that last? He'd cross that bridge later if Eliza Blaxland came out of the tunnel alive and ready to be a bride.

Brenley offered his approval. 'Just be sure you get the job done if she says no. There can be no room for sentiment and it must be done soon.' Yes, speed was of the essence. He and Brenley could agree on that. They needed to act before the new shareholders were in place.

Miles gave a grim, satisfied nod. 'I'll go tonight.' One way or another, everything would be settled at last. This time he would make Eliza Blaxland a proposal she couldn't refuse.

She'd refused Eaton. It was the only thought that had claimed her attention since the moment she'd left the garden. Eliza sat in the front parlour, half-heartedly listening to Sophie practise her piano as the afternoon faded into evening. A whole day gone and nothing accomplished, no decisions made. She hadn't just refused Eaton. She'd hurt him. He'd told her he loved her. He'd been devastated last night despite his stoic show of strength to the contrary. When she'd not said the words in return, he'd not stopped fighting. Another man would have walked away and licked his wounds. But Eaton had come back for more. He'd opted to reason with her, to appeal to her pragmatic side. And she had wounded him twice. She'd equated him with Miles Detford.

She'd made a mess of something beautiful and well intentioned. His offer was nothing like Detford's. She'd not seen it at the time. She'd been too busy protecting her independence. It had not been her intention to set him up for failure or to demean his offer. Quite the opposite. She'd wanted him to see that she loved him, too, enough to give him up, enough not to trap him into a marriage that would ultimately disappoint him. She'd wanted him to see reason as well, that two people should not marry because one of them relied on the other. It created a toxic cycle of dependency. Her mother had never been more helpless than when she was married. For all her independence, Eliza feared marriage would strip her freedom away, wear it down over time until she, too, was entirely dependent on a husband. It was a solid reason. She had no real protection of her independence under the law. So, why did she feel as if she'd made a terrible mistake? Why did she feel as though she'd thrown happiness off the cliffs of Porth Karrek and it was drowning in the sea while she dithered?

'Shall I play another song, Mama? I have a new one from Eaton.' Sophie turned on the bench to face her.

Eliza nodded patiently. 'Please, play another.' Sophie started on the lullaby, encouraged by the praise, and Eliza smiled regretfully to no one in particular. How would she ever forget Eaton? Was that even possible? Eaton, whose presence was stamped all over the dower house and not because the house was his property to begin with, but because he'd tried so very hard to make them feel at home. Over the weeks, he'd brought dolls for Sophie from the nursery at Falmage Hill, sheet music looted from Cade Kitto's stores at the school, flowers sent down from the main house to decorate the tables and consoles.

It had worked. The place had taken on a comfortable, lived-in feeling. At some point they'd stopped becoming tenants and become residents.

More than residents, a dangerous wisp of thought curled in her mind. *You became a family here. Eaton gave you a family and you gave him one. You had a child with no father and he was a man thirsting to be one to your daughter and a husband to you. Together, you both were enough, you both had enough.* She'd taken that hope from him when she'd refused him.

Eliza made impotent fists of her hands. How could she not have seen it? His proposal wasn't only about Detford and Brenley and the mines. It was so much bigger than that. There'd been a chance to have more than a marriage of convenience. She'd thrown more away than just a business deal when she'd refused Eaton. She could have given him the family he wanted and he could have given her a family, too, although smaller than the one she'd imagined for herself. That would have been enough if she had Eaton beside her.

Eliza stilled, shame filling her. Eaton didn't know that. Did Eaton think he wasn't enough for her? That she'd refused him, using the business as a smokescreen for the issue of his infertility? Did he think she didn't want *him*? That he could never be *man* enough for her?

Just the opposite was true. She'd never known a man like Eaton, a man who was so thoroughly *enough* in every way. But there was no going back now. She'd made her position clear and he would not come for her again. She'd hurt, humiliated and walked away from the man she loved. It was enough to make her want to break down and sob, but if she started, Eliza feared she might never stop. She had lost Eaton. Now she was truly alone in a way she'd never been before and it was all her own stubborn fault.

Eliza swallowed hard. She would not give in to despair. She would move on from this and bury the hurt a little deeper every day until she could feel nothing at all. She'd done it before when Huntingdon died. She would do it again. She needed action, plans. She was not unlike Eaton in that regard. What did she do now? Her mind was occupied forming scenarios and options. Should she pack up Sophie and return to Truro and her comfortable town house, to the routine of her days? Life in Truro might not be exciting and it might be lonely, but at least she understood it and who she was in that life. She'd been gone too long. She was missing her bed, her office, her own things. But simply going back couldn't make things the way they'd been before. There would still be the business of the shareholders to deal with. But, to do so from the luxury of her own home, surrounded by her own things, might bring some balance. The sooner she got back to her routine, the sooner she could forget Eaton.

Sophie would miss the house when they left, but not as much as she'd miss Eaton. Her daughter adored him, not just his adventures, but *him*. Children had an innate sense of a person's inner character, they knew when they were sincere and when they were just attempting to flatter and win affection. Perhaps she should take her cue from Sophie? What could be so wrong with a man who was adored by his dog and her daughter? A man who had done nothing but empower her with the gift of his time, his home, his resources, even the resources of his friends? He'd not hesitated to introduce her to his parents. She could only imagine what the Duke had had to say about her.

It seemed unfair that Eaton had to defend her to his own father after having already had to defend her to so many others. Another reason why she should pack her trunks for Truro. Soon, Eaton would realise how much trouble she was for him. He'd realise, too, that she would always be trouble. His kind would never accept her. His beloved family would never accept her and she wouldn't allow him to give up his family for hers. Eaton deserved so much more than she'd bring him. Yet, there would be moments of wonder: picnics on the beach, rambles in the woods, suppers in the orangery, Sophie laughing as he cavorted with her, priceless moments. There'd be pleasurable moments, too, intimate moments just between them: lying abed in the mornings spooned against his hard body, endless nights of lovemaking, days of watching him flash that smile of his. Those moments would be worth the sacrifice. No. She could not be tempted and she would be if she stayed.

Sophie finished playing the lullaby and Eliza called

her over. 'I have something to tell you, my darling.' She pasted on a smile. 'We are going home to Truro. We will leave in the morning. Isn't that great news? Tomorrow night we'll sleep in our own beds and you'll have your own toys.' She hoped she sounded excited. If she was excited, perhaps Sophie would be excited, too.

Sophie looked crestfallen. 'But I don't want to leave. I want to stay with Eaton. We haven't found the treasure yet.'

'It will be winter soon and far too cold for treasure hunting. Besides, Lord Lynford can't always be on hand for adventures.'

'He was going to take me up to the conservatory for the holiday concert,' Sophie put in with slightly more diplomatic tact. Darn Eaton for making promises he knew he was unlikely to keep. Now she'd have to dry the tears left in his wake.

'Will we get to say goodbye?' Sophie asked.

'I don't know. You can leave a note for Lord Lynford, if you'd like.'

'He likes to be called Eaton. Not Lord Lynford,' Sophie corrected her with a slightly accusatory tone as if she was to blame for ruining their fun.

'Mrs Blaxland—' one of Eaton's loaned maids bobbed in the doorway '—you have a caller.'

'Who is it?' Eliza rose to her feet, clumsy with her skirts, her mind slow to shift gears between discussing leaving Eaton and trying to figure out who would call on her.

'Mr Detford.' The woman's tone was full of disapproval. The visitor was calling too late in the afternoon;

it was nearly five o'clock, well past visiting hours, especially when the visitor in question was a man who was not Lord Lynford.

What was Miles Detford doing here now? Instant worry overcame Eliza. Any number of issues might have brought him out. Was something wrong at Wheal Karrek? Was this about the mines? About Brenley? The shareholders? Surely things could have been handled during polite calling hours. He would not call at such an hour without reason, which meant something was wrong at the mine. 'Where is he? I will see him at once.'

'I've put him in your office, ma'am.'

'Thank you. Will you have Miss Gilchrist come down for Sophie? And instruct the maids to start packing. We need to leave for Truro in the morning.' She hoped Miles's business wouldn't take long. She wanted to have dinner with Sophie. With any luck, the visit would take ten minutes and she would send him on his way with an answer.

She reached the office door, straightened her shoulders and sailed into the room. 'Miles, what are you doing here?' He looked worried and that worried *her*.

'No good news, I am afraid.' He came to her, taking her hands in his. 'I want to talk you out of this madness of replacing the shareholders. This is Lynford's plan. He's using you. You've only known the man for a month. I've never known you to be reckless. I fear he must have some hold over you.'

Eliza pulled her hands away. 'Miles, I know what I am doing. Lynford has no sway over me.'

'Perhaps it's you who has a hold over him, then? I can't believe either of you have thought this through.' Miles drew a folded paper out of his pocket. 'Especially after the pamphlet. I assume you've seen it? Then you know how foul it was. I warned Brenley to hold back, but he would not. He's gone after Lynford, too, and that school of his.'

'What?' Eliza reached for the handbill, scanning it rapidly. Eaton had not told her the entirety of Brenley's treachery. There it was in black and white—Brenley was indicting the conservatory for taking funds and direction from the immoral Lynford and his mistress.

'I'm sorry, I thought you knew.' Miles took the handbill back while her mind reeled. She was not going to cost Eaton his conservatory. Not only Eaton, but Cade Kitto and his new wife. Perhaps it was indeed best that she was going home tomorrow. Just in time, it seemed. Perhaps being out of sight would put her out of mind, at least long enough to save the school. 'My dear, this is a deuced difficult situation and I dislike heaping more bad news on it all, but there is something else. The new tunnel at the mine. I think you should come with me, there is something you should see.'

'Now?' Eliza tried to steady her mind. All she could think of was Eaton and his precious school: his legacy, his boys, his memorial to Richard Penlerick. She was ruining everything she touched.

'Yes, I think now would be best. The fewer people around to notice the better,' he pleaded with her. She understood the need for exigence and even for secrecy.

Eliza put her hand on his arm. 'Yes, of course. I

don't forget how difficult it is for you to walk a fine line. Brenley and I, we've put you in an awkward position.' Over the years he'd had to balance his friendship and loyalty to her against his business association with Brenley as a shareholder. He was her friend now, wanting to warn her no doubt about Brenley's latest attempts to push through the tunnel against her express wishes. Dinner would have to wait and she would likely miss Eaton's evening visit—if he was even coming. But the mine needed to be dealt with. If Brenley had fuses down in the tunnel, or if Brenley had been giving orders again, she would put a stop to it. 'I'll just be a moment. Let me get my things and say goodnight to Sophie.'

Eaton was going to ambush her. He swung off his horse in the drive of the dower house, nerves drawn tight. He had the upper hand, but he also knew he was down to the last of his chances. He was risking everything on this final roll of the dice. Once the initial miasma of his disappointment—nay, his devastation—had lifted, he'd seen the flaw in his proposal. The formality of occasion, of his very invitation, had made her wary. She'd sensed something was afoot from the start and she'd been braced for it. She would not have that luxury tonight. He would catch her by surprise when she didn't have time to marshal her responses or be on alert. It was her own tactic, after all.

He'd given Eliza the day to sort through her feelings as he had sorted through his. Her rejection had cost her something. She'd not refused him lightly. He could see that now with the benefit of a day's distance. Refusing him had hurt her as much as it had hurt him. That recognition gave him hope enough to try one more time. There must be a way to get past her defences, her assumptions about what she needed. He'd searched all day for the words. He reached for the flowers in the saddle holster and for the small present he'd brought for Sophie. He dusted off his breeches and straightened his coat. He pushed a hand through his windblown curls for futile effect. No matter, he rather thought Eliza liked him wind-rumpled. The thought gave him courage. Eliza liked him. Eliza *loved* him.

He knocked at the door, taking a final deep breath as the door opened, an excited Sophie ducking past the footman and throwing herself at him. 'I knew you would come to say goodbye!' Eaton knelt down and she wrapped her arms around his neck in a hug. 'I don't want to go, Eaton. Won't you persuade Mama when she comes back?'

Eaton stood up and stepped inside, his mind fumbling over the words. Sophie had imparted so much information all at once. 'I'm afraid I don't understand. You're leaving?' His earlier confidence began to slip. Eliza meant to do it then, she meant to cut ties with him completely. If he'd waited another day, he would have missed her. The truth of it was in evidence everywhere. Trunks were open, maids were folding clothes and running up and downstairs precipitously to retrieve items. The pace at which the maids were working suggested there was an urgency to the task, that it was newly assigned. Eaton knew his staff. They were organised, they never gave the appearance of rushing anywhere because nothing was left to the last minute. They would not have deliberately delayed packing.

Eaton looked about, realising what else Sophie had said. 'Where's your mother? She is gone?' She was usually never far from Sophie, not with dinner so near.

'She's gone.' Sophie pouted. 'She said she'd be back for dinner but she's not. She never breaks a promise,' Sophie said solemnly. 'It's all Mr Detford's fault. I bet he breaks lots of promises,' she said sulkily.

'Detford was here?' Eaton squatted down again and drew Sophie close. 'Did your mama go somewhere with him?' Why would Detford come here? Why would she leave with him? And why was she not back yet?

'They were going to the mine,' Sophie supplied. 'Mama said it was urgent.' On Detford's word. But that might be enough for Eliza. Eaton's mind raced. She'd always viewed Detford as an ally and still did despite their recent quarrel. Eaton didn't like it. There were too many variables to consider. Detford would have received the letter regarding the new shareholders joining the board. And Detford had yet to publicly declare a side in the little war between Brenley and Eliza. The bounder was likely playing both sides as it suited him. The man had already tried once to marry Eliza. Eaton didn't think the proposal had stemmed from affection for her as much as it had from an affection for the money and influence that would pass to him once they wed.

A few mad scenarios ran through Eaton's mind. Was Detford the lure? Did Brenley think to pressure her into some sort of deal through less than gentlemanly means? He didn't allow his thoughts to wander in that direction. There were all nature of dastardly pressures that could be brought to bear: kidnapping, threatening Sophie, dragging Eliza to the altar to marry Detford against her will and murder her if she did not. He could not stop his mind from raising questions: Who would inherit everything if Eliza were dead and Sophie so young? Probably Eliza's feckless uncle and her delicate mother. They would be easily overcome by the likes of Brenley and his cartel. The Blaxland fortune wouldn't last long in their hands.

Eaton's gut began to churn with his imaginings. If Eliza were to die before she were wed, Brenley would have a clear path to the holdings. Eliza's majority would be nullified and the new shareholders would be unable to stop him from taking control of the mines. But that was the least of Eaton's concerns. Eliza was out there somewhere with Detford. There was no guarantee they'd actually gone to the mine. That could be a ruse as well. At the moment, only two things mattered. Finding her and marrying her immediately to remove her—and Sophie—from such harm.

Unless he was wrong. Perhaps he was overreacting. Perhaps there was no evil lurking behind Detford's visit. Eliza valued her independence. She would not appreciate Eaton following her or interrupting the meeting. She would take such an interruption as proof that she'd lose her autonomy through marriage, that he would never truly let her run the business on her own. Did he wait here? She had been late before, like the day

Sophie had been ill. Did he go to the mine and hope she and Detford were there? Hope that he'd be in time to stop any nefarious undertakings? Hope that he'd have a plausible excuse if all was as it should be? And then he would take her to task for leaving him.

He rose and dusted his breeches. 'Shall I go after her?' he asked the darling face looking up at him. Sophie was worried. He'd caught her glancing at the clock, marking every minute her mother was late.

'Yes, please,' Sophie answered. 'One day Papa went to work and didn't come home. I want Mama to come home.'

Sophie would have been old enough to grasp the rudimentary details of that day. No wonder Eliza had sent for Sophie when her stay in Porth Karrek had been extended; no wonder she was never far from her daughter. Fears that were only somewhat irrational could play havoc with the young mind. That settled it. He would go to the mine and bring Eliza home, even if it meant bearing the brunt of Eliza's anger. He looked down at Sophie, thinking. He could not leave her here with only Miss Gilchrist for protection. Miss Gilchrist had been useless on the road when he'd discovered them. If there was trouble afoot, it might come here. Detford might be a decoy so that the way was clear to snatch Sophie.

Eaton called to one of the maids, 'Betty, get Miss Sophie's coat.'

'Am I going with you?' Sophie brightened at the prospect of an adventure.

'No, you are going somewhere far more exciting. The big house where I live. My parents are there and they love children. There are games and toys in the nursery and there's a beautiful banister to slide down.' Betty brought her coat and Eaton bundled Sophie into it. 'Betty will take you up to the house.' Over Sophie's head, he gave Betty strict instructions. 'Go straight to the house, have Sophie explain to His Grace what has happened. Stop for no one. Run if you have to.'

Betty would be loyal. Betty would follow directions. Eaton saw them off and swung up on his horse, going as fast as he dared in the dark, and hoped he wasn't too late—or better yet that he wasn't late at all.

Chapter Twenty-Two

It was getting later by the minute. Eliza had the distinct impression that Detford was stalling. Upon arrival, they'd gone to the office to discuss shares, a superfluous discussion that had had no urgency to it, in Eliza's opinion. Soon, the last of the crew would be gone, the mine empty. Perhaps that was what Miles was waiting for. Perhaps he didn't want to be seen by anyone. It spoke volumes about his fear of Brenley and even about the depth of his friendship for her, Eliza thought, that he would risk so much to alert her to whatever waited in the tunnel.

Sophie would be disappointed. Dinner time had come and gone. 'Can we go down now?' Eliza prompted. 'I need to get home. I did not realise this would take so long.'

Detford turned from the window with a mild smile. 'Yes, we can go now.' He took a lantern from the hook and she followed him downstairs, relieved at last to be making progress. But Detford seemed nervous, agitated or excited. Did she imagine a falter in his step? Once inside the shaft, he swung the lantern around, letting the light glance off the walls. All was in good order: strong timbers gave support to the rock; the floor was as free of debris as possible. She prided herself on safe working conditions, as safe as mining could be.

The shaft was deep and the deeper they went, the warmer it got. They reached the junction where the new tunnel had been started. Miles hung the lantern on a nail. 'This is what I want you to see, Eliza. Look at this rock.' He took up a pickaxe and a chisel from where they'd been propped by the wall and set to work, carving into the rock until the surface was chiselled away. 'Look at this. The copper is even more plentiful than suspected. It's right here on the surface, just waiting for us to pick it out. Every indication suggests the lode extends further than we have plans to dig.'

'You mean further than I have plans to dig.' Eliza met his gaze with a stern one of her own.

'Yes,' Miles conceded. 'We are leaving money on the table, Eliza. It's no longer just a hypothesis about what might be out here. This is the richest lode any mine has seen for some time.'

'And the riskiest,' Eliza argued.

'The technology exists. The Levant mine is using it—ventilation fans to help with heat, the pumps to disgorge the water. It can be done,' Miles pressed politely. These were old arguments. Ones she'd considered before.

'I don't know that submarine mining is right for us. The technology is still new, it is fallible.' Even now, she could hear the sea overhead, proof of how far out they were, how very close to disaster. Should a wall give way, no one would survive such an accident. There wouldn't be time to think, let alone to escape. She could not commit men to working under those conditions for hours and hours every day.

'If you pay them enough, they'll dig.' Miles read her thoughts.

'I will not bribe poor men to risk their lives just to feed their families.' Eliza knew the money would indeed entice men. She *could* pay them to take the risk. She *would* not. A man should not have to live in jeopardy simply to make a living.

'Don't be stubborn. You were right to get steam power in here to replace the horses. You know technology makes us more efficient.' Miles was cajoling now, flattering her. 'I thought if you could see the proof of the lode, you might reconsider.'

Eliza narrowed her eyes. 'Did Brenley put you up to this?'

'It's good business, Eliza.' He evaded the answer. 'As your friend, I felt duty-bound to show you the proof.'

'Now that you have, we may go.' Eliza turned to start the long walk back to above ground, but Miles's hand closed about her wrist.

'There is something else, Eliza.' The warning in his voice stopped her as effectively as the grip on her wrist. There was a hard edge to Miles Detford now. The cajoling friend was gone. 'Brenley will not appreciate your intractability on the tunnel. If you will not make the decision to extend the tunnelling, perhaps you would allow me to make it for you, as your husband.'

The thought was so outlandish Eliza almost didn't grasp it. 'What are you saying, Miles?' It was worded like a proposal, but it sounded like a threat.

'Marry me, Eliza, as you should have years ago. We could have avoided all of this. I have Brenley's word he will post a retraction about Lynford and his school and about you. Allow me to take the decisions regarding the mine from your conscience. I will consult you, of course.' She knew what that consultation would be like: patronising and useless. Detford would report to Brenley and Brenley would do what he wanted. Miles could not be her hero under those circumstances. Didn't Miles see that? As her friend, how could he think she'd even consider such an arrangement beneficial?

'Do not refuse me. It will go poorly for you,' Miles warned.

'I am not afraid of Brenley.' She wanted to get out of the shaft, back up above ground where she had space. She felt trapped, crowded by Miles and the rock walls.

'It's not Brenley you should be afraid of at the moment. It's me.' He pulled his coat back, revealing the weapon in his belt.

Dear heavens, Miles had a pistol. Didn't he know the dangers of firing a gun inside a mine shaft? Her heart hammered. 'Miles? What are you doing? What is this?' But she knew. Eaton's voice whispered again, *He is not your friend.* 'You can't fire that in here, you will kill us both.' A gunshot could bring down loose rocks, enough to block the way out.

'That's up to you. Don't make me use it.' He advanced on her until her back was pressed into the rock, his voice cold. 'I will ask one more time. Marry me. I have papers. You can sign them before we walk out of here and announce our happy news to the world. Or refuse and I will be the only one walking out of here.' Of course he had papers, something legally binding to ensure she couldn't lie to save to herself.

She was thinking fast now, realisations piling up in her mind. All these years, she'd thought he'd accepted her rejection when he'd really just been biding his time. She needed to get out of the tunnel. A new twist of fear turned in her stomach at the thought. Was Sophie safe? Should she have ever left her? Had this been an attempt to lure her away?

'Don't be stubborn, Eliza,' he admonished, the back of his hand skimming her face, his gaze dropping to her mouth. 'Marry me and all will be forgiven. You can walk out of here and into a new life. In time you will see that I am right, that it is for the best. This is not worth dying for.' His hips pressed into hers. She felt the hardness of his sex. Dear lord, this horror aroused him. 'Marry me and live.'

For a while. A cold chill came over her despite the heat of the depths. He would kill her first. A dead wife was so much more easily managed, her assets more easily acquired. The true danger came to her for the first time. Detford would not let her leave alive. 'We would be happy together, Eliza, if you would just allow it, if you would just allow me to show you.' He was fumbling with her skirts, his mouth slanted over hers, seeking a kiss.

She turned her face away, thrashing about. Detford pressed her to the wall, holding her captive between the rock and his body. His mouth came at her again and this time she couldn't avoid it. But she could fight him. She bit down hard on his lip. Detford cried out in surprised pain, losing his focus. Eliza shoved at him, hard, pushing past him, and began to run, scrabbling over rocky terrain in a dark landscape. She wasn't fast enough or far enough. She went down with a thud, something sharp in the darkness cutting her lip, scratching her cheek as Detford tackled her from behind. She screamed. Detford swore, the blow came and her world went even darker.

It was still dark when she found consciousness again. Her head throbbed, the waves throbbed. Then panic pulsed. The mine! She was in the mine! And she was alone in the dark, deep under the earth. Through the pain, she forced herself to think. How long had she been down here? Did it matter? Knowing the answer to that question seemed like a luxury. Light would be more useful than knowing the time. But neither luxuries were forthcoming. Did she dare call out? Would anyone hear? Or rather, would the right people hear? Someone who wasn't Detford or Brenley?

Eliza struggled to her feet, but only made it to her hands and knees. Whatever Detford had hit her with had left her dizzy and queasy. A sharp-edged rock, maybe? The butt of his pistol? She never should have come down here with him. She should never have trusted him. What a fool she had been! Her first clue should have been his insistence on secrecy, on waiting until everyone had left before they'd made an appearance in the shaft. She hadn't understood he simply hadn't wanted witnesses while he carried out his crime.

She crawled forward on all fours. She couldn't risk standing up, couldn't risk passing out again. Progress was slow and dangerous. She didn't know where she was going, or what she would find. Mines had all sorts of crevices and cracks one might fall into, or twisting turns one might accidentally take. People could be lost down here in this dark world and never recovered.

She would not think about that now. She would think positively. She would think about Sophie and how much her daughter needed her to get home. Sophie must be worried sick. Eliza calmed herself. She would not panic. She would think about Eaton and how grateful she was for everything he'd done. She'd never felt about any man the way she felt about him; here was a man to be relied on, to be trusted, who cared for the well-being of others, a man who loved her daughter, who loved her. A man she loved. A man she loved enough to give him up, yet she had not told him so. She had not said the words. She'd been too stubborn, too determined to be independent, to see that loving him didn't make her weak, didn't make her dependent. Why hadn't she seen it before?

To her left, gravel fell away beneath her hand. She reached out and felt only air. She stifled a scream. She was on a ledge. Horror rose. To her left there was nothing but darkness and emptiness. She'd taken a wrong turn. There'd been no ledge on the way down. Eliza picked up a pebble and tossed it, hoping to hear it clatter on other rock. Perhaps the ledge was really a slope, which was only somewhat reassuring. But she could not hear it land. How far did the ledge extend? Did it curve or go in a straight line? She didn't know. She couldn't see. Did she dare go on and hope the ledge didn't end? That it curved back towards the safety of two walls?

Eliza assessed her options. If she was wrong, she could pitch off the end into nothingness. If she stayed where she was, crews would return in the morning, she could call out and hope they would find her, hear her over the throb of the waves and noise of the tools.

The thought of spending a dark night in the mine carried a horror of its own. Eliza felt for the rock wall to her right and huddled against it, hugging her knees tight to her chest. It would be a long night either way. Morning was likely a long way off. She'd left home at five. It had been seven when they'd entered the mine. She would be missed by now. She was hours late. Would Sophie or Miss Gilchrist sound the alarm? Would anyone answer? Her one hope was Eaton, but she'd refused him in no uncertain terms. Would he come or had he washed his hands of her?

Eaton was alone in the yard of the mine. He wheeled his horse in a circle, letting the animal breathe as he took in the deserted property. He'd ridden as hard and as fast as he'd dared in the dark to reach Wheal Karrek, only to find it deserted. What had he expected? It was well after working hours. Then he saw it, a covert flash of light in the office window, hidden away quickly. Someone was up there and they didn't want to be seen. Likely, they'd already heard him ride in. He couldn't assume he'd escaped detection.

Eaton swung off and headed up the steps. With luck, the person in the office was Eliza. But he didn't feel that lucky. He reached for his pistol. Eliza would not have dithered at the office, knowing Sophie was waiting. That left Detford. Eaton didn't like what that implied. If Detford was alone, that worried him a great deal.

Eaton barged through the office door, deciding to use brawn and surprise as his best weapons. 'Where is she?' he demanded. He let the door bang off the wall for effect. Detford looked up from the desk startled, frightened. He had the ledgers out, but that was the least of Eaton's concerns.

'I don't know what you mean.' Detford rose, putting the desk between them.

'You left the house with Eliza hours ago,' Eaton growled, advancing on Detford. Detford might have the desk between them, but Eaton had the door behind him. Detford would have to get through him first to reach it. Detford wasn't leaving anytime soon.

'What have you done with her?'

'Does it matter? It's far too late.' Detford eyed him, trying to concoct a plan and failing.

Eaton cocked the pistol and drew out his other one.

He fired the first at Detford's feet. Detford swore. 'You could have hit me!'

'The next one will. Consider that your warning,' Eaton ground out. 'I don't know how much Brenley is paying you to do his dirty work, but it cannot be enough to die for. It's probably not even enough to be wounded for.' With a pistol he didn't need to jump the desk, Detford was just now realising that. Eaton grinned as Detford paled. 'Now, let's try the question again. Where's Eliza?' He could see Detford weighing his options. But a man like Detford only ever arrived at one conclusion.

'She's in the mine. I didn't kill her,' Detford offered as a belated defence. 'I just left her there.'

Eaton's blood began to surge. He should shoot the bastard now. Detford had taken the coward's way out. He'd left Eliza in the dark, hoping she'd do the job for him. She just might. Eliza was too stubborn. She'd kick and claw her way right onto a ledge, or over a drop-off, and be lost for good. Eaton waved the pistol. 'You first, Detford. Lead the way and know that I'll shoot at the first sign of any trouble.' He nodded towards the lantern by the door. 'You carry the lantern.' He wanted one hand free in case Detford tried anything.

The mine was an eerie place to be after hours, the lantern throwing shadows against rock walls. Eaton fought back a bout of panic when he thought of Eliza without even the comfort of a lamp. They reached the tunnel and Eaton stopped. 'This is where you brought her? This is where you fought with her? Shine that lantern down there,' Eaton directed, his eye catching something dark on the ground. He bent down and tested it with his fingers, careful not to take his eye or pistol off Detford. The man was sweating and not just from the heat of the lower levels. He held his fingers up to the light and cursed. 'This is blood, Detford. What did you do?'

He steadied himself against the rage. Detford had harmed her. She was down here, hurt and lost. 'Let's retrace our steps, shall we?' Eaton ground out, shoving Detford before him. At each junction he paused and called out, 'Eliza!' But the only sound that came back was his voice. At the third junction he heard it, a faint answer. It was wide, a fork in the shaft, really. It would be easy in the dark to turn left instead of staying on the main path.

'Eliza!' Eaton called again, pushing Detford forward.

'We are not going down there,' Detford protested. 'It falls off into nothing.'

'I can shoot you here, then,' Eaton offered. If Eliza was down there, they were going even if it were the bowels of hell.

'You won't shoot. It might destabilise the roof.'

'Would you like to bet on that? You'll still be dead and the roof looks well timbered to me.' There was no way he was leaving Detford behind to wreak any kind of mischief while he located Eliza.

Eaton called instructions, hungry for the first sight of her, 'Eliza, wait for the light. Don't move until you can see.' He swung the lantern, his hunger for the sight of her turning to clammy horror when light hit the pathway. It was as Detford had claimed, narrow and dangerous, falling away entirely on the left. It was a miracle she was still out there. Then he saw her, pressed against the rock wall, and his heart leapt. 'We're almost there, Eliza,' he called out. 'Can you move towards us?' The path looked unstable to his eye, as if too much weight would send it collapsing. He didn't want to risk the three of them out there.

Eliza began to move, crawling slowly, each inch taking an eternity. She was being careful, Eaton realised. She knew the path wasn't reliable. Eaton kept talking, kept her focused on moving forward. She was nearly there, just a few feet to go when Detford turned on him, swinging the lantern at his face. Eaton jumped back, the lantern missing him, but Detford's motion caused the lantern to go out, thrusting all three of them into darkness. Eaton heard Eliza scream. Where was Detford? The darkness was the great equaliser. He didn't dare shoot for fear of missing Detford or hitting Eliza or starting a rockslide in the dark.

Eliza screamed again and gravel rolled. He could hear the sounds of scuffling. Detford had her. If he wasn't careful, they would both plunge to their deaths. Eaton fumbled for a match, desperate to relight the lantern. The wick flared and he raised his pistol without hesitation but there was no shot that didn't risk Eliza. Detford held her against him like a shield with one arm, his own pistol raised with the other. 'Put your gun away, Lynford. You will get us all killed,' Detford drawled. 'I'll throw her off the ledge.'

'You throw her off the ledge and you'll be dead before she hits the bottom. 'Where's the victory in that for you? All your hard work for nothing. Best to come up to the ground and take your chances at a trial,' Eaton reasoned. But Detford was beyond logic.

Detford's eyes narrowed. 'You say that because I am the only one with a decent shot.' And he took it without warning. The pistol report echoed throughout the cavern. Eaton felt the bullet take him in the left shoulder. He went to his knees. Eliza screamed as a rumble began in the depths of the mine. She was struggling, trying to reach him. The rumbling was getting louder. The ground began to shake. The path beneath Detford's and Eliza's feet was disintegrating, increments of shale sliding away. Detford couldn't hold her and maintain his balance at the same time. On his knees, Eaton levelled his own pistol, his left shoulder burning. If he could hold steady long enough, he'd have a clean shot and he could free Eliza. 'Eliza, stay down!' He called his warning and fired. Detford crumbled, clutching his arm, his pain consuming him entirely.

'Eliza, honey, come to me now!' Eaton held out his good hand, his eyes riveted on Eliza, lending her the strength of his gaze. The path was dissolving fast. Another shudder of the mine threw Eliza to her knees. She crawled towards him one lunge at a time and then he had her hand. He closed his grip around it as the ground beneath her gave out. She screamed, suspended in air with only the strength of his arm as an anchor. The rumbling was all around them, rocks falling everywhere. Detford was trapped on the other side, desperate and bleeding as his footing grew smaller, the path falling away beneath him. 'Help me, man!' Detford cried as the last piece of solid ground fell from beneath his feet, but Eaton could do nothing to help the other man as Detford's grip failed him and he fell into the abyss.

'Eliza, hold on! Look at me! Keep your eyes on me. Give me your other hand!' Dear lord, let him have the strength. Let his wounded shoulder hold. All he wanted was to get Eliza out of the mine, to see her safe. What happened to him didn't matter. Eliza would be free. That would be enough.

The tunnel was collapsing. One moment she was falling, the next Eaton's hand had gripped hers, the only piece of stability in the chaos around her. A body passed her and she was screaming as Detford fell, his hands clawing vainly for purchase. For a moment he had a fistful of fabric and part of her skirt tore away, but Eaton's arm held steady. How could it be enough? Already her fingers were slipping, sweaty and unsure. He was calling to her, his other arm bloody and slick as it reached down to her, his voice instructing her to look up, to give him her other hand. But to swing her body, to gain the momentum she needed, required courage. Any movement might cause her other hand to slip.

'Come on, Eliza! I won't let you fall!' There was urgency in his voice. She had to act now or she might doom them both. She was counting on Eaton as she'd never counted on anyone before. She would only get one chance. She drew a breath and swung her other arm. Eaton's strong grip closed about her wrist and he began to pull her up, hauling her against him, shielding her from the falling rocks with his body, ushering her to the sanctuary of the main shaft.

'Are you all right?' Eaton's arms were tight about her. She was trembling, but there was no time. The cave-in would trap them if they didn't move.

'We have to go!' But she stumbled, her efforts not able to match her words. She was hurt, sick, her head wound making it impossible to walk. She was going to die here. She hadn't the strength left to get out. 'Eaton, go. You can't stay here with me.' Already the corridor was a thunder of falling rocks.

'Not without you.' Eaton was grim. 'You carry the lantern and I'll carry you.'

'But your arm…'

'No arguing, Eliza. All I need is one good shoulder to sling you over.' He swept her up and lumbered towards safety, strong enough for both of them.

Eaton staggered only at the last, collapsing as they emerged into the fresh evening air of the mine yard, surrounded by people and noise. *Help had come.* It was the only thought Eliza could register. She was dizzy and unsteady. Bude was there with Inigo and Cassian. Someone draped a blanket over her shoulders, someone else pressed a glass into her hand. She wanted none of it. 'Help Eaton, he's hurt. He's been shot.' She wanted to stand up, wanted to go to him, but she couldn't. 'Where's Eaton? Is he all right?' But no one would answer.

'Shh…'

Someone—Inigo, perhaps?—soothed her.

'We've got him. We're taking him home. He's unconscious. A doctor will be waiting.'

'And Sophie? My daughter?' Eliza fought the urge to want to sleep. So many people needed her.

'She's fine. She's with my wife.' Bude knelt before her, taking her hands. 'We need to get you both home. I have my carriage.'

She was going to be all right. Eliza woke late in the afternoon the following day at Falmage Hill. Her head hurt, but she wasn't dizzy. That was an improvement. Sophie was beside her. She reached for her hand and smiled at her daughter, but Sophie didn't smile back. She went straight to the point. 'Mama…' her face began to crumple '…the doctor says Eaton might die.'

Eliza struggled to sit up, black spots swarming before her eyes from the effort. No, Eaton could not die. He would not die for her, or because of her. 'Sophie, find me a dressing robe and find someone to help me. Get Cassian.' She wouldn't be able to manage the walk alone. She needed someone to lean on. 'We must go to him. We're his family.'

The doctor had not lied. Eaton was pale and unmoving in his bed. She'd never seen him so still, this man who was filled with energy. Cassian helped her into a chair. 'He lost a lot of blood. An inch to the right and he would have died in the mine. The bullet was close to an artery,' Cassian reported. 'He developed a fever last night. He hasn't woken since we brought him home.' Cassian gave her a long look. 'It is my opinion that he'll wake for you, if you could find it in your heart to give him a reason.'

She heard the reproach in his tone. So he knew. Eaton must have told him she'd refused his offer. 'I was mistaken in that decision,' she whispered.

Cassian was tired and drawn from a long night spent at his friend's bedside. 'He is like a brother to me. I have known him since birth. Life has not always been fair to him, but he's never let it stop him. He would give his all for those he loves. He proved that last night. I know of no better man.'

Neither did she. Eliza's throat was too clogged for words. Eaton had protected Sophie last night with his quick thinking and he had not hesitated to come for her. 'I'll stay with him awhile. You should go and rest.'

Cassian took Sophie and closed the door behind him. Alone, Eliza reached for his hand where it lay atop the blankets. There were things she needed to say to him, things she'd realised in the mine—or perhaps she'd always known them and had been too afraid to admit it. 'Thank you, Eaton, for saving me, not just last night, but even before, by helping me see that I don't need to be alone.' She threaded her fingers through his, alarmed at how stiff they were, how unmoving. 'Thank you for looking after Sophie.' Her voice cracked and the words seemed inadequate. She would be dead now if not for him. Instead, it was he who was in danger. She laid her head on his chest, feeling the fevered warmth of him. 'Eaton,' she whispered, 'I love you. I need you to wake up so I can tell you I've changed my mind. I will marry you if you will still have me.'

* * *

Eliza was safe. Eliza was free. His mission was complete. He could go now, on to whatever was next. The next world, perhaps. There was nothing in this one for him now. Eliza didn't want him, didn't need him. Maybe this was why nothing had pricked his interest since the school opened. Maybe he *was* done here.

My boy, you're wrong. You're too young to be done.

'Richard!' He couldn't see anyone, but he could hear his mentor, his old friend's voice.

She loves you—aren't you listening?

'She doesn't want me. I can't give her a child.'

You can give her more than a child—you can give her hundreds of children. Open schools. Adopt. Make Falmage Hill a home again. I never thought you would give up so easily, Eaton. She's already lost one man. She can't stand to lose you, too. She needs you, her daughter needs you. Wake up, be a husband, be a father. Listen to me...

There was a new voice now. Eliza's voice, begging him, wanting him.

I want to tell you I've made a mistake, I want to marry you. I don't want to do it alone any more.

He pushed against heavy eyelids and coaxed his hand around warm fingers. He forced sound over his dry throat and was able to form a single word. 'Eliza.' And she was there, beside him, crying, kissing him, holding his face between her hands.

'Eaton, I was wrong. I made a mistake.' She was babbling through her tears.

'I know,' he managed to say hoarsely with a smile. 'I heard you. You want to marry me.'

'Yes. As soon as you're able.' She clumsily poured him a glass of water, slopping some of it on him as she tried to help him drink.

'You pour water the way I pour champagne in moving carriages,' Eaton rasped. 'What changed your mind, Eliza?'

'When I was lost in the mine, I realised I wanted to marry you not because I needed you or was dependent on you, but because I loved you. I. Loved. You. That's the only reason.'

'It's the best reason.' Eaton pushed back her hair with his good arm. 'It's the reason I came back. I wanted to have a life with you and with Sophie, and any children we might accumulate on the way, more than I wanted to die.'

Eliza smiled, the sweetest sight he'd ever beheld. 'You must be feeling better already. You're making plans.'

Eaton grinned. 'Can you plan a wedding in three weeks? The moment I am well enough to walk down the aisle, I want to marry you. Every minute counts, Eliza. I don't want to waste a single one.'

Epilogue

Not a moment was wasted. Three weeks to the day, Eliza stood at the doors of the school's grand salon, dressed in a gown of pale blue velvet, a veil of cream lace on her head. Blue for loyalty. Blue for truth. Blue for eternity. Today, she was breaking one vow to take another, far more important one. She'd sworn never to marry again, but she'd not sworn never to love.

'Are you ready?' The Duke of Bude offered her his arm. Eaton's father would give her away to the man she loved in the place where they'd first met, the place where Eaton had proposed, the place where Eaton had given so much of himself to so many.

'You look beautiful, Mama.' Sophie twirled in her new dress, blue as well, her hair done in long thick curls. 'Is it my time to scatter the rose petals?' She was excited for her part in the ceremony. Eaton had insisted she be part of it. 'Today, I am getting a papa,' she told the Duke proudly.

'Yes, you are.' The Duke bent down to tweak a curl.

'And I am getting a new granddaughter and a daughter-in-law. Who do you think is the luckiest? I think I am.'

Eliza disagreed. She was the luckiest of them all. She'd found love when she'd least expected it. She'd also found a partner, a man willing to be her equal, willing to fuse her dreams with his. Eaton had been true to his word, scrambling for a special licence as soon as he managed to get out of bed. He was marrying her three weeks after he'd awoken from his fever and she was ready. She didn't want to wait a day longer to start their life, not when she'd nearly lost the chance altogether.

From inside the grand salon, chords sounded on the Sébsastian Érard and the doors opened to a wedding march Cador Kitto had composed just for them, another three-week wonder. But love made so many things possible. Sophie went before her, happily spreading rose petals down the ribbon-festooned aisle, guests rising as she made her way towards the front. Eaton's friends were there; Inigo and Cassian smiled, the Duchess of Bude wiped tears from her eyes as she passed.

Reverend Maddern waited for her alongside Eaton but she had eyes only for her soon-to-be husband. Eaton stood dressed in a blue morning coat and fawn pantaloons, dark hair already unruly just as she liked it; his arm in a sling, a reminder of his bravery—a reminder, too, that whatever came their way, they would face it together.

She heard little of the service and would remember even less except the part where Eaton kissed his bride. The Reverend pronounced them husband, wife and family as Eaton gave Sophie his good hand and led them back down the aisle. Eliza did not think the world could feel any more complete. But Eaton had another surprise for her.

On the way to the wedding breakfast at Falmage Hill, the carriage turned towards Wheal Karrek, stopping a short distance from the mine yard. She tossed Eaton a questioning glance. She'd not visited since the night Detford had died. Inigo had kindly—and temporarily—taken over the reins of the business in addition to quietly investigating Brenley's attempt at creating a mining monopoly among other financial considerations. There was no proof Brenley had done anything illegal, yet, but it would take time. Already, she could see the effects of Inigo's efforts. He'd organised the recovery and stopped any further tunnelling. The damaged section of the mine from the rockslide was being pumped out below. Above ground, a section of land had been quartered off with stakes and string. She threw Eaton a glance. 'What are we doing here? What is this? No one said anything about a stop.'

'Consider this an ambush.' Eaton grinned and looked mysterious. 'Be patient. I have a wedding gift for you.' He jumped down and rang the bell, calling all the miners to assemble, all work forgotten for the moment as Eaton climbed back in the open carriage and stood up for all to see. 'Attention everyone! Today I celebrate my marriage to this woman, the new Lady Lynford and the future Duchess of Bude. In honour of that marriage, my gift to her is the Wheal Karrek school for miners' children, where everyone will be able to learn to read and write.' He turned to her. 'Eliza, would you do us the honour of breaking the ground?'

Eliza swiped at her tears. A school! He was giving her a school. Had there ever been a more wondrous gift? The gesture overwhelmed her as so many of his gestures often had from the start. She took the shovel from Gillie Cardy and dug out the first scoop of dirt to a rousing cheer from the miners. 'Thank you,' she whispered to Eaton.

He beamed. 'It was your idea.'

Her new husband certainly didn't waste any time. But she knew what he'd say to that. There wasn't any time to waste. There never was when you were in love.

* * * * *

Whilst you're waiting for the next book in
The Cornish Dukes miniseries,
why not check out Bronwyn Scott's
Allied at the Altar miniseries

A Marriage Deal with the Viscount
One Night with the Major
Tempted by His Secret Cinderella
Captivated by Her Convenient Husband